The Raja Is Dead

The Raja Is Dead

Shivani Singh

HarperCollins *Publishers* India
a joint venture with

New Delhi

First published in India in 2006 by
HarperCollins *Publishers* India
a joint venture with
The India Today Group

HarperCollins *Publishers*
1A Hamilton House, Connaught Place, New Delhi 110001, India
77-85 Fulham Palace Road, London W6 8JB, United Kingdom
Hazelton Lanes, 55 Avenue Road, Suite 2900, Toronto, Ontario M5R 3L2
and 1995 Markham Road, Scarborough, Ontario M1B 5M8, Canada
25 Ryde Road, Pymble, Sydney, NSW 2073, Australia
31 View Road, Glenfield, Auckland 10, New Zealand
10 East 53rd Street, New York NY 10022, USA

Typeset in 11/13 GoudyOldStyle
Nikita Overseas Pvt. Ltd.

Printed and bound at
Thomson Press (India) Ltd.

To GM, for the notebook and pen

Prologue

Sirikot is not all gone.

I remain.

I am the quiet sky over its politely decadent landscape. I am the desiccated flower between the covers of its gilt-edged diaries. I carry the knowledge of Sirikot. Knowledge of all that should not have happened, but did; and all that should have happened, but didn't.

There is such a thing as too much knowledge. It tires you. There are stones that you must carry. I am the oldest living member of Sirikot's clan and I can feel the breaths left in my body. They are limited, countable. Death's crooked finger is pointing at me.

Yesterday, I saw my dead husband's image behind me in the bathroom mirror, a sign that my afterlife was here to receive me, to take me away. When I came out of the bathroom my family found me shaking. I trembled at the finality of completion, at the impermanence of all that I have known and loved.

'I don't have much time. He's come to get me,' I said.

There is life and there is death, that much we know. But do we know what to do with the time in between? Where did my life go? Where did Sirikot vanish? I am tired. I must put the stones down. I must try and remember, sort out the chaos of my existence. As always, I keep coming back to Sirikot and all those from Sirikot who populated my life, my memory.

Sirikot, my mother's parental home, where I dreamt my childhood dreams. Sirikot, palace of laughter and illicit love and the warmth of family close by, like a fire in winter. At a time when ordinary mortals were kings and queens, and kings and queens were ordinary mortals.

My mother's father, my Nana Sahib, was the raja of Sirikot. I remember him as only a grandchild would — big in every respect. He had large eyes, a huge head, a great mane of hair and a prodigious beard dyed vigorously with henna and parted in the middle. The gems and stones adorning his body were the grandest I have ever seen, bigger even than what Nani Sahib, my grandmother, wore. He had a booming voice. His presence filled a room. His laughter resonated. His anger was the stuff mythologies are made of. Yet the soles of his feet were as pink as a newborn baby's. With us, the children, he was capable of immense gentleness. He was a big man, my grandfather. To me he will always be king.

Ma, his first-born, the first princess, and Nani, my grandmother — strange how I always remember them together — Ma was a finer, more sophisticated impression of her mother, both of whom I associate with fire — one consuming, the other consumed. Nani was the great womb, a giant receptacle. She was mother to eight children and some miscarriages. She had lustrous long black hair that never greyed and a diamond stud that sparkled on her upturned nose. It was she who taught me how to smoke. 'Inhale!' she would command and laugh when my head reeled over her hookah.

My mother had three sisters whose beauty was legendary. Though they were all married by the time I grew up, I had heard that when they were younger, people walked miles just to catch a glimpse of them. I can still see them, in their bobbed Audrey Hepburn haircuts, defying age, smiling their exquisite, nicotine-stained smiles. Their warmth reached out to me from the three corners of the country, where they went to live after they were married.

They were not there that crucial year of 1947. The year time tested Sirikot and found it wanting.

It was the beginning of Independence and the abolition of the princely states. It was the year of the brightest of festivals, and of death and darkness. It was the year of murder and the loss of innocence.

In 1947 I turned thirteen. I was ready for womanhood and the secrets of adult people. I saw human nature bend and twist like will o' the wisps to every societal pressure. A lot of what happened then changed my girlhood, and my life.

Perhaps my memories may seem irrelevant in today's time. This new millennium, that I thought I'd never see, has no time for the antiquities of yesterday. It is a generation obsessed with immediate gratification. But I see in it the same follies. I see them in the news, in the government, between man and woman, between parent and child. Times change, human nature doesn't.

My mother's brothers were in Sirikot that year, with their wives and children. All except one, a pale young uncle who I always remember in a sola topi — so set in his English ways that he always spent his time in Calcutta or away at shikar camps, far from the intensity of Sirikot. But the other three were present in Sirikot that fateful year, of whom the youngest, Uday Mama, was younger than me by a year. I called him Baby Uncle. He was my closest confidant.

That year I lost him too.

~

Rajraj, my eldest uncle, born after Ma, was the next in line to the throne. He was yuvraj, heir apparent, and Yuvraj Mama Sahib to me. A man so complicated that even now it is very difficult for me to pin a personality trait on him. I cannot say for sure whether he loved his family or hated it, whether he was an atheist or a believer, a cuckold or a misogynist. Though his favoured status in Sirikot and the adoration resulting from it kept him in general good humour, he looked bloodless and pasty, insipid even, somehow incomplete. His tendency to fidget vaguely irritated me. He was a self-professed teetotaller who drank in secret. He reminded me of water collecting surreptitiously in a corner. In his obsession for his wife I saw the final debasement of human spirit.

His wife, Gayatri, was the yuvrani of Sirikot and Yuvrani Mami Sahib to me. My mother believed she was a greedy grasping woman who lacked the breeding and culture that behooved a yuvrani of Sirikot. She had a crazy kookaburra laugh and reserved a stock of bitter chocolates in her rooms. Somehow the taste of bitter chocolate always reminds me of her — full of dark mysteries and pungent secrets. Sometimes just a chance reference, a rich brown smell or the colour of polished teak, can start a veritable deluge of memories in me, and shake me to my core.

Bhavani, Ma's second brother, was the Rajkumar Sahib of Sirikot and Kumar Mama Sahib to me. He too had a tendency to compulsions, but in his later years it shifted from wine and women to the loftier realms of spiritualism — as if he was picking up where his brother left off. Stockier, sturdier than Yuvraj Mama Sahib, he wore a permanent smile, as if smirking at his own rakish good looks. He had the best collection of funny faces and ghost stories and always smelt of the outdoors. Though he was criticized as a wastrel I remember that he smiled often, that his jokes were many, and that he lit up a room when he walked into it.

His marriage to Kumud Mami Sahib was an unfortunate one. They were a mismatched pair — a rock married to rarefied air. She seemed to be made of nothing at all. Disconnected, a homeless waif walking about the labyrinthine zenana, her head full of strange ideas. It did not take her long to lose her tenuous hold on reality.

Then there were the others, those who served us. Our nurses — Dhaima and Santoma; their children Pushpa and Shanti who were our companions; the gardeners, the guards, the one-eyed water-bearer, the priests, and scores of others I don't even know, who were the glue that held Sirikot together. Their loyalty made our ruling family what it was. They buttressed us, and the more they held us up, the more contingent we were on them. In their unconditional devotion was so much shrewdness; in our lordliness so much vulnerability. Together fief and serf ruled for four centuries in the ancient little kingdom of Sirikot in the Eastern Province of India.

We'd endured; we prevailed.

~

The Sirikot palace was a jewel shining at the foot of the Mangala mountain, like a forest goddess's toe-ring. Majestic stone lions guarded ornate gates in four auspicious directions. A cornucopia of flowers bloomed in the vast green stretches of Sirikot, as if the sun shone only for them. Lovebirds and lal-munias lived out dainty lives in the bird house. There was never a speck of dust in the acres of garden or stone or concrete. Chandeliers depended from ceilings like an encroaching glass forest. In the kitchens, cooks fried puris from dawn to dusk. The granaries were always full of rice. The iron rooms of the ganta ghar were never empty of gold and silver.

You knew when it was winter in Sirikot. The dull slap of heavy Persian carpets being rolled out in the immense corridors resounded in the palace. Well-dressed women attendants with flowers in their hair walked softly in a row, overturning brass pitchers of hot scented water for the rani's bath. The durbar hall was witness to the breathtaking spectacle of the sirapawa ceremony, when landowners touched the feet of the raja with their vividly coloured turbans before wearing them and turning the hall into a proud dazzle of multicoloured turbans and voices raised as one in allegiance to the raja of Sirikot.

Around the ivory table, in the billiards room and the banquet hall, inlaid French beadwork glittered on the walls. In the ballroom, starchy English gentility wearing the jewellery presented to them by the successive rajas of Sirikot waltzed to the strains of Johann Strauss, as we, the children, waited politely to show them our paintings of the English countryside.

Sirikot, that fabled land, where the birthdays of elephants were celebrated in ritual detail; Sirikot, where blue-carpeted corridors ran through the wings of the palace like veins through the leaves of an ancient tree. Sirikot, full of marble and stained glass and precious stones, governed by age-old traditions and the laws of heredity.

And it all came tumbling down.

❧ PART I ❧

One

It was March, two weeks before the madness of Holi. At the Sirikot railway station, Nana Sahib's personal bogey, emblazoned with the royal coat of arms, detached from the train into a cordoned siding.

My grandfather, Nana Sahib, the raja of Sirikot, was very proud of his railway station. It made him feel modern and glad that his womenfolk and children could travel across India through the railway's remarkable connectivity, while still remaining in purdah and *en retinue* of cooks, khansamas, dhais and servant girls. We alighted and were immediately surrounded by a tight circle of canvas screens to shield us from curious eyes.

It is tradition that the brother should receive his sister on her visit home. Since, as heir apparent, Yuvraj Mama Sahib's status was too exalted, Kumar Mama Sahib, the second eldest, had come to receive us. He unearthed Ma under the canvas screens and greeted her in his typical humour. 'Send word,' he said. 'The walking mosquito net is here.'

My mother's pleasure was evident in the foolish grin she gave him. My younger sister Dakshyayani and I were more demonstrative. We ran squealing into his welcoming arms.

'Now,' he admonished, staring at the threatening red spreading across the tip of Ma's nose. 'No waterworks in the station. Save it for your big reception in the palace.'

'Quiet, Bhavani, you ass,' Ma decreed, beside herself with joy.

'Yes, HH, whatever you say,' Kumar Mama Sahib solemnly saluted.

Traditionally, we would have proceeded to the palace in palanquins but given the new spirit of liberation my grandfather had sent his metallic-blue Chrysler Windsor. Holi festivities were imminent in the town square. There was joy in the air. Festooned halwai shops selling all sorts of sweets and others peddling the objects of religion did brisk business. Everywhere, Sirikot flags and pennants shivered when they caught the breeze. Like an enthusiastic infestation, the buntings and decorations had crept right up to the polo ground outside the palace. Whirling dancers kicked up a storm of dust. Strings of mango leaves and marigolds were everywhere. Alpana decorations, depicting a myriad mythologies, were stamped on the freshly whitewashed houses that fell on our route. Somewhere in the corner of the post office, the new tricolour flag — incongruous, solitary — waited forlornly for a snatch of wind.

In the front porch of the Sirikot palace, across the busy colours of the gardens and the busts of his ancestors, Nana Sahib waited. Alongside him were the ruling ladies, their heads discreetly covered, a supernatural contingent of stillness and modesty. A gaggle of my cousins, agog with anticipation, had gathered around too; their servant companions standing somewhat apart, at a respectable distance.

My mother's reunion with her father was intense. Nana Sahib had never touched his daughter in both their lives except to put his hand in blessing a few inches over her bowed head. Conversation between them was too full of reserved propriety and deference for any informal affection but the tone in his voice made it clear that, among his numerous children, she, his first-born, was his favourite.

'Munna Ma,' he said. 'Your mother has missed you.'

Embarrassed by Ma's public struggle for emotional equilibrium, I quickly moved to touch Yuvrani Mami Sahib's feet. She did not hug me but gave me a tightly benevolent smile, making it obvious that she had still not forgiven me. During our last visit I had fallen from grace over a silly incident, when I had innocently disclosed that Yuvrani Mami Sahib had added some temple jewels to her collection. Temple jewellery belonged to the God Trust and no member of the ruling family could rightfully own it. Ma, who brooked no nonsense over Sirikot customs, had apprised her of this fact in no uncertain terms. Hence, the benevolent smile laced in arsenic. But Kumud Mami Sahib's warm embrace compensated for Yuvrani Mami Sahib.

Baby Uncle would not stop talking. I was distracted from his chatter and my cousins' insistent hissing into my ears just long enough to register the slight shadow that darkened Ma's face when she noted that her older brother, Yuvraj Mama Sahib, was absent from the reception. But then my cousins were everywhere, excitedly whispering something about a killing. Dhaima, Ma's nurse, directed me towards the arti and pujas. Nani waved lights around our faces and anointed vermilion paste, turmeric and rice on our foreheads. Village women sang reunion songs. Some of them ululated. The high-pitched singularity of their tone made the words breathed into my ears sound more like a lament than the intended invocation of good luck. The rajpurohit, the palace priest, stood by holding a salver of prasad from the morning puja in the palace temple. Later we would visit all the temples and pay our respects. But for the moment it was enough to meet every member of the receiving family, giving each affection and respect according to their age and station.

The assembled women waited for Ma to give the cue — her famous chin wobble. She complied. Promptly eyes moistened and the sniffing began, unheedful of Kumar Mama Sahib's friendly jibing. Sirikot was well known for its hospitality, its tearful reunions and its melodramatic farewells. And it was not just family — even if a casual visitor left Sirikot without a sufficient display of grief it meant that there had been some glaring oversight in the hospitality extended and was cause for grave concern.

How different it is today. In my time, it was considered rude if you didn't postpone your departure at least twice.

After the reunion, a procession of chattering relations, servants, Baby Uncle, Nani, Ma, my sister Dakshyayani and I proceeded through the maze of palace courtyards. We were moving towards the nursery.

I was loath to leave the mardana, the men's chambers, where we had been received. Its scalloped arches opened onto the outside world. One could look at the sprawling pleasure gardens, the elephant corral, the horse stables and the summer house by the palace pond. Beyond, was my grandfather's zoo. I asked Baby Uncle in a conspiratorial whisper whether the white peacock was still around.

Keeping pace beside me, Baby Uncle was a blur of excited skips and hops and bobbing head. 'Yes, Leela, it is. And I have to show you more. Much more. There are secrets, many secrets.' He was an amusing sight, practically sizzling with some badly restrained gossip. The killing was probably an act of vengeance by a disgruntled cook who had throttled his pet parrot's neck, or something. Still, it would be worth investigating.

Suddenly, with an angry start, I realized that the moustachioed duwari who guarded the inner zenana was right in front of me. 'Wait!' I said. 'This is not the way to the nursery.' We had gone right past the nursery, situated between the mardana and the zenana.

Ma and Nani exchanged looks. 'You'll be staying with Nani and I,' my mother said in that nonchalant tone parents use when they know there is trouble ahead.

I stamped my feet. Ma's dark eyes flashed and she raised a warning finger. All these years later, I still remember Ma's hands. Soft, incredibly soft — like butter. The hands of a woman who never used them for any physical work besides writing letters. She was quite a woman, my mother — soft hands and nerves of steel.

'I'm staying with Baby Uncle,' I announced, bravely making my stand.

'He's not Baby Uncle. He's Uday Mama Sahib. You be careful to address him that way. And the nursery is no place for a young woman like you.'

I was flummoxed. I didn't know what to do with this new-found status extended to me, like a peace offering. With all eyes on me I hesitantly took capitulation as the political choice, 'But the zenana is so boring. Where will I play?'

'You do have a zenani bagh here,' said Nani Sahib deeming it safe to intervene now.

'But it's so boring!' — I thought it appropriate to continue my tantrum to a respectable point — 'You don't have a durbar hall like the men do.'

That elicited general amusement. 'Yes, but we run it anyway,' my mother laughed.

'You see, Jemma Sahib, we don't *need* a durbar hall,' Dhaima's cackle became a wheeze. She was maybe a few years younger than Nani. Swarthy and fulsome, like all the other women attendants, or vas gharianis, she smelt of 'Evening in Paris' and wore thick silver anklets around her feet and flowers in her hair. She did not do any menial work like the lower class of servants except for helping us with our baths and toilette. She was not remotely connected to the family or the extended family of patidars. Her elevated status, like that of so many other dhais and their children, was a mystery to me. Still, I decided she was only an exalted servant, a glorified nurse, just a dhai.

'You shut up,' I told her. 'Always buttering up Nani and Ma.'

The procession smiled indulgently and we carried on.

~

Afternoon-siesta time. It was imperative that we pay our respects to my eldest uncle, the Yuvraj, and visit the temple and call upon all the elderly granduncles and aunts living in the various wings of the palace. But all that could wait. It was nap time first.

Dakshyayani had already been packed off to the nursery with Baby Uncle to be cared for by Baby Uncle's dhai, whose children were to be their companions. I had to content myself by extracting a promise from my mother to be allowed to spend the night in the nursery. Just this once.

But it was still afternoon. My mother and Nani settled comfortably back among the antimacassars to the soft rustle of peacock feather fans and the clinking bangles on the arms of the vas gharianis as they pressed their feet. Cool rose sherbet and the pleasant sound of the gold nutcracker demolishing betel-nuts lulled me. Outside a mild sun blazed.

Dhaima's two daughters must have received news of our arrival because they were ushered in. Her elder daughter Shanti was to attend on my mother. She was around my mother's age and wore a permanent sulk on her face; a sallow woman whose pinched face and disaffected air annoyed me. 'She thinks she's the queen of England,' I grumbled to Baby Uncle later in the evening. In spite of her sullen demeanour she could have been a woman of rare beauty, had it not been for a livid childhood scar that had deformed the left side of her face. Dhaima's younger daughter Pushpa was a few years older than me and friendly enough. She seemed genuinely pleased to see me. I smiled lazily at her and sank into the silk cushions when Dhaima instructed her to press my feet.

Lying back amongst the bolsters, Nani needed to spit out some betel juice. Her silver spittoon was in the furthest corner of the room. Dhaima sprang to her feet and sped to fetch it, but it was too late. Unable to find a suitable receptacle in that fraction of the moment, Nani grabbed Dhaima's older daughter's hand and spat into her palm.

Shanti looked first at her palm, which she had instinctively cupped, and then at all of us sprawled on Nani's massive, canopied bed. She gave us a look of such disgust that it stopped our breath. When we collected ourselves, I laughed. Shanti left the room. My mother turned to Nani and said, 'Really, Ma, you are too lenient. Did you see that look?'

Nani and Ma sat cross-legged, facing each other, their long hair loose on their backs. They looked like clones. They had settled down for a long gossip session and were baring their hearts to each other, catching up on lost time. Dhaima and Pushpa sat on the far corner of the bed like inanimate objects, wearing the carefully expressionless faces of the mindless. My eyes were growing heavy.

'I folded my hands before Raja Sahib and begged him,' Nani was saying. 'I said that I have become a grandmother now, no more, Lord, no more. My body cannot take the pain of another birth. He was gracious, your father, he forgave me. He said I had done enough. I had given him more heirs than a raja and the state could desire.'

'He has a new favourite now!' Dhaima suddenly roused herself from her comatose listening; her venom unexpected.

'Who?' My mother asked with studied indifference.

'Phulwati they call her. She plays the sitar. She is beautiful, young, only eighteen they say. And she has a bloated head. The other day I caught her wearing the same set of kundan earrings I had seen Yuvrani Sahib wear. Can you imagine?' Dhaima said. 'The lady is pissing fire.'

My mother digested the news. 'Things are changing, Ma,' she said thoughtfully. 'And I don't like it. All this would not have happened in your time.'

The languor of the afternoon had me paralysed by now. My eyelids drooped till I could see the blackness behind. My last thought as the afternoon heat claimed me was a sneaking suspicion that all the fanning and foot-pressing was a premeditated design to lull me to sleep, so that the others could get on with the palace gossip. But I think I managed to catch some fragments uttered by Dhaima. 'Cheetah', I caught and 'marks on the throat'. My curiosity jumped at the words but my brain had gone to sleep. My last thought was that Baby Uncle had been speaking the truth after all.

There had been a murder.

~

My mother's older brother, Yuvraj Mama Sahib, was a vaguely handsome man. He had inherited Nana Sahib's height and fair colouring and wielded a beaked nose that had lain recessive in previous generations only to show up again in Baby Uncle and him. All his good looks couldn't take away the effeminate pallor of his face and a certain furtiveness of expression that dishonest moneylenders have. He had an unconscious habit of wringing his hands as if he were washing some imagined sin and laughed heartily when he was nervous. He talked without showing his teeth and spent the major part of his day and night in fasts, pujas and esoteric rituals. To a critical adolescent like me, his religiousness seemed entirely fraudulent. He was too tainted and flawed for the pedestal Ma, Nani and the people of Sirikot had hoisted him on.

I had once heard a strange story about him. It had struck me immediately as being both fantastic and commonplace. After the birth of my mother, Nani had visited a renowned sage living in a cave on the Mangala mountain behind the palace. He was a fakir of some siddhis or powers and certain eccentric habits, one of which was eating off the floor. He recognized Nani as soon as he saw her and greeted her by her honorific, 'Rani Sahiba of Sirikot'. 'In my next life, Rani Sahiba,' he declaimed, 'I will be born from your womb. You will know me from a purple birthmark on my left thigh. You must ensure that I am made the raja.'

He did die soon after, so the legend goes, and Nani faithfully produced a son bearing the fakir's purple signature. Most people believed the story. And Yuvraj Mama Sahib's eagerness to be coronated was explained thus – he was actually an old soul, elevated in the spiritual ladder but still dragged down by vestiges of desire for earthly gratification.

Incredibly, there was a similar story attached to Nana Sahib. Before my great-grandmother gave birth to him, a wandering sage had proclaimed, 'You will give birth to a boy. You will know him by a birthmark between his shoulder blades. When the birthmark travels down to his backside he will die.'

Considering the way my Nana Sahib's life ended, I take birthmarks very seriously.

~

After my siesta, Ma and I set off to meet my uncle, the heir apparent. Runners scurried ahead of us to inform Yuvraj Mama Sahib that we were on our way. Approaching his chambers, we heard the heart-rending shrieks of men being whipped. Yuvraj Mama Sahib's distant shouts at them sounded like the bark of an animal. It made my blood run cold.

Our runner informed us that a week ago, during a hunt, Yuvraj Mama Sahib had encountered some tribals wearing the sacred thread ordained only for brahmins and upper-caste kshatriyas like ourselves. On being questioned they had told Yuvraj Mama Sahib that an old seer in their tribe had bequeathed the right to wear the sacred thread on them. Yuvraj Mama Sahib had invited them into the palace saying that he would conduct a proper sacred thread ceremony, in keeping with the ancient scriptures. The poor forest-dwellers had complied, only to be branded with hot irons: a permanent imprint of the loop of sacred thread burned on to their bodies.

Yuvraj Mama Sahib met us in his spartan quarters. His pranam to my mother was like him — not too warm and not too cold. I liked to imagine that brother and sister had been close till their respective marriages replaced that intimacy with the burden of different responsibilities. I think his fondness for me was genuine, though, as with most things about him, I couldn't be sure. He had taught me how to wink, and had once gleefully encouraged me to cut Ma's hair when she had been sleeping. But his pale imitation of the gauraiya joke was a source of chagrin to me. 'Gauraiya' or 'little partridge' was an endearment Kumar Mama Sahib used for me and I disliked Yuvraj Mama Sahib's intrusion into the privacy of our little game. 'Ram Din,' — he predictably called out to his imaginary cook as soon as he saw me — 'no need to cook mutton for dinner. I'm going to have this little gauraiya.' I squealed dutifully and hid behind Ma, wishing my uncle would stop being such a dolt.

Yuvrani Mami Sahib received us in a loud sari that spoke eloquently of how unused she still was to the subtleties of high living. My mother's respectful enquiry after her well being and my aunt's measured response was indicative of the fact that though Yuvrani Mami Sahib was younger to my mother in years, as the Yuvraj's wife she was elder by status. Yuvrani Mami Sahib imperiously told my mother that her cook had made Ma's favourite venison pickle and she would be sending it across to her. The conversation between them was perceptibly limited.

Sometimes I felt sorry for Yuvrani Mami Sahib. She knew she would never be accepted in Sirikot. Not so much because her father was only a big zamindar from Uttar Pradesh — technically a non-royal — but more because of the anonymous letter received a month before the wedding that had claimed she was an easy or 'faisha' woman who had filled the neighbouring gutters of her parental home with unwanted foetuses. But perhaps she was hated most of all because Yuvraj Mama Sahib had trashed the letter, saying that all marriageable girls were susceptible to vicious rumours and had insisted on marrying his doe-eyed, moon-faced beauty. It was believed that she had used tantras not only to get into Sirikot, but still actively practised the black arts to keep Yuvraj Mama Sahib in her control.

'So, Apa,' my uncle said to my mother after a strained silence. 'Now that you are here our father can leave the running of state affairs to you.' If there was sarcasm in his voice there was good reason. The last time my mother had been in Sirikot she had an ear to Nana Sahib when he quelled an uprising of land squatters. It was she who had installed the new rice and flour mills. It was she whom he'd consulted about his visit to Delhi to meet with the Chamber of Princes. She, who had laid the foundation of a primary school and ordered the whipping of a patidar for making insulting remarks about Nana Sahib. Given Yuvraj Mama Sahib's eccentric religious habits and irrational temper (some called it a cruel streak) and Kumar Mama Sahib's inability to govern because of his celebrated licentiousness — at least one Sirikot progeny was needed to uphold the mantle! Nana Sahib relied heavily on Ma's visits to her maternal home. The flash of her dark eyes evoked more respect than even Nani's could muster. Baby Uncle, needless to say, was too young to make a difference. Yuvraj Mama Sahib, it seemed, was succumbing to a bout of sibling rivalry. I watched my mother closely for her response.

Ma smiled playfully. 'So, Rajraj, *that's* why you didn't come to receive your poor sister even though she was coming home after two years?'

Instantly, Yuvraj Mama Sahib was profusely apologetic. His white teeth peeped sheepishly through his fine lips, probably the only set of teeth in Sirikot unstained by the abuse of tobacco. 'You must excuse me, Apa. I came down with a bad attack of gout. You know how it is this time of the year.'

'How will you rule Sirikot with gout like that?' Ma was teasing him; like all siblings he was acclimatized to a little harmless bullying, yet I could feel him squirm in his seat.

A renowned Muslim vaidya adept in the treatment of gout lived in Sirikot. Nana Sahib regularly used his compresses and unguents but Yuvraj Mama Sahib had been vehement about his refusal to accept treatment from him because the vaidya was Muslim. This bothered me. At the age of thirteen I did not know a great deal about religion. But I did know that in the eyes of god Hindu and Muslim were one. I found Yuvraj Mama

Sahib's religious position not only untenable, but also frankly idiotic.

His face, meanwhile, had darkened. Perhaps the playful barb had hit home. 'Ruling Sirikot is a joke,' he said. 'Everybody knows that Sirikot, like all the other states in this region, is run by women.'

'Really?' My mother raised an eyebrow. 'Are you saying that it is not Baba, our father, ruling Sirikot but maybe — Phulwati?' She gave a short laugh at her own joke.

'Speak to the English governess, she will give you perspective,' — Yuvrani Mami Sahib's interjection was uncalled for — 'in England and in Europe the sons of ruling families are educated in Eton and Harrow. In the hostels there, princes are not followed by a trail of elephants and cooks —'

'— and they serve time in the army, navy and air force,' Yuvraj Mama Sahib finished for his wife. I could see that his obvious show of marital harmony had offended Ma. 'Here, we are trained under the command of first-class nautch girls from Lucknow.'

I watched my mother trying to regain her composure with clinical detachment. Her brother and sister-in-law's arguments, so sudden, so unconversational, had shaken her. And then, as if a crude discussion on Sirikot administration was not enough, Yuvraj Mama Sahib took it upon himself to summon their old governess, Mrs Wood.

Mrs Wood was a dearly loved tutor of the ruling family. A portly white woman in horn-rimmed glasses, she always wore a floral-print petticoat which I found hilarious, it was as if she had not dressed yet. She joined them readily, corroborating what my uncle had said.

'It is true,' Mrs Wood said in her mellow, Indianized accent. 'In spite of Raja Sahib's best efforts, Sirikot is dangerously close to becoming a historical misfit.' And her words launched them into a vociferous examination of the history of Sirikot.

Though situated in the heart of the Eastern Province of India, Sirikot was founded by warriors from the western frontiers of Rajasthan. More specifically, by the Kachchawa Rajputs, nobility from the Amber fort in Jaipur. Four centuries before, they had turned their attention to the peace and plenty of Sirikot and, beheading the peaceful brahmin rajas of the region, had built a brand new palace after razing theirs to the ground. It was said that the earth around the Govinda temple was still stained red with brahmin blood and that a mound of sacred brahmin threads lay buried in some forgotten shrine, to this date.

Subsequent centuries of easy living and no wars saw the men pickled by wine and smothered by women. Their allegiance to the Marathas through marriage had kept the British at bay and though they were unable to secure the 'Ruling Chief' title, they continued to enjoy the untrammelled glory of their royal lineage. By this time, the women of the family had discovered it was convenient to keep the men in their moronic state. The instruments of power in harem diplomacy were the raja's sons, most importantly, the next-in-line for the succession of the throne. These the women prevented from too much exposure, making sure they were not given much education. Whatever they learnt of history and mathematics was within the confines of the palace. This was true. I could vouch for it. Sirikot had a fleet of tutors. They taught us English, French, the arts and sciences.

'But that is not enough,' Mrs Wood said. 'Inside the palace we can teach you how two plus two add up, but we cannot teach you the other levels of learning that come along with it. We cannot teach you independence and self reliance, because your environment precludes such learning. We cannot give you the thirst for knowledge that headmasters can give. Here we are not your masters, we are your servants.'

Yuvrani Mami Sahib exclaimed, 'The only competition my husband had in his childhood was his older sister! And they say he shouted at the arithmetic teacher when he got his multiplication wrong. He said, "I am the Yuvraj of Sirikot! Whatever answer I get when I multiply two numbers, is the correct one."'

I giggled. I had felt that way many times. The Hindi teacher in Sirikot, I remembered, would start almost every other sentence with, 'Praying at the feet of your royal personage, I humbly request, that if it does not hurt your esteemed and most beloved cheeks too much, would you, ever so kindly, repeat the syllable "Aa".'

'Ma didn't even know when I had a full set of teeth,' Yuvraj Mama Sahib complained. 'Because the dhais, instead of brushing my teeth, were still trying to clean my mouth with cotton gauze and honey when I was eight years old —'

'— and after much singing and cajoling, when a poor dhai would hesitantly approach his mouth with her finger wrapped in gauze and honey' — Yuvrani Mami Sahib piped in as though she too had lived her husband's childhood in great detail —

'— he would bite her finger,' Mrs Wood finished wryly. 'Do you know,' she continued in the same mien, 'what happened when the Raja of Lalnagar died? The Yuvraj was only seven years old. The British decided to coronate him anyway. During the coronation ceremony he was carried into the durbar. The British asked the women to set him down so he could at least walk up to the throne. When the women put him on the floor, he wobbled and fell over. He was a seven-year-old human child who could not walk because he had never been set on the ground!'

'That's what mollying and coddling does to you,' Yuvraj Mama Sahib observed.

'Mollycoddling,' Mrs Wood corrected, despite herself; Mama Sahib gave her a sharp look.

'But you weren't brought up that way,' Ma protested. 'You could walk by the age of ... umm ...'

'— four,' supplied an impassive Mrs Wood.

'You studied in Raj Kumar College for two years. You took only two cooks, a dhobi and an elephant with you. Then you went to St. Xavier's College. Of course, Baba bought you a house in Calcutta for your studies, but everybody does that — ' Ma looked at Mrs Wood for approval and she responded with a strained smile.

Yuvraj Mama Sahib sighed. 'The sad part is, after the heady adventure of my college education in the outside world, I couldn't wait to come and sink back into the feminine laps of Sirikot,' he said and fell into a pensive silence.

The silence extended long enough for Mrs Wood to take it as her cue to leave the room and then Yuvrani Mami Sahib announced she was retiring to the zenana. I sensed my mother relax. Now brother and sister were in a more convivial mood. Suddenly, for no particular reason, without turning her head in my direction, my mother asked me to go and play outside. I knew that tone. It meant she didn't want me to hear what she was going to discuss next. Pushpa was half asleep at my feet. I gave her a gentle kick to wake her up.

Pushpa and I went outside into the grey shadows of the giant colonnade. I could see her pale face lit up by the yellow light of the tallow burning on the walls. Far on the ramparts the watch-keepers beat the nagaras. Their booms echoed till the neighbouring forests. It meant another hour had passed. Our lifespan was now an hour less. Our ages an hour more.

I ordered Pushpa to stand against the wrought iron railing and sing the naughty limericks I knew she had picked up from the village. Petrified, she sang, her voice gravelly and tuneless like much of folk music. I crept behind a pillar near the window and listened to Ma.

'I still think it was an accident,' Ma was saying.

Yuvraj Mama Sahib was looking at her closely. 'I have seen the corpse,' he said. 'It was not an accident. If it had been an accident his throat would have been ripped off. His throat had been slashed. Only his body was mauled.'

My mother chewed her lower lip. 'You can't be so sure. He could have wandered inside the zoo in a drunken haze. It is known to happen. Remember how, a few years ago, the elephant Bhoothnath trampled an inebriated mahout?'

He looked at her evenly. 'This man was a teetotaller. Didn't you know him? He wasn't a nobody. He was a patidar. His father was at the sirapawa ceremony last year. He was a young man, full of life. He had two small children. His wife applied henna on the Yuvrani's hands during our wedding. Have you forgotten?'

My mother absorbed this. 'Then who could it have been?' she asked lamely.

'He was a patidar, for god's sake! He had the blood of the family. But why am I saying this to you? You, who have had patidars whipped.'

My mother was indignant. 'I have never had them whipped! Really, Yuvraj, sometimes you say the damnedest things.'

'Why? This is not the first blood on Sirikot's hands. We've burned villages. We've decimated families. A hundred kilos of sacred brahmin thread lies buried under the Govinda temple.'

Ma was breathing heavily. She was agitated. 'That was political. That was necessary. Those were the casualties of battle, of the system. *This* is murder!'

Yuvraj Mama Sahib's eyes glittered angrily. 'Who knows what secrets these walls keep? Who knows who is the enemy?'

Though her jaw snapped into a hard pugnacious line, a vein in my mother's neck throbbed in giveaway nervousness. 'Why don't you find out? Why don't you investigate?' she said.

'I don't want to find out who is responsible,' he said, the immobility of his body eerie. 'It could be Baba, it could be Ma. It could be one of my brothers, or sisters.'

~

'Leela!' A sharp call jangled my nerves. Pushpa stopped her terrible singing mid-syllable. A hand fell lightly on my shoulders and I jumped out of my skin. Yuvrani Mami Sahib was standing behind me. So she hadn't retired to the zenana after all.

'Hasn't your mother taught you that it is bad manners to eavesdrop?'

Her whisper was a light breath in my ear, like a passing zephyr.

Two

Talk of the dead patidar filtered through the palace walls like spreading damp, escaping Ma's censorship and seeping into my ears. The death, like all other Sirikot gossip, had taken on the fantastical proportions of a folktale. I postponed my visit to the nursery to hear all that was being said in the zenana. The serving class yammered the most and I heard conspiracy theories of an evil plot against the ruling family and macabre stories of the patidar's ghost moving through the corridors at night holding his head in one hand and dragging his severed leg by the other. I heard that a renowned tantrik had predicted the death as a precursor to other deaths. 'Wrong, wrong, wrong,' he had said, touching his ears in expiation. I heard that the British were investigating the death and that Nana Sahib was locked up in consultation with them.

All other gossip had taken a backseat in the zenana. Over and over again, the poor dead patidar was talked to death.

The one person who was certain who the killer was, was Kumar Mama Sahib. 'It's the British,' he said with stubborn truculence. 'When in doubt, it's always the British.' He was visiting Ma *en famille* in Nani's chambers. Kumar Mama Sahib's wife, Kumud Mami Sahib, and his two large-eyed daughters greeted us and then everybody settled down to discuss the topic of the hour.

I knew relations between Kumar Mama Sahib and his wife weren't particularly cordial — I had rarely seen him visit his wife's chambers or speak to her. Not even when they were among informal company; not even when they were alone with their two young daughters who carried about them the air of stunned helplessness that children from broken homes have. They had come to visit us after dinner.

Nani had been unusually quiet since evening, when Ma and I had gone up to her room, and Dhaima, who had been sitting with her, had left hurriedly. Her daughter Shanti had not been around for the last two days. Perhaps she had been chastised for her impertinent look. She was way too hot-headed; her arrogance had to be curbed. Dhaima had actually named her 'Rajeshwari' meaning 'the one who rules' when she was born but Nani had found the name too presumptuous and re-christened her a more modest 'Shanti', meaning peace.

Nani sat shrouded in the darkness, only the deep gurgles of her hookah betraying her troubled thoughts. She had resisted all my mother's efforts to cajole her into conversation, finally warning her with uncharacteristic graveness that she was acting like a truculent child. Then Dhaima had returned with bowls of rose water and Ma and Nani lit up their cigarettes — held in ivory-handled cigarette holders — and immersed their feet in the cool rose water.

The evening sky was as if stained by the spillage of a giant inkpot. The evening breeze wafted up, perfumed by the jasmine blossoms of the zenani bagh. Plaintive tunes on the flute and the winsome melodies of the vas gharainis drifted up from Yuvrani Mami Sahib's chambers, which were adjacent to Nani's chambers in the great octagonal beehive we called the zenana. I'd relegated Pushpa to the task of giving me the exact number of stars in the sky.

When Kumud Mami Sahib came in my mother ordered an enamel bowl of rose water for her but she politely declined. 'I prefer doing my ablutions myself,' she said.

This was a direct hit at all the ruling ladies of the zenana. None of them bathed alone. They were helped with their bathing, brushing, oiling, scrubbing and combing by the vas gharianis.

My mother's reply was curt: 'I am not asking you to take a bath. I am just asking you to soak your feet, Kumud.' Since both Kumar Mama Sahib and Kumud Mami Sahib were younger than her they did not enjoy honorific suffixes.

'No, thank you,' she said again, her eyes downcast. Kumud Mami Sahib's wayward scent of old roses distracted me. I looked at her. She was trying hard to be still so that the nervous jangling of her bangles would stop. An odd kettle of fish, as Mrs Wood would say. Of Nepali and Himachali extraction, she was, I imagined, a mountain girl at heart. She had spent a few years in Europe. For a long time I had thought that was where she had got her peaches and cream complexion. But I was young then and did not know that it was also the colour of the Himalayan people.

I considered Kumud Mami Sahib the most beautiful among all my Mamis. She had an absent-minded air about her which I adored. It was so different from the canniness I saw all around me. She was vociferous in her protest of the purdah and had an embarrassing habit of making dire predictions about the end of monarchy in public. It had taken all of Nani's authority as a mother-in-law to put her in place. I liked her. She was a rebel, unlike Yuvrani Mami Sahib whose criticisms of Sirikot were vested in the interests of her husband. Kumud Mami Sahib wrote poetry and played the violin divinely. Whenever I wandered into her chambers she offered me revolutionary pamphlets written by freedom fighters. But she was the least popular of all my aunts. Some said the streak of insanity in her family had surfaced in her and she was capable of violent outbursts. I found this difficult to believe because though she had strong political convictions she was mostly mild mannered.

Perhaps it was in an attempt to steer the conversation away from a potentially dangerous moment between the sisters-in-law, that Kumar Mama Sahib had broached the topic of the patidar. 'It's the British,' he said again, trying to provoke Ma, drawing away her line of fire.

'Hah!' Ma snorted.

'But it has to be. He was a freedom fighter involved with the Bengal revolutionaries.' My uncle had beautiful fish-shaped eyes which clouded over in confusion when his older sister insinuated that he was a dunce who could only hold one idea in his head.

'So I've heard.' My mother was being deliberately vague, preoccupied. This could only mean two things. The first, that she hadn't heard but did not want to display her ignorance. The second, that she had heard but wanted to know more. My guess was the first.

'You do know there is a freedom struggle on?' Kumar Mama Sahib raised an eyebrow.

'Don't be rude,' Ma retorted. 'I believe in the freedom struggle as much as your wife does. I think Mahatma Gandhi is a true saint. I think Nehru is a charismatic leader and ... and ...'

'There you go roaring like paper tigers,' Nani interjected irritably. 'Let's put our own house in order first.'

But Ma was too impressed by her own nationalism to stop. 'And ...and... I believe in democracy!' she concluded lamely.

'Don't you think democracy will strike very close to home?' Kumud Mami Sahib probed.

'Why should it? Nana Sahib will continue to rule, but he will rule democratically. That cannot go away. We have been ruling for centuries. Even a democracy needs rulers. It will be a democracy, right? Not an anarchy?'

Kumar Mama Sahib suddenly looked very dejected. 'But they may require new types of rulers. Not rulers like us, but rulers like Nehru and Vallabhbhai Patel.'

'Nonsense,' Ma said, speaking with confidence about a subject beyond my comprehension. 'Rulers are rulers. They have no reason to disturb us. The Indian princely states have agreed to accede to the Indian dominion. It will be a peaceful transition.'

'Ma,' I asked, dangling my feet from a Chippendale couch, 'why are we called "princely states"? Isn't Nana Sahib a raja, a king?'

'There, you see!' Ma waved her hand towards me. 'It is independence for us too. For two hundred years we have been under British yoke, pledging allegiance to a king we have only seen in paintings. This is our country. This is *our* freedom too!' Ma was impassioned; in the mood for a state declaration. Nani's hookah grumbled on.

Kumar Mama Sahib, enthused by Ma's rhetoric, hoisted me onto his lap and squeezed me tight. But the next moment his shoulders flopped. He gave a belly-sigh, his stomach inflating like a tight pillow behind my back and rattling his chest until he exhaled slowly. 'Who knows what the winds of change might bring?'

'Well, I just think it was wrong of the British to kill the patidar in my backyard.' Nani was irritated for reasons entirely her own.

'And by the way,' Ma rounded on her brother. 'How do you know it was the British?'

'The estate manager said that the Collector had confessed to him that the patidar was getting too big for his boots,' said Kumar Mama Sahib finally managing to get across what he had been trying to say for some time. 'He was becoming a threat to their administration.'

'What administration?' Ma queried. 'They will be leaving this country soon.'

'You know what the Collector is like,' Kumar Mama Sahib shrugged. 'He doesn't really believe the British are leaving.'

'Thank god for one thing,' Ma said. 'At least that means there are no murderers inside the palace.'

'It's the curse,' Kumud Mami Sahib spoke up suddenly in the gentlest of tones. 'Every ruling family has a curse. The bloodline finishes after nine generations, or eighteen, or twenty-seven; always a multiple of the number nine.' Her tone thrilled her audience into a chilly stillness that only encouraged her to go on, making her give a little laugh and intone, as if in her sleep: 'Maybe that's the time it takes for the pot of sins to spill over. Nine generations, or in more righteous lineages, eighteen. Yuvraj Sahib will be the eighteenth ruler of Sirikot. The number nine is here. It means after Yuvraj Sahib, there will be nothing. The time has come.'

The courtyard was deathly quiet. A stray scent of jasmine blossoms caught the wind and made my spine tingle. I was spellbound. I couldn't take my eyes off Kumud Mami Sahib's face, aglow in the moonlight.

Pushpa was still counting the stars.

~

Ma granted me permission to stay in the nursery for a few days. The rooms were larger than those in the zenana and opened out onto gardens on all sides. There was a huge courtyard where the children could play. Posh bungalows for the English tutors, governesses and doctors flanked the garden's edge. When I reached the courtyard, Raghavendra, Yuvraj Mama Sahib's older son (Yuvraj-in-waiting, we called him) was perched inside a broken wheelbarrow. He was an obese child whose teeth had rotted from eating too many apples. He wore a yellow paper crown. Baby Uncle and Yogendra, Raghavendra's brother, were on all fours trying to drag the wheelbarrow and its contents around the courtyard. I assumed Raghavendra was playing Nero again.

'Come on, Black Horse!' Raghavendra said imperiously, poking Baby Uncle with the end of a broken stick. 'Come on, White Horse!' He prodded Yogendra, who was as emaciated as a street urchin.

When the three of them saw me they let out girlish yells, the sort only boys can make. 'The witch is here! The witch is here!'

Dakshyayani and my other girl cousins came out shrieking from a room. It was a surprise ambush in my aid. Arms crossed,

I held my ground as the boys circled me. I gave Baby Uncle the Steady Eye. He wavered guiltily and his look of confused betrayal was a moral victory for me. But then with a rallying war cry of 'Let's drown the witch!' I was dragged to the biggest canopied bed in the dormitory and bounced, hands and legs flailing, up and down on the spring mattresses. In the general hullabaloo it was not clear who was drowning whom and who was winning. Pandemonium prevailed.

Mrs Wood stopped us with a booming, '*Quiet!*'

After a sombre lecture punctuated with much glaring, Mrs Wood stood us along opposite walls, girls and boys confronting each other like two firing squads. We waited for Mrs Wood to leave the room and the moment she was out of sight Raghavendra started again. He twisted his hands so that only the stumps of his fingers were visible and showed them to us. I knew what he meant. He meant, 'You are lepers.' Not to be outdone we did the same from the opposite end of the room, making a few innovative faces as well, for good measure. Soon choice abuses breached the ranks.

'Daughter of a pig,' came a salvo.

'Grandfather of an owl,' went the retort.

'Communist,' Dakshyayani swore, using a newly heard word.

Mrs Wood walked in looking suitably aghast. 'Would you believe that these are the boys and girls of cultured families? I am extremely taken aback,' she said giving us the benefit of the sternest expression in her collection before striking home with: 'What is the difference between you and the gharianis' children?'

She had played her trump card. We looked at each other in genuine, but fleeting, contrition before she marched us off to an English dinner of mulligatawny soup, shepherd's pie, bread baked in the English kitchens, vegetable cutlets and caramel pudding.

~

In the dormitory, after dinner, Baby Uncle and I elected to lay down together on the largest canopied bed, with his dhai, Santoma, fanning us till we fell asleep. My eyes were beginning to dim as I watched the fireflies synchronize a neurotic dance around the mahua trees through the window. Baby Uncle was probably lying stock-still waiting for Santoma to leave because the moment she did he shook me furiously, annoying me no end.

'Quit that, Baby Uncle!' I said, turning on my side. 'Go to sleep, this is the hour of the ludbudiya ghost.'

'Leela,' he said in a hoarse whisper. 'Somebody is turning down the flame. The lamp is ready to go out.'

Immediately I froze, paralysed with fear, eyes wide open.

'Got you,' he giggled.

I was just reaching for my pillow to whack him when, with a flourish, Baby Uncle produced a torch which I suspect he reserved for just such occasions. He held the bright end under his chin to make his scary face. 'I'm ready to tell you my secrets,' he said.

I was immediately interested, because the way he was going on I knew it would be good.

'You know Yogi, the gardener boy?'

'Yes,' I said trying to remember him.

'He's my brother.'

'What?' The room, the whole world, spun around me.

'And he's not the only one. I have many brothers and sisters,' he said enigmatically; a saint espousing universal brotherhood.

'What are you talking about?'

'You know the vas gharianis in the palace? In the zenana and the mardana?'

'Yes? What about them?'

'Their relationship with Baba is the same as Ma's relationship with Baba.'

'You really are a crackpot!' I said hitting him on the head for his indiscretion. 'Nani is the Rani Sahiba of Sirikot, you idiot. How many Rani Sahibas of Sirikot are there?'

'Yes,' he said, shushing me down, speaking in whispers, 'there is only one rani — but that other part, the thing between man and woman, you know the sex thing, he has it with all the vas gharianis.' Then his forehead funneled in a suspicious frown, 'You do know about the sex thing, don't you?'

'Baby Uncle,' I said with the crushing certitude of an Absolute Truth. 'Whatever you know, remember, I know better.'

He was put out but curiosity got the better of him. 'Really? Who told you?'

'Yuvrani Mami Sahib,' I confessed. 'She took me into her chambers some years ago and showed me this really dirty book. You know she is very weird. She told me in great detail how she and Yuvraj Mama Sahib do it.'

'What did she say, what did she say?' He prickled with anticipation.

'About how they' — suddenly embarrassed, I pushed him away — 'I'm not going to tell you.'

Baby Uncle snickered in a wicked, mannish way. 'I know for a fact,' he said, 'that before Yuvraj Dada visits her he has all the linen changed. He sprinkles himself with holy ganga-jal afterwards. So if her description is too vivid, then you can safely presume her paramour is not Yuvraj Dada.'

'How mean, Baby Uncle!' I defended Yuvrani Mami Sahib. 'What a scandalmonger you have become. And who could her lover be?'

'The gardener, the tailor, the cook,' he shrugged. 'There is no dearth of males in the zenana. Do you know that most of the women in the zenana are so frustrated they get excited looking at a dog in heat?'

I looked askance at my uncle, convinced that since I had last met him, two years ago, he had grown into a bad boy with a wicked imagination. 'And why are you telling me sick stories about Nana Sahib? Your own father?'

'I'm sorry to disappoint you, Leela,' he said in a sarcastic, grown-up way, 'but what I said about Baba is a fact.'

At that moment I felt the first twinge of sadness that had, in all probability, been lying in wait for Baby Uncle and me all this while. Suddenly, at that moment I wanted Baby Uncle, the child, back. 'But why would he want to? He has Nani.'

'I know,' he said thoughtfully.

'Does Nani know?' I suddenly remembered, aghast.

'Of course she does.' He was growing impatient. Nani's knowing was a foregone conclusion. 'She's not bothered. It's something all rajas do. The women are only concubines, after all. This is just a duty they perform. It's the system.'

The system of course. The anomaly fell into place neatly. The world was in order again. I was relieved. 'So what's the problem? He's just doing what rajas are *supposed* to do. His father probably *asked* him to do it. It must be a state policy or something. It's not his fault.'

'No, it isn't.' Baby Uncle had grown bored with the topic now and turned away. Maybe to think, maybe to sleep, I couldn't tell. A distance had crept in between us. I knew it would be gone in the morning but I moved a few inches away from him.

'Baby Uncle?' I ventured after a while, speaking into the darkness without turning around.

'Yes.'

'Does that mean my father has concubines too?'

'He probably does,' he said.

I thought of my mother and squeezed my eyes shut.

'What happens to the children?'

'The vas gharianis who produce a daughter get better living quarters than the other servants. They don't do menial work like the others but continue serving the royal family, mostly in the zenana. They are the dhaimas. The ones who produce sons are the santomas.' Clearly, he had figured everything out: 'They get a house and land and are more respected than the dhaimas. They serve the sons of the royal family. Their sons, you know the ones they call the antars, get important positions among the staff. Some of them even attend court. Haven't you ever wondered at the term antar, so different from the santos and the patidars? Antar means bastard.'

He laughed in sudden glee, turned on his side and shook my shoulder. 'Do you know why my nurse is called Santoma? Because after one generation my family will become a santo, borderline royalty, till in a few generations, my family becomes a patidar, no longer technically royal at all! Get it? My nurse is called Santo-ma. She's playing mother to a potential santo!'

My spirits lifted, not quite comprehending the direness of his knowledge. All I understood from his playful tone was that Baby Uncle — the baby — was back. 'Oh, shut up,' I said happily, 'and go to sleep. Dream about all the concubines you'll get when you become raja.'

Baby Uncle sighed. 'You are such a duffer, Leela. Don't you understand? How can I ever be raja? I'm the fourth son.' Then he spoke again slowly, mockingly enunciating each word: 'My children, you haven't been listening,' he said with great satisfaction, 'are santos. They will end up as patidars.'

And having had the last word he fell sound asleep.

~

I stared at the darkness ahead of me. My family seemed to flit in and out of its shadows, full of reason and purpose beyond my understanding. They seemed taller, opaque, darkened by mystery and a hint of menace. For once, the fear of the ludbudiya ghost did not shut my eyes and slip me into oblivion. I have always suspected that the ludbudiya ghost was a product of the collective imagination of all my Mama Sahibs. The spirit of a quartered man, the ludbudiya is a headless, limbless torso. When he rolls up to you in the middle of the night, the place reeks with the stench of rotting flesh. He also shrieks as he rolls along.... This was the point we children, consumed by fright, always forgot to clarify. How does the ludbudiya ghost shriek if he has no head? But Kumar Mama Sahib had mastered the shriek to a practised finesse,

sending shivers down our spines during the ghost story telling
sessions. Tonight even the ludbudiya ghost paled before the
monotonous litany of one frightening thought: *Pushpa is my aunt.*

My eyes were wide open. My brain was a tangle of nerve
endings. I decided to go to the toilet. For that I needed to walk
down the corridor. It looked very dark from where I lay. I lifted
the heavy lamp by Baby Uncle's bedside and walked outside.
The fireflies were still doing their crazy dance. In the corridors,
the tallows on the walls had burnt low. My eyes burned from
lack of sleep.

Baby Uncle's nurse, Santoma, was sleeping on a mattress in
the corridor. She slept there at night in case a child getting up
at night needed her. There was a row of vas gharianis sleeping
farther down. I bent to wake her up.

'Jemma,' she said addressing me in local dialect as princess.
I had not even touched her. Her tone suggested alertness. I was
taken aback. Had she heard us speak? I thought we had been
whispering.

'I need to go to the toilet.'

She was on her feet in a trice. She took the heavy lamp
from my hands and we walked down the corridor side by side,
she stooping from her waist, a little distance away from me.
That is how the serving class walked alongside us. Stooping to
show they had no presumptions to be taller than us; a little
distance away so that their shadow did not fall on us. I gave her
a slant-eyed look. The lines in her cheeks looked deeper. Her
drooping lips gave her an evil countenance. My blood suddenly
ran cold.

By the time we reached the lavatory I was paralysed with
fear. The row of open thunder-boxes presented themselves to me
as if arrayed for terrible battle, like the gaping maws of the
severed heads of the ludbudiya ghost. 'Leave the door open,' I
said in a strangled voice.

'All right,' she said and sat down to wait by the door, the
lamp in her hand.

I sat on the thunder-box and heard my urine clink against the aluminium pan. I was urinating between the ludbudiya ghost on one side and an evil concubine on the other. I finished my business as fast as I could and fled back to bed.

Santoma tucked me in and massaged my forehead, her hands small and amazingly strong. 'You think too much, Leela Ma,' she whispered, her hands and voice sending me into a hypnotic trance. 'Birth is not chance. It is not coincidence. Birth is one's own choice created by the karmas of our past lives.'

~

The next morning I was in a foul temper without knowing why. I had booked the enamel bathtub with the golden tiger claws for my bath and when I reached there Baby Uncle was already splashing in the water with his clothes on while Santoma looked on indulgently. Because he was whooping in a moronic fashion, I tried to brain him with a brass mug.

He stumbled out of the bath and fled. I ran after him brandishing the mug in a way that genuinely frightened Baby Uncle. Santoma's hands had meanwhile flown to her face and she was trying to tell me something. I suddenly understood what she was saying. 'Jemma,' she was protesting. 'You are naked.'

I grabbed a towel and holding it in front of me with one hand continued giving chase.

The courtyard erupted in delight. My cousins split their sides looking at me. I turned around and realized what the problem was. My behind was completely exposed. Baby Uncle had collapsed on a swing, crying for joy. After summoning my clothes and my dignity I made my entry again a while later. My audience was exhausted with all that laughing.

For no particular reason I marched purposefully towards the fountain. A now quieter Baby Uncle fell in step with me.

Santoma followed.

'Don't follow me,' I spat at her. 'You old prostitute.'

Smiling, undeterred, her steps did not falter.

Further behind me Dakshyayani quizzed Raghavendra. 'What does prostitute mean?'

I turned around briefly to catch his expression of sagacity. 'It's somebody who sells carrots,' he told her.

As the oldest child in the nursery, the sudden burden of knowledge weighed heavy on me. I had read Charles Dickens and Munshi Premchand. I knew that outside the palace walls there was a remote but real possibility that the world was different. That other world haunted me by day the way the ludbudiya ghost haunted me in the palace at night. Instinctively I feared and respected the other world as much as I feared and respected the ludbudiya ghost. I sat on a grassy patch around the fountain and sulked.

'Remember what Mrs Wood says,' — Santoma was not placating me so much as exorcizing me — 'she says that fairies live in grass patches that are greener than the others.'

I had kept strict vigil on the greener patches throughout my childhood and had not seen one miserable fairy. But I was damned if I was going to tell her that. It annoyed me that she was unfazed by the magnitude of my insults. 'Shut up, you old fool. There are no fairies.'

'Look there's one,' Baby Uncle exclaimed but was immediately disappointed. 'No, only a rose petal.'

Considering that my exercise in offending Santoma was getting nowhere, I decided to sneak a look at the fairy thing anyway. I thought maybe today, upset as I was, a fairy might take pity on me and show herself. We all looked intently at the green grass for a while.

'They call him the Breeding Bull,' Santoma said finally.

'Who? Who is the Breeding Bull?' Baby Uncle fell for the bait.

'Raja Sahib. The Breeding Bull. The Mardand Sand,' Santoma intoned, sitting cross-legged, in the lullaby-singing position. Soon she held us riveted as she narrated the life of my Nana Sahib to us. She told us about his daily routine. I listened intently. For all the years I had spent in my grandfather's palace, I knew nothing of his daily routine.

My grandfather lived in the Chandramahala. That I knew. It was the set of rooms above the highest ramparts of the palace. I had heard it had a great view of Sirikot though I had never seen it. He woke up early, around seven o'clock, and started the day to the music of the shehnai. Then the vas gharianis brushed his teeth. After his morning ablutions, he went down to the Kund for his massage and bath.

'I have been there,' I said. 'I have heard laughter and the music of daphlis coming from deep within the wells. I had wanted to go nearer and investigate but the duwaris, the guards, never let me.' Baby Uncle pointed his beaky nose at me to show me he had had a similar experience.

'During his massage and bath,' Santoma giggled, 'he polishes off two vas gharianis.'

'During his massage, or during his bath?' Baby Uncle wanted to know. 'And two as in two together, or one after another?'

She tut-tutted and continued with Nana Sahib's itinerary. 'He is very fond of his masseur,' she said. 'Only yesterday he presented him a gold necklace.'

'That fond,' Baby Uncle noted.

'After his bath he goes to pay homage to his ancestors. He offers them tarpan everyday.' Santoma proudly confessed that it was her job alone to clean the puja items. 'He looks very handsome pouring water to the gods from the tamb patr,' she added affecting the coy way of the vas gharianis.

After the puja, she said, Nana Sahib had an English breakfast, details about which she could not give us, since it was not really her department. But that was a part of his day we were familiar with because we had breakfasted with him several times. He went from there to the durbar hall at eleven.

'You have seen the four gold thrones for his sons there? You do know that a santoma's son can never sit on his lap while he holds court?' Baby Uncle asked turning to me.

I knew now.

'Well, I've been sitting on his lap for a month,' Baby Uncle said proudly, announcing it like a rare accomplishment.

'Considering all his other sons are too old and heavy ...' I shut him up.

'In the afternoon he goes to the zenana,' Santoma continued. 'The rani is the first choice for his siesta. Whether the rani is willing or not, the raja polishes off an average of another two women in the afternoon. From four to eight or nine o'clock he stays in the durbar hall. I do not need to tell you how many schools and hospitals get built in those four hours.' She pronounced it like an admonishment. 'After durbar, his bathing ceremony lasts till nine when he polishes off two more vas gharianis.'

'That's six!' said Baby Uncle. 'He polishes off vas gharianis the way I polish off moti-choor laddus. What does he eat?' he exclaimed.

'Your father,' Santoma said, 'does not touch alcohol. In the morning he has a glass of thickened milk, garnished with almonds and some other ingredients I have never been able to discover ... well, then he has dinner in the harem. After dinner he visits the nursery. Then it's back in the harem where the first choice is again the rani. Depending on her mood he comes back to his quarters in the Chandramahala and —'

'— polishes off two more vas gharianis!' Baby Uncle and I chorused.

'You call him the Mardand Sand. The Breeding Bull?' I said, sickened. 'He sounds more like a dog in heat to me.'

'No, no,' — nothing would stop her from singing my grandfather's glory — 'he is the most virile man I have seen! I have known other men in my time but he is all Man. You do not know how women fight to spend a night with him. I have never known anybody like him. And I speak for all the vas gharianis. He is not like your Dada Sahib,'— she pointed to me — 'your paternal grandfather.'

'What's wrong with my Dada Sahib?' I was stung. 'I'm sure he can polish off as many vas gharianis as Nana Sahib can.'

'Your Dada Sahib,' she said with uncharacteristic anger, 'is a pervert. I know. I went with Badi Rajkumari, your mother, to her sasural with her dowry. I came back in two years. He is a sick man. He makes the vas gharianis look at filthy photographs. He has lewd paintings on his wall. He uses instruments. He is a lecherous and dirty man.'

Baby Uncle and I were silent. It was taking us a long time to understand the difference between the two men.

'Your Nana Sahib' — she tried to make us understand — 'serves us. Look at the number of families he has created. Look at the number of livelihoods that exist only because of him. Look at the number of antars in the court. Royal blood flows in them. He irrigates us like a gardener would irrigate his flowers. See the schools and —'

I got up to go. I'd had enough. I looked out one last time at the greener patch and knew the fairies were not turning up after all.

'Jemma Sahib,' Santoma called after me. 'Please don't take all this too much to heart. Concubinage is an age-old, god-blessed tradition. Do you know, one of your great-great-grandfathers was averse to concubinage and did not want to uphold what he considered a depraved practice? His wife, your great-great-grandmother, a wise and just queen, continuously tempted him with nubile and young girls till he relented.'

I shut my ears to her words and decided to go in and study Sanskrit. After all, the Sanskrit master had been waiting for me all day.

Three

It was rare for Nana Sahib to visit us in the nursery three nights in a row but we were too young to suspect his motives or look for reasons and looked forward to his visits as fervently as devotees to a darshan of god. When he sat among us we showered him with the unconditional adulation of the young. The memory of the time we spent together that spring has stayed with me, sharpened and made even more vivid by the events that were to follow.

For some unknown reason, a doll, an English clown, was wound up at night and placed strategically outside the nursery door. Whenever it was touched it would clap its hands and make a horrible din, enough to drown out the noisiest outpourings of children. When Nana Sahib visited us he would stand at the door and kick the toy. The ensuing racket was the herald that proclaimed he was with us, and we would burst forth with shouts of glee, in an uninhibited and rousing welcome.

I can still recall my grandfather, sitting amidst us, regaling us with the most perfect imitation of animal calls I have ever heard. We sat spellbound as he transformed himself into a peacock and then a hyena and then a roaring tiger. We clambered all over him in our excitement when he was done. Dakshyayani made plaits in his long hair. I ruffled his beard and ran away before he could catch me.

My standard exchange with Nana Sahib was the bridegroom game. 'What kind of bridegroom do you want, Leela Ma? A pink one or a green one?' My Nana Sahib would ask me.

I would think for a moment. 'This time I want a yellow one, with purple polka dots,' I would sparkle at him.

'What a bright little penny our Leela Ma is,' Nana Sahib would beam at me, all the while holding Baby Uncle firmly in his lap, as if not wanting to let him go.

One day, Malini, Kumar Mama Sahib's older daughter, fondled his moustache. 'Dada Sahib,' she said, 'your moustache is so hard, like wax.'

'That's because it is waxed, my little pigeon. You know what else, I can dangle lemons from it too.' And he beckoned to the vas gharianis who stood around wearing obedient smiles. Immediately one of them hurried out and, returning with two lemons, went about the intricate process of dangling them from his moustache. Nana Sahib made a great many faces to complement the look. We beat our fists against the cushions and beds in hysterical laughter at his antics. Suddenly Baby Uncle put his hand against Nana Sahib's cheek and exclaimed in shock, 'Baba, you are crying.'

All at once the laughter subsided. The nurses looked at each other worriedly. Nana Sahib held Baby Uncle close to him and kissed his forehead. His gesture brought up the bile of suspicion in me. Men in our families rarely made such public displays of affection. 'Don't be silly, bevakuf. These are tears of joy,' Nana Sahib said gruffly, wiping his eyes.

Baby Uncle's beaked nose drooped. 'No, Baba Sahib, you are sad.'

Nana Sahib hugged him tight and said, 'Don't blame me, child. What can I do? Our fates are sealed at birth.'

Baby Uncle looked up at him, cross-eyed in confusion.

The mood had changed in the room. The children were suddenly wide-eyed with anxiety and craned their necks to look up at the adults. Were they looking for answers or were they just manifestly bewildered? I don't know. But I do know that when grown-ups are anxious their eyes cloud over. When children are anxious their eyes widen and become a crystal-clear gaze. Like a doe's full frontal stare when caught unaware in the floodlight of a hunter's torch.

Nana Sahib asked for his harmonica. It was brought to him on a silver platter. He played 'Auld Lang Syne'. Some of us knew the lyrics of the song. Mrs Wood had taught us.

Dakshyayani started to cry. Irritated, Nana Sahib abruptly stopped playing, jarring the last note. He threw the harmonica on the bed and left. Malini wet herself. The vas gharianis attended to her while Mrs Wood tried to shush the rest of us down. A rash of complaints suddenly erupted across the room. A pall of gloom hung over us. As if we had just heard a story with a sad ending.

~

The next morning we met Nana Sahib for breakfast. We sat around him at the twenty-seater dining table and ate omelettes and chakli peethas fried lightly on a steaming hot tava. We had fried green peas and potatoes roasted in their skins. There was chutney and pomegranate juice, crackers and jam, butter and cream. There was toast and bread brought in from Calcutta and topped with Marmite. There were large silver glasses of milk and Horlicks which we had to drink perforce. There was no room for fussing today. Not in front of Nana Sahib.

As Nana Sahib's oldest grandchild I had the privilege of sitting immediately to his right. Usually Nana Sahib would have showered a major part of his attention on me. But not today. Today he was busy cutting his six-egg omelette into little pieces and placing them on Baby Uncle's plate. For Baby Uncle, receiving even a morsel from his father's plate was a moment of glory. A stab of jealousy twisted inside me. Children took precedence over grandchildren, I made note.

'I hope all of you have mastered the art of eating with forks and knives,' my grandfather said, his hawk eyes surveying us from under thick bushy eyebrows.

'Yes, we have,' we muttered as we fumbled with our cutlery. Liveried attendants stood behind us refilling our plates every time we finished a bite; my scowling at them did not help.

The waiting governesses and dhais were about to usher us out after breakfast when Nana Sahib insisted we join him in his courtyard, which adjoined the dining hall. We trooped out after him and soon got busy among ourselves, creating our usual ruckus while Nana Sahib settled down under a pipli-embroidered beach umbrella to go over his correspondence. His estate manager stood behind him with his head bowed, his hands folded behind his back.

'Huzur, there is an urgent matter regarding the death of the patidar.'

I pricked up my ears.

'We will discuss it later,' Nana Sahib said. It sounded like a firm evasion of the topic to me. 'I want to discuss the security committee today. Applications for new appointments have been passed without my seal...'

'No, no, no, huzur,' denied the ingratiating manager, his straggly moustache quivering with every vehement gesture of appeal. My grandfather listened calmly to what seemed like a bureaucratic oversight, but a botch-up nevertheless. And I lost the thread of their conversation.

Baby Uncle and I got busy admiring the view of Sirikot from the terrace. My jealousy was forgotten. I drank in the waving rice fields, the emerald orchards and the glistening ponds. It was so different from the view from the zenana. All we could see from there were the zenani bagh and the boundary walls of the palace. The trees and ponds looked minuscule from where

we stood, like the colours and lines in a map. Malini and I
walked to the verge and looked down the vertical drop of the
wall. A man was walking inside a door at the bottom of the
palace. Something white glinted in his hands. Squinting down
at him made me giddy.

'Not so close, Malini Ma,' Nana Sahib called out to my
cousin. 'You are too close to the edge.' He gave her dhai a sharp
look and she ran to fetch Malini.

The estate manager continued with his supplications. I suspect
it had reached a point where Nana Sahib was not even listening.
He was just sitting there, soaking in the balmy morning air.
Metal clanked in his private bathroom adjoining the courtyard.
The noise carried to us.

'What?' Nana Sahib started, betraying a jumpiness that was
quite alien to his nature. 'Oh, it's the mehtar,' he exhaled relaxing
visibly.

I looked at Nana Sahib very carefully. Beads of sweat dotted
his forehead. Why? I asked myself. These days the sun was at her
most compassionate, with just a hint of warmth at noontime;
there was no reason to sweat. My poor grandfather! I thought.
What burdens he must carry. What untold miseries he must
keep hidden from all of us so we continue thinking he is the
indefatigable, invincible raja. His imperious countenance
poignantly belied the sweat on his forehead. I remembered a
lesson Mrs Wood had read us about Damocles' sword. That is
how my grandfather looked to me that day. As if a sword hung
over his head by a horse's hair.

The mehtar went about his business in Nana Sahib's lavatory.
It was his job to replace the dirty pots with fresh ones, leaving
through a tunnel that opened out near the ground directly below
us. Before he left he would fill up water for the washbasin and
the silver spouted canisters placed on the left side of each thunder-
box. The water was for Nana Sahib's avdust. Avdust is the water
used for washing off excreta. Many westerners and even Indians
have remarked on this, asking why we have a term for such a

lowly act. I would imagine the term is a subliminal reminder that the left hand should not be used for any other activity. I heard in the zenana that the one time Nana Sahib severely castigated Mrs Wood was years ago when she was caught trying to teach his children how to use toilet paper. 'What's next, Mrs Wood,' he had apparently shouted. 'Will you be telling us to bury our dead? There are fundamental differences between us. You should know where your boundaries lie!'

When Yuvraj Mama Sahib had been studying in London he had complained bitterly – not of the weather or the people or the food, but of his inability to take avdust. 'The water is frozen in the morning. So I have the water heated and melted before it can be used for avdust. I can't bear it. I'm coming home,' he wrote.

Avdust had always been a hot topic of discussion between Baby Uncle and I. We had both concluded that if the English and we were so radically different in conducting the most fundamental ablutions how different we must be in, say, sexual intercourse.

'We don't kiss. They do,' Baby Uncle had pointed out.

'And how do you know?' I'd asked, aiming my dangerous query straight at him.

He remained unfazed. 'I've read the *Kama Sutra*. And I've read their books. They are kissers, we aren't. Leela, I've realized that with all their hoity-toitiness they have no sense of hygiene. They don't wash their mouths after meals. They don't clean their tongues while brushing.'

'No!' I demurred.

'Yes! They don't know what a tongue cleaner is.'

'No-o!'

'Yes! And sometimes they don't take a bath for months.'

'That couldn't be true!' I defended the English against such a preposterous accusation.

'Yes, it is. Haven't you read their books? They change their collars and wash their hands and feet. I always wondered why they changed collars. And then I realized they change collars because they never take a bath. It is to hide their scruffy necks!'

My hands flew to my face. 'And *these* are the people who have ruled us for three hundred years!'

'And all that kissing. Without even brushing properly, without a tongue cleaner!' Baby Uncle touched his ears making the sign of Shiva. 'Now you know why their colonization never worked. It is best for us to part ways,' he ended in a philosophical tone.

We looked down the verge again and our attention reverted to the mehtar. Peering down together, Baby Uncle was able to predict the exact time that the mehtar, having finished his job, would appear at the exit directly below us. 'Now,' he said, and a second later the mehtar crawled out, carrying chamber pots full of night-soil.

Pleased with his unerring acumen, Baby Uncle hopped to Nana Sahib's side. 'Baba Sahib,' he said, 'I have heard that the mehtar goes through your faeces looking for gold.'

'And why does he do that?' Nana Sahib was amused.

'Because they say a raja, because he is raja, does not shit like other humans. He shits gold.'

Nana Sahib patted Baby Uncle's head and gave a nasty laugh. He walked up to where I stood looking down at the mehtar collecting his white aluminium pans. 'I have a feeling they won't be thinking that for very long,' he said.

We all looked down together and the mehtar, perhaps because he subconsciously felt watched, looked up. Seeing Nana Sahib he fell prostrate on the ground in a long pranam. Above him Nana Sahib nodded.

I could see the muscles bunched together on the mehtar's shoulders. His dhoti was dirty and ragged; he wore it in the manner of the labour class, barely covering his knees. His calf muscles were on display, like meat in a butcher's shop. I was suddenly moved to pity. And puzzled by it. I saw many levels of cruelty in the palace every day. So why should a mehtar move me? Was it his humanity — because I knew that in the eyes of god we are all born equal? I think it was because the lowliest duties of the untouchable community were being performed not by a woman but by a handsome specimen of manhood.

At the undeveloped age of thirteen I knew that the female gender was more resilient than the male; she had an almost spiritual level of tolerance, far exceeding that of her counterpart. A social status such as this would diminish but not extinguish her. This man, I was sure, was already completely emasculated. He would soon wear the blank expression I had seen on the faces of the older mehtars. As if they had switched off from the task of living. Then I thought — when you spend the major part of your life looking at a person's shit, if your livelihood depended on cleaning it, it wouldn't be surprising if one day you start looking for gold in it.

My nagging sense of guilt was mitigated by the remembrance of the rajdhobis in the zenana. Some of them were also young men. Their job was to collect the used sanitary napkins of the ruling family women, clean them, press them and put them back. This accursed and unholy Greek God was not alone. There were others like him. When the oppression of one is quantified by the oppression of many it becomes just another social phenomenon.

Another radical thought reared its head. It's not as if the ruling family women couldn't afford to throw away the napkins. Why create an entire community to clean them? There were even separate dhobis for the soiled garments of the vas gharianis.

At the time I was too young to know the answers. I know them now. Such was the economics of untouchability. By creating a cleaning industry their status was maintained and reinforced.

Nana Sahib was a shrewd man. When I turned around I saw him looking at me. From his great height he placed his bejewelled hand on my head. 'The rajdhobis and rajmehtars do well for themselves. In comparison to others in their community, they are wealthier and landed. I wouldn't worry about them.'

I wondered whether he knew what I had been thinking. Could it be, my naïve mind thought, that one of the powers one gained when one became raja was the ability to read people's minds?

At that point, Baby Uncle, knowing his father was more kindly disposed to him than usual, decided to risk a boldly familiar question. 'Baba, do you really shit gold?' It was a genuine question. Baby Uncle was not being ingenuous.

Nana Sahib laughed and turned back to his chair. 'I've never thought about that. Maybe I should check next time.'

My glance strayed back to the ground. The mehtar was looking up straight at me, a black-eyed stare of pure venom. I stepped back as if hit by a poisonous dart.

Baby Uncle caught the visual exchange between us. 'Don't worry, Leela.' He set his chin, his babyish jaw bones contrasting oddly with his grim expression, 'I'll see to it that he gets whipped for that look.'

But the mehtar had gathered his pans and was lost in the foliage of trees.

'Let it be.' I was surprised to hear my own voice; it too sounded oddly grim. 'He looks beyond punishment to me.'

~

That evening an incident occurred which completelty transformed my early, girlish impression of Nana Sahib. For the first time I saw him not as my grandfather or even the raja. I saw him in his most primitive form, a male animal. Time has softened the shock of the moment. All these years have buried the memory under the rationality and weight of other memories. But when I dust off the accumulated nostalgia of that era and its people I cannot shake off the lingering disgust I'd felt when the event unfolded before me. As if I had, by accident, stumbled upon my grandfather with no clothes on.

All arrangements had been made in the courtyard outside the durbar hall for a drama troupe from Lucknow. The show

was to be open to a section of the public. The patidar in charge
of social affairs had even shifted the brocade curtains in the
durbar hall to the proscenium.

'He'll have hell to pay tomorrow. Today everybody is too
excited,' Raghavendra had noted gravely.

I had seen the patidar-in-charge in the corridors flirting with
the excited vas gharianis. He was in his element, drinking in the
attention lavished on him, raving about the fashionable women
in the troupe and promising the vas gharianis foreign liquor
after the drama was over. Then he became even bolder. 'And
then I will take all of you for a motor ride in the Vaitary forests.'

I thought the vas gharianis would swoon in ecstasy. Some of
them were affected enough to carry smelling salts, the way Ma
and Nani did. And I had even caught them complaining about
the heat and flies in the manner of my mother and grandmother.

I dressed with care that evening, favouring a pink embroidered
sharara and begged Ma for some of the make-up she had bought
from the catalogues of *Vogue*. That would show the fashionable
girls of the troupe, I thought. My pleading was to no avail. I was
informed I was too young.

'Do you want the village girls to think that the daughter of
the rajkumari is a country bumpkin?' I railed, distraught. Tears
rolled down my eyes ruining the carefully applied kohl. 'The
shringari dresses your hair for two hours. And I can't wear some
lipstick?'

'No,' Ma was firm in that stubborn way of hers.

Dhaima was clasping thick gold payals around Ma's ankles.
And here I was begging not to look like a street urchin. The
unfairness of the system loomed in front of me, unbearably
large. I hated her. 'You are an evil stepmother.' The cry came
from the depths of anguish.

My mother, impatient to be ready and on her way, relented.
Just when we had reached a compromise on a touch of lipstick
and some rouge on my cheeks, Shanti entered. She had reappeared
in the zenana, back as Ma's attendant, after a few days of sulking.

And though the serving class was not supposed to look us in the face while speaking to us, she would now sometimes stare back in direct insolence. A tiny tic acted up in the sides of her mouth whenever she spoke. I tried to punish her with some of my own masterpieces from the withering looks department, not that she ever noticed. For once she looked animated. Her eyes shone. 'Phulwati has arrived first for the drama,' she said knowing she had delivered a masterful blow.

'What?' Ma flared. She peeled Dhaima's fingers off her pallu and stormed out of the room, the chiffon in her sari rustling in delicate protest. Entering Nani's room, she kicked aside the yards of unfolded sari that my grandmother was about to be draped in and confronted her. 'Ma, I've been warning you for such a long time! Baba has lost complete control of his harem!' she shouted and then repeated what Shanti had told her.

Nani's make-up looked really awful to me. Her sallow complexion was chalky under gobs of face powder. I wondered whether the vas gharianis had made her up funny on purpose, to show Nana Sahib how old and ugly Nani was compared to them. But Nani stared at Ma in a dignity so quiet it calmed my mother. 'Let it be, Munna Ma,' she said. 'She's just the current favourite. They are so young. It goes to their head.'

'But, Ma, how can she arrive at a public function before the rani?' My mother protested in confusion.

'It's fine, Munna Ma, don't bother about these little things. She's probably heard that Raja Sahib and I are not sharing the marital bed any more. It's given her a bloated head, poor thing. Just like Raja Sahib's last favourite, who accompanied him to Delhi for his meeting at the Chamber of Princes. She threw such tantrums in the hotel, flinging plates at bearers and things, that it didn't take him long to get rid of her.'

Nani's calmness showed her vast experience in concubinage. The wisdom of her acceptance lent an unearthly sheen to her face. It was a serene glow, which the chalkiness of her face powder could not take away. 'We will go for the drama performance, and

I will not allow any scenes.' Nani spoke to my mother in exactly
the same tone that my mother had used with me a few moments
ago.

The excited throng outside the theatre was being kept at bay
by stick-weilding duwaris. I could hear the tinkle of ghungroos
behind the proscenium curtain. The troupe was ready to perform.
A few patidars and managers and the patidar-in-charge were
flitting about the aisle whispering last minute instructions. The
front row, of silver chairs upholstered in maroon satin, was empty,
waiting to be occupied by the ruling family.

There she sat in the second row, with a companion. There
was no mistaking her even though I was seeing her for the first
time. A young girl, barely in her twenties, with sly eyes and a
winning smile. At least she did not have the temerity to sit in
the first row, I thought. She had the courtesy to stand up and
pranam Nani, Ma and me. She was tall, much taller than Nani.
The face of a nymph and the body of a goddess, I noted. The
small muscles of her shoulders rippled under her silk blouse.
And though she wore her sari to show off her body to full
advantage, it was clear that, not too long ago, she had been
accustomed to hard physical labour.

Then my mother gasped. I followed the direction of her
gaze. It had fallen on the gold karghani around Phulwati's
waist. It was exactly like the one Nani had gifted to Yuvrani
Mami Sahib. This was sacrilege! I looked at her feet, and then
I gasped too. She was wearing gold payals. It was an unwritten
law that only blue-blooded women could wear gold on their
feet. The vas gharianis wore a lot of jewellery, but it was mostly
silver.

As if the gold karghani made in the design of the royal
daughter-in-law was not revolt enough! I ground my teeth in
anger and sympathy for Nani. I looked at my mother, a picture
of darkly seething dignity. She waited for Nani to take her chair
and then followed suit. We all sat down, one by one, in order
of seniority. Pushpa sat at my feet.

Once we were seated, the public was released from the tight cordon of lathis. After the throng had settled in and the noise had died down, the drama began. The songs, the skits, the music and the dance were a rousing call for freedom and the liberation of the motherland. Fidgety under the prickle of silver embroidery and face powder I could not follow nor appreciate the subtler nuances of the drama.

Suddenly, Nana Sahib entered the courtyard, like a character making an entry in a play. His face was livid. He covered the aisle in a few giant strides, his silk sherwani flapping against his knees. His strides were so long that from where I sat I could see the inner seam of his pyjamas and the pyjama string between his legs. All of us cringed instinctively as he loped towards us, his face red with coagulated rage.

But he didn't even look at us. He stood in front of Kumud Mami Sahib, who cowered before him, and reached a hand behind her to grab a fistful of Phulwati's hair. Like a rat dragged out of its hole by the tail. Phulwati stood up squealing in pain.

Chairs scattered about him. The music in the drama stopped. The performers stood rooted to the spot in a tableau of mortified silence. Nana Sahib pulled Phulwati out and then tossed her to the ground where she lay at his feet, whimpering as he rained blows on her. 'You dare appear at a social function before the rani? You think you take precedence over the rani?' Nana Sahib kicked Phulwati's supine body with his pointed sandals and she screamed with every blow. Her body writhed and contorted. My initial gloating at her plight gave way to pity and shock at Nana Sahib's unrestrained violence.

'Mercy!' Phulwati screamed as if she was being slaughtered. 'Mercy! O Lord, mercy!'

Nana Sahib raised his hand, his eyelashes fanning out under the strain of his widened eyes. He looked around him as if searching for a stick or something hard to beat her with. Then Nani got up and caught his hand. The public, the drama troupe and the women of the zenana looked on, mesmerized by the real-life drama unfolding before them.

'Raja Sahib,' Nani said quietly. 'She's only a child.'

Maybe it was the chilling quietness of her tone or just the restraining hand of his wife that stopped him. He let his hand drop to his side. He was breathing heavily. But Nana Sahib was not done yet. 'These women,' he screamed, pointing a ramrod finger at the crumpled girl. 'They become my favourite for two days, wear a few jewels and develop the airs of a rani.'

A dance performer tried to sidle up to the side of the proscenium for a better view. The ghungroos on his feet betrayed his movement and he froze in his spot. Nobody dared disturb the dramatic tableau. My mother was now also by Nana Sahib's side making placatory noises. They were turning away to leave when Nana Sahib turned round to shoot his last volley of abuse. 'I piss everywhere,' he raged. 'That does not mean where I piss is important.'

Nana Sahib, Nani and Ma walked out of the courtyard. Everybody else followed suit. The crowd dispersed whispering furiously. I glanced around looking for Pushpa but she was nowhere to be seen. Probably hiding behind Dhaima somewhere, I thought. I remained seated on my chair beside the fallen girl, horrified by Nana Sahib's last statement. He had reduced Phulwati to a piss pot!

Phulwati lifted her shoulders off the floor, her contorted face partially visible behind wet strands of hair. 'You old debauch!' she spat at the long-gone Nana Sahib. 'All it takes is a little poison in your milk.'

'Oh, really?' I said getting up from my chair, feeling dainty and imperious in my pink embroidered sharara. 'Then who will buy you gold karghanis?' I flashed my fakest bright smile and added — 'Memsahib Phulwati!'

I knew her eyes followed me as I flounced off to find Pushpa. A few paces from the exit I turned to sneak a look at her. She was still half-raised from the floor, her eyes black coals. Her lips twisted in a bitter smile.

Four

Holi was finally upon us, arriving amidst much fanfare, like a state guest. After all that waiting and preparation, Sirikot succumbed readily to the need for a climactic celebration. It was time for abandon.

The zenana resounded with village women singing their guttural songs as vas gharianis flitted about like nectar-sick butterflies, skirts swirling in a dizzy dance to their rustic tunes. The chameli-entwined swings on the boughs of the zenani bagh trees were in perpetual motion. The gardens seemed to have gone mad with colour. Dining tables groaned under the weight of new dishes. Stomachs were sick and heavy with sweets. Coloured drinks were passed around, quenching some thirsts and slaking others. Coloured water flowed from fountains. Heaps of coloured powder waited in the courtyard. Brass water pistons were kept on the ready. Curd waited in tubs to be dyed with gulal and smeared on willing faces. Soon the revelries would begin. Each of us would be dunked, sprayed and smeared in colour by our friends and loved ones. An unstained face would be a sad face. Today all was forgiven. Today it would be the primary colours of love.

I was done with my filial duties. As quickly as I could, I had bowed before my elders with folded hands and anointed their

feet with colour. After much cajoling I'd even grudgingly touched
Baby Uncle's feet and addressed him as Uday Mama Sahib in
an ungracious mutter. Then I'd concentrated on counting my
hoard of gifts. Nani had gifted me a mango orchard. Nana Sahib
presented me with a bazaar. Ma gave me a necklace and earring
set of kundan diamonds. Yuvrani Mami Sahib had parted with
a ruby ring, Kumud Mami Sahib gave me a book of Aurobindo's
poetry. And Baby Uncle gave me a dunk in the fountain.

The revelry at Holi always came with a subtle sexual undertow
to the merry-making. Maids and duwaris dressed as Radha and
Krishna made fools of themselves acting out the ras lila — the
Lord's love play. Nana Sahib sat on a marble chair in the middle
of the courtyard. An attendant filled his mouth with coloured
water which he spat out on the screeching vas gharianis. A subdued
Phulwati was among them. This was one of the rare occasions
that allowed him a public show of affection for his concubines.

Earlier, in Nani's quarters, during a mock water fight, I'd
watched Nana Sahib make a grab for Nani's hand but she'd sped
away, her clothes clinging to her body, seeming amazingly light
on her feet. I saw my grandfather smile at her and bestow a look
of such fondness, it could only have come from the shared
sweetness of a difficult and long life. But when he drew her close
to him, I saw that my grandmother's face was stony under the
caking Holi smears. 'What is it, Rani?' He lifted her chin and
asked her with great tenderness.

'We can never be good spouses, Raja Sahib,' she had replied
stiffly, 'if we cannot be good parents.'

Yuvraj Mama Sahib could not allow his younger brother's
wife to touch his feet because of the system of purdah between
them. He gave his blessings to Kumud Mami Sahib without
looking at her face. But there was no customary purdah between
his wife, the yuvrani, and his younger brother, Kumar Mama
Sahib, her devar. The two took full advantage of the leniency of
this custom. He carried the full-bodied and not unwilling Yuvrani
Mami Sahib for a dunk in the fountain. Their clothes clung to

their skins. Every line of his shoulders was visible under his stained white kurta; every curve under her bodice. They disappeared for several seconds under water, their clothes bubbling up to the surface. I caught a glimpse of a bare watery leg but nobody else cared. A married woman was allowed a little flirtation with her devar on Holi day.

I have always wondered at this custom. It was years later that I pieced together its logic: though purdah is prevalent in many communities, it is most stringently observed among the Rajputs. More so, among the Rajputs of the western frontier where war and therefore interaction with Muslims was more frequent. Purdah is not a Rajput custom but acquired from Islam. This came as a shock to me when I learnt of it, but the logic is unbeatable. In warring communities, like those of Muslim invaders, womenfolk are more susceptible to the 'foreign eye' and must be kept away both from invading males and other males of their own community who might take advantage of an absent warrior husband.

No wonder the Rajputs adopted this custom as a relevant and necessary one. An elder brother is kept away from his younger brother's wife because she may be younger and therefore prettier than his own. His wife, though, is allowed some latitude with his younger brother because in all possibility she is older and probably harbours maternal feelings for him. A little harmless flirtation would not go beyond releasing a little sexual tension.

If that was what Kumar Mama Sahib and Yuvrani Mami Sahib were doing under the surface of the fountain water, I thought, they were doing it well. I could sense that same release in the scores of men who had suddenly appeared in the zenana. For this one day the zenana was not out of bounds. Men entered as if the gates of heaven had opened to them, their faces black with congealing colour, their bodies straining from a denied emotion I could not understand. I saw a vas ghariani wrapped around a palace guard behind a pillar. I even saw a couple atop the branches of a tree! Chasing, grasping, clawing, grabbing

hands and running feet, blurred in high velocities of movement.
A cook lay groaning in a suspicious looking puddle with his
dhoti undone in a psychedelic haze of bhang-induced
intoxication. Bhang — the leaves and flower tops of cannabis —
was added to food and drink like salt and sugar that day. Though
the children were not allowed to eat it, even Ma had bhang. In
the collective grip of the despotic God of Bacchanalia, bhang
altered minds and freed them from the shackles of quotidian
existence. Surrendering to a primitive but final delirium of
celebration, the palace hallucinated, wept, laughed, dreamt,
rambled, fought, in the deluded insanity of a Holi afternoon.

Only peripherally aware of the intricacies of adult merry-
making, I was among a band of children who sprayed, caught,
scratched, and ran after each other like happy whelps of hyenas
after a small kill. Screeching at and chasing each other we found
ourselves in the gardens bordering the mardana and the nursery.
The delineations of status had broken down among us. Levelled
out by celebration, we did not distinguish between royalty and
the servants.

A strong hand dragged me under the water spouting from
a stone dolphin on a small promontory. The hand held fast
while I spluttered and spat under the heavy cascade of the
dolphin's spume. When I finally shook myself free I tried to
gasp, laugh and open my eyes from under dripping eyelashes. I
shook my hair and looked at my playful offender. He was older
than I, probably sixteen. He had curly black hair. The mask of
colour on his face could not hide his chiselled features. Beneath
the wide swathe of a green fingerprint on his cheekbone I saw
fair skin. He looked as if he had walked out of an oil painting.
His eyes were fixed on me. Then Baby Uncle was between us,
breaking our mutual gaze, and the spell.

'And who is this?' I asked him gesturing at the youth in
casual disdain.

'Oh, him? Syce — the stable boy,' Baby Uncle said, before
loping after a cook's daughter.

We were left alone again.

The stable boy reached out a finger and touched my wet cheek. For many nights after, I stayed awake agonizing over how my cheek must have felt to his touch. Even now, when I allow myself — and I often do — I can recall with shameful clarity the feel of his firm hand brushing my face. That day, I shivered. His face was so close, his look so intense, it burned right through my body.

'I dream that one day I will marry a princess like you.'

When I opened my mouth to speak he was gone. I was alone now, standing foolishly, looking after him, my hair dripping wet, my face painted like a monkey, my gut churning slowly like fresh butter, hurting me with every turn. That was one of the few times — perhaps even the only time — I truly felt like a princess. Just as suddenly a thought hit me between my eyebrows and I was smitten with horror. I sank down on the stone steps near the waterfall. They felt cold, like a tombstone. There was no denying the bitter voice of reason. *Oh god!* I thought, *what if he's my grandfather's son?*

Sirikot was in the interiors of the eastern frontier. The local population had dark skin and fleshy features. Chiselled features and a fair complexion ran strongly in the ruling family and in some brahmins. A few days ago Baby Uncle had told me that it was sometimes considered a proof of paternity. If he was not Nana Sahib's son he could well be the bastard child of any of my Mama Sahibs, or even the sinful fruit of Yuvrani Mami Sahib, her promiscuity, to my imaginative mind, now an open secret. And any product of these unions would not get legitimacy under any law. He would have to be abandoned.

The inexorable laws of fate closed in on me like garden walls. Shame and guilt were rubber bands contracting my body. I walked back to the zenana, alone, shivering.

~

The Holi durbar convened in the evening. It was a solemn affair with a subdued show of regalia. People moved slowly, still heavy with the after-effects of the morning's carousing and bhang. They were washed and scrubbed and consciously overdressed. Overdressing was an important norm, its extent decided by the exigencies of status. Dressing up more than the raja would be an insult to him; underdressing would be an insult to oneself. Nana Sahib sat resplendent on his gold throne with a plumed aigrette on his turban — the mark of kingship. Baby Uncle was perched on Nana Sahib's lap wearing the unctuous expression of a spoilt cat resting on a silk cushion. My older uncles sat, moustaches a-bristle, on either side of their father, on their smaller gold thrones, their shoulders held broadly, their hands resting lightly on the arms of their thrones, one foot raised on a cushioned foot-stool. They sat under richly embroidered chhatris or parasols while behind them impassive servants swirled peacock feather fans with unflagging motion. The potency of their combined masculinity was increased not only by their elevation from the floor but also by the presence of the smaller landowners and zamindars, all milling to pay homage to the Raja of Sirikot.

Behind Nana Sahib were platters bearing gifts covered with silver-embroidered yellow silk. A paan leaf with an areca nut and coloured abir powder was placed on top of the gifts. The womenfolk thronged the balconies and terraceways that led out of the mardana into the halls and stairs and met in a courtyard and a garden back in the zenana. The women of the ruling family sat on chairs with the best vantage to the thrones. Seated among them I peered at the gathering through the bamboo curtains fixed in front of us to protect us from roving eyes. I could see the colours of Holi still trapped in the French glass beads on the walls and the glinting chandeliers and in the overlooked, tricky-to-spot region behind the courtiers' ears.

The men came up the stairs one by one to pay tribute or nazar to Nana Sahib. They anointed his feet (conspicuously placed on a foot-stool for the purpose) with coloured abir and handed

him a silver guinea, the symbol of allegiance. They pranamed
Nana Sahib and received his gifts. There was much hand folding,
there was much dye still trapped under fingernails, there was
much tittering and commenting from the balconies.

After all the rules and norms of politics were conducted and
observed in accordance with the prescribed decorum of durbar
etiquette Nana Sahib began his speech. At the time, I was sitting
on the edge of my seat, my hands tracing the pattern on the
railing, fidgeting restlessly. I remember only the drone of Nana
Sahib's stentorian voice and Baby Uncle's bleary eyes as he strained
to stay awake.

'People of Sirikot, friends, esteemed neighbours and relations,'
my grandfather began. 'We are gathered here on a joyous occasion.
But this year I feel differently about Holi. I feel, we are poised
on the eve of another, much bigger, celebration. The celebration
of the freedom of our motherland.

'Many doomsayers say that this will never happen. We will
never shake off foreign yoke. Many do not want it to happen.
Many believe that the English are a necessary evil for the
continuation of our way of life; they deem them imperative for
the survival of monarchy.

'I say that they are wrong. I say that monarchy will always
survive. Because all political systems follow intrinsically the tenets
of monarchy.

'What is the most fundamental tenet of monarchy? The
most fundamental tenet of monarchy is the ability to rule.
Whatever the political system be, there will always be rulers. A
political system without rulers is anarchy. We all know that anarchy
is not a viable political system advisable for any community in
the world.

'We are safe. The monarchy is safe. But my fellow rajas and
rulers and zamindars, all of them, in every generation, must
look at the changing face of the times and decide to adopt what
is best for them. Unwillingness to change is the readiness to
perish.

'Democracy is a new word, used more and more frequently these days. Freedom fighters like Nehru and Mahatma Gandhi use it. Do not be scared of this word. Make it your friend. Soon it will serve your purpose. Democracy will free us of the English. The English have used us for too long. They have kept us tied to their purse strings with silken threads. We have been puppets to their throne. Fighting for their gun-salutes. What is a gun-salute but a consolation toy that the English have given to Indian rajas to fight over, while they busy themselves leaving their footprint over the face of Mother India?

'Sirikot is not a "Ruling Chief". The British denied us the title because we refused them a hundred elephants to quell an uprising in a neighbouring state. And I am glad. We do not need a title that is worth only a hundred elephants and treachery towards our neighbours. Sirikot rajas have been carrying our hereditary title for seventeen generations. And we will continue for another seventeen. We are not scared of the whispers we hear around us. Whispers of a new disease called Communism. This disease became an epidemic in Russia. We must watch out for it, pluck it out root and branch when we see it. These elements exist in India too, yes, even in Sirikot. Communists are strange irrational creatures. They want to grab and rape the land we have nurtured for centuries. To this ungodly evil I have only this to say, "I am not afraid."

'We are Rajputs. We are warriors. We know how to fight even ideological dacoits. They cannot hurt even a hair on my child's head. If god didn't want us to be rajas he would have seen that we were born as peasants. But he didn't. He saw to it that rajas were born. That is why my sons were born. That is why my sons' sons were born.

'Do not be scared of democracy. Remember, Nehru and Mahatma Gandhi are people like us. They are rulers. The rulers of democracy. In fact, every great freedom fighter, every revolutionary, every shaheed — from Bhagat Singh to

Chandrashekhar Azad — is a true Rajput. Like us they are true warriors! Like us they are true rajas!

'So on this auspicious Holi let us raise the war cry for freedom.'

And with Nana Sahib leading, the durbar followed in chorus:

'Jai freedom of the motherland!'

'Jai democracy!'

And lastly, and most poignantly, 'Jai monarchy!'

The uproar shook me out of an unearthly stupor as I trod between dream and wakefulness, my thoughts with a multicoloured stable boy who walked through a garden of white flowers.

When the noise died down, a white-haired elder got up from his chair and addressed Nana Sahib. He bent low in a long pranam that was exaggerated enough to make it insolent. His face was pitted with small pox and wrinkles crowded the rest of his visage. 'Pitamber,' someone in the crowd whispered in an involuntary introduction and I heard a feminine suspiration of fear in response. I had heard the name before. He was the bastard son of Nana Sahib's grandfather. An antar of renown, he was known for his vicious hatred of the ruling family. Now he waited for Nana Sahib to give him permission to speak.

'Speak,' Nana Sahib said finally, with equally exaggerated imperiousness, a master permitting his dogs to eat.

When Pitamber spoke, his words were twisted and sardonic: 'Normally, I would not bother His Esteemed Person with irrelevant questions, considering how well the administration of Sirikot is handled. But, of late, there have been rumours about the death of a patidar, a close friend of many. It is important to dispel these rumours, to put the doubting minds of Sirikot at rest.'

'And what are the rumours, Pitamber?' Nana Sahib's beard moved to accommodate his chin as his head sank into his chest. His thick brows were furrowed. I thought, this is how Blackbeard, the pirate of the high seas, would have looked.

'The rumours are,' Pitamber ground out his words slowly to fuel the suspense, 'that the orders to kill the patidar came from inside the palace.'

Immediately, the durbar broke into a buzz of agitated whispering. Furious hums rose and fell like the delicate movements of a symphony.

The patidar's death was three or four weeks old. The dust had almost settled. Even his ghost didn't feel like a concrete presence in the halls and corridors any more. Why was Pitamber bringing this up now? Had he deliberately waited for a full Holi durbar to put his cat among the pigeons? Nana Sahib's silence made me suddenly alert and very scared.

The chief of security separated himself from the whispers. He raised his voice so that it could be heard above the din: 'I submit before the durbar,' he said loudly, 'the full report that has already been presented to the Esteemed Personage of the Raja Sahib of Sirikot.'

'Let him speak!' Nana Sahib roared as the crowd broke into furious whispering once again. The crowd fell silent. Not once had Pitamber taken his slanted gaze from Nana Sahib.

'The patidar,' the chief of security said in a loud, clear voice, 'was a confused man. His head had been turned by strange and conflicting philosophies. We know for sure that he had joined a ragged band of brigands in Calcutta. They call themselves soldiers of the Indian National Army. They espouse a doctrine that goes against everything the English believe in. That includes monarchy and the ancient traditions of zamindari. I knew him. He did not even believe in the freedom cause of Nehru and Gandhi. He was a young man whose blood was hot. He had totally defected to the other side. I know for sure that he and his gang of followers were involved in looting and plundering the houses of some English Lords in Calcutta. He was a thorn in the side of the English and they were planning to remove him. He had no love for Sirikot. Whenever he was here from the city he was known to make incendiary comments about the ruling family. He was also involved in the land squatters' uprising two years ago.

'But I also know that though he had been a constant nuisance for the Sirikot administration, he never overstepped the mark.

He still had some respect for the ruling family. He still believed in god, whatever his Communist teachers may have taught him.

'I knew him personally. He presented no real danger to the royal family. So why should anybody within the palace want to get rid of him? It was the English he was after. It was the English who were after him. They slit his throat and threw him to the cheetahs in the Raja Sahib's zoo to deflect attention from themselves. The English Collector Sahib was heard to publicly announce that, finally, a big headache had been taken care of.

'The case was closed three weeks ago. I wonder at my Esteemed Brother's intention in raking up this subject now, on such an auspicious occasion,' the chief of security concluded.

I scanned the durbar for white faces. There were none. In fact, the absence of a British presence on a formal occasion such as this was conspicuous and irregular. The chief of security looked at Pitamber, waiting for his rebuttal.

Pitamber, who had not once taken his eyes off Nana Sahib's distant figure perched above, spoke as if he had been waiting for a long time to say what he was about to say: 'Then let me give you the results of my own observations. When I spoke to the patidar's widow she was distraught but still in full capacity of her senses. She told me that, two days before the patidar's murder, four men in black cloaks had come to the house. Their faces were wrapped in the cloth of their turbans. One face was unravelled in the ensuing scuffle and she chanced to see it. That face belonged to a palace duwari.'

The entire durbar broke into agitation, weighing the value of Pitamber's words. But Nana Sahib did not move. He didn't even turn his head; he kept looking straight in front of him, like the blind King Dhritrashtra when the drama of the Mahabharata unfolded in his court.

Then Kumar Mama Sahib was up on his feet and shouting 'Pitamber!' warning the enemy, as once Nana Sahib must have warned Pitamber's father when he was young: 'Before you speak, assess the magnitude of your words! You dare take the words of

a mindless widow to cast aspersions at the palace! How can she
be so sure that it was a palace duwari? How many times has his
widow even been to the palace? It was night. The invaders were
hooded. How can she be certain of what she saw? Unless what
she saw is what she wanted to see. We all know of Pitamber's
hatred for the royal family. Maybe he paid her to see what she
wanted to see.'

The chief of security broke into a nervous laugh. But a few
voices were joining in the dissent. The timbre and decibel of
their collective tone rose like the rumble of an imminent storm.

'Raja Sahib,' a voice separated from the crowd. 'Settle this
dispute once and for all.' The voice found a face, visible to all
now — a big moustache and honest clear eyes. 'Bring the widow
in for questioning.'

'This is a serious allegation.' A high soprano from the back.

'A raja is not above the law.'

'A raja is responsible to his people.'

'If this is a palace conspiracy against a poor patidar the
palace should remove the stain of doubt.'

'It should clear its name.'

'Other patidars could be next.'

'The patidar disappeared two days before his murder.'

'Where was he?'

'The palace must clear its name.'

'Pitamber is not alone. The rumours are everywhere. All of
Sirikot is talking.'

Words came up from different ends of the durbar like the
rehearsed lines of a chorus. A group of dissenters could be
identified now. They seemed to share a common purpose, as if
bonded by a secret. They confronted the throne with an air of
defiance. Pitamber stood out from them, diminutive in height,
but large in his single-mindedness, carrying his animosity like an
unwieldy weapon, his face contorted in hate.

My Mama Sahibs were arguing with the dissenting voices.
Even Baby Uncle looked like he wanted to speak. The durbar

had become a verbal battlefield. No individual words could be distinguished any more; only the incoherent babble of infernal noise.

'There is more!' Pitamber shouted to raise his voice above the din, his throat throbbing from the volley of his words. 'Junta of Sirikot, there is more!' He paused dramatically to pull the audience into a vortex of suspense.

My Mama Sahibs no longer sat with one leg languorously resting on their foot-stools. Their feet were planted on the velvet carpets on the floor, ready to spring up at a moment's notice. Only Baby Uncle's eyes betrayed the fear they all must have been feeling. He looked what he was — a scared eleven-year-old boy. A palace murder did not augur well for the family in this politically fraught time, more especially the murder of a patidar.

Patidars were strange animals. Neither royal nor common, they seemed genetically wired to foment trouble on both sides. Their bitterness was legendary, their cunning hated by common and royal alike. Once, at a similar durbar a year ago, I had had a brief glimpse into a patidar's psyche in my paternal grandfather's court. What he said had shone like a little pearl of truth: 'Why have you made us?' was his impassioned cry to Dada Sahib, the Raja. 'We are pariahs of the palace, your stray dogs without shelter. Better than us are the untouchables. At least they know their place.' To which Dada Sahib's younger son, Ma's devar, had replied, 'You see me sitting on a throne today. But my children won't be any different from you. So be careful whom you call a stray dog. Primogeniture is the system. Who are we to question it?'

When the audience had quietened down, Pitamber stepped forward to make his parry. 'A day after the patidar's disappearance I was in the manager's office to discuss the revenues of the year's harvest. For those who are not familiar with the palace, the palace dungeons lie just beyond the office. The manager was not in his office, so I decided to wait for him. I was walking near the dungeon —'

'You had no authority to be there,' the chief of security suddenly intervened. 'Who let you enter?'

'Call the duwari responsible!' Kumar Mama Sahib said jumping into the fray, but his voice was drowned in the confused babble of voices that began to claim the durbar.

Then Pitamber's voice rang out sharp as a knife: 'I found a crumpled letter thrown from the dungeon window. It was lying in the grass.' He took out the letter from his sherwani pocket. Like the patidar's death, it looked as if too many hands had mauled it. 'It has been signed by the patidar. It says' — the dull tone of Pitamber's reading voice went against the impassioned plea with which that one line must have been written — 'Let me go, or let me die!'

I felt my throat constrict. The letter fluttered from Pitamber's hand, the pathetic testament of an unlived life. What physical tortures did the patidar undergo? Did they bleed him? Did they burn him? Did they starve him? I knew that in Sirikot starving was a popular form of torture. It was easy. The torturer's hands were clean and probably so was his conscience, a sin of omission rather than commission.

There was a story the dhais told us when we refused to sleep. 'The jokho will come and get you.' They said that the treasures of the rajas were hidden in certain spots within the palace compound. To guard the treasure a child was tied to a stake at the exact spot and starved to death, care being taken to ensure that the child's last sight was food kept away from its reach. When the child died its spirit became a spiralling light, the jokho, ready to seize any trespassers on the site, thinking that they have come for its food. But the patidar could not have been starved. He died a day later. What they did to him was mercifully or mercilessly short-lived. It was over before the cheetahs got to him.

'Let me go, or let me die.' I squeezed my eyes shut, knowing I was doomed to carry those lines with me, always.

Nana Sahib aroused himself from his stupor. He moved to speak but Yuvraj Mama Sahib had already pre-empted him. He stood up and addressed the durbar, which looked on with one malevolent eye. 'The patidar had been brought in for questioning, that day. But he had been released the same day. The chief of security had personally seen him off. He was alive and well. Nobody knows what happened to him later.'

Pandemonium broke out. Nana Sahib and the chief of security looked at Yuvraj Mama Sahib in horror, taken aback by his damning statement. After all the denials of any connection of the palace with the patidar, Yuvraj Mama Sahib in a glaring volte-face had exposed the palace's dirty underbelly.

Nana Sahib and the chief of security took on the dialectical exercise of confusing arguments, reasoning and explanations. Another hour elapsed. Minds were frayed by contradictions and elliptical logic. As if to defuse the explosive situation, the issue of 'palace leftovers' was brought up as a welcome reprieve.

Some voices piped up from the balcony. The servants in the palace had been protesting for a while against the system of eating the leftover food, scraped from the plates of the royals. They found the custom demeaning. However, some of the older servants — women mostly — had tried to quell the revolt by proclaiming, 'If we never found this custom offensive there is no reason for the younger servants to complain.'

A few of the older servants were ushered in to present their case. A couple of vehement younger ones were heard out too. In the end, Nana Sahib decreed that eating leftovers was not to be considered a mandatory custom. Those who felt strongly about it need not do so. The palace was capable of feeding its people. However, those who felt eating leftovers expressed their sentiments to the royal family, could continue to do so; they should not be frowned upon.

The durbar was too spent to either agree or disagree. They filed out and the meeting was dissolved in a state of emotional exhaustion. The balcony emptied out in a jangle of bangles and tinkling anklets. For me one image nagged on, like a premonition.

It was the expression of horror on Nana Sahib's face when Yuvraj Mama Sahib had made his damning statement.

~

Holi evening, full of dull gloom, was an anticlimax. The palace seemed lost in thought, conflicted, reasoning with the brooding ghost of the patidar. Feet dragged as if bogged down by a ball and chain. Like a contagion, children caught the feeling of oppression. We moved around in lackadaisical whispers, quiet, not wanting to get in the way of the preoccupied adults.

Baby Uncle and I were trying to play chess on Kumud Mami Sahib's jade chess table, in the veranda outside her quarters. We communicated through looks, trying not to speak, as if speaking would unleash some terrible event. From her bedroom we could hear Kumud Mami Sahib's soft keening. It wafted up to us, a slight stench of madness. She always cried under the effect of bhang on Holi. Some people laughed; some cried. It did not disturb us. The effect of the drug stayed longest with her. Her children were also playing in the courtyard. Malini, eight years old, rocked with mind-boggling precision on a wooden toy horse. Vaishnavi, six, sat on her dhai's lap while the dhai pointed at the moon and fed her kheer from a golden bowl. 'Chanda Mama Sahib door ke ...' she crooned in the cracked monotone of a witch.

Knight to King 4. My turn. Suddenly a maid ran out from Kumud Mami Sahib's bedroom in a flurry of petticoats, the air exploding around her. 'Bahurani Sahib is having a fit!' she shouted, then yelled to Vaishnavi's dhai with the authority of a midwife who was about to deliver a baby, 'Go get the vaidya! Inform Rani Sahib immediately!'

Without looking at each other we children rose as one and made a silent entry into Kumud Mami Sahib's bedoom where we stood in an orderly row about her bed, watching wide-eyed, drinking in the images, colours and smells that would shape the rest of our lives.

The bed on which Kumud Mami Sahib tossed and turned looked as if it had been mauled by a superior force. She writhed and contorted her body like a ferocious animal in its last throes of life. Like a snake being beaten to death, like she was fighting the devils from an unknown hell. I thought she was giving birth to some monstrous creature, a demon or rakshas that would explode from her body to confront us. Five maids held her down. One put a spoon between her teeth. Her cheeks stretched in a macabre grin. Spit gathered on her chin as her body continued its ugly dance.

By the time Ma, Nani and the vaidya came running in her eyes had rolled and her body had gone limp. Before they turned their attention to her, we were shooed out.

Outside, in the moonlight I gave Malini's shoulders a rough shake. 'Hey, Malini, what's wrong with your mother?'

'Is she mad?' asked Baby Uncle.

Malini looked at us, her luminous eyes big but calm with the intrinsic acceptance of the cruelty of our generation. 'No, no, not mad. It's lelipepsy.'

Hearing raised voices from the bedroom we sneaked in again, in ones and twos, but stayed clustered near the door. As always, in a crucial moment, the grown-ups had forgotten our presence. We were invisible; it was okay.

Nani was at the head of Kumud Mami's bed. Ma sat by her side. The maids sponged her forehead with cold water. Her hair hung in wet strands. She was pale, speaking in tired whispers, full of the urgency of a dying person giving last instructions, running her tongue over her parched lips. Her lips never stopped moving, never stopped uttering those fatal words, even though she shut her eyes from time to time to rest, talking half in sleep, half in waking. 'It was a dream, Apa, such a strange dream. As if it happened in front of my eyes. So clear, My god, so clear. Apa, Ma, you know how prophetic my dreams are, how accurate. They are never wrong. Never, not once. I see the past and future through them. I get my messages through them. He was a black man, so black.... Black as coal, black as night. And he was brahmin. I know he was brahmin. Don't ask me how I know, I know. Maybe he was wearing the sacred thread around his body. I don't know whether I saw it, but I know he was the brahmin beaten in the granary. You know the granary, near the Lion Gate? He was beaten there. How he was beaten, with what mercilessness! Have you ever seen a man being beaten to death? It is more horrible than seeing them hanged or burned. I am sure, though I've never seen hangings or burnings. How he cried for help. My god, those cries still reverberate in my ears. He was beaten to death, Apa. Ma, I saw a black brahmin beaten to death in front of my eyes! I have seen murder in front of my eyes. We have to find out who did it, such a merciless killing. The murderer has to be punished!'

She closed her eyes as if she never wanted to open them again. 'Such sins have been committed here. Such sins, the grossest, the most impure! How will we live them down? How will we do penance? How will we wash them away? Terrible things are going to happen. We cannot stop the wheel from turning. Penance, we must do penance.'

All I heard from Ma and Nani was a soothing refrain, like a witch doctor's litany. 'Go to sleep. It's nothing. Everything will be all right. Now go to sleep. Just go to sleep.'

~

Normally, I loved the preparation for sleep in the zenana. The pattering of feet, the rustling of clothes, the urgency to finish last minute chores, the clinking of utensils in the deep well of the night gradually growing quiet like the chattering of birds settling in, the linear movement towards business reaching culmination. Some quarters would plunge into darkness sooner than others. Others would still carry late-night whispers that whistled through the corridors across courtyards. Servants gathering up in corners to relax, share a confidence, a laugh or a smoke. Secret affairs were discussed. A few hours of freedom before a slumber that would awaken to another day of service. Late night was their time. The last sound I heard was always their muted voices in the corridors, like chimes in the wind. My mother had been insisting for the last couple of nights that I sleep in the nursery, making me mildly suspicious of her change of heart but I didn't want to question her lest she change her mind. Anyway exhaustion was crushing my bones to powder.

That night I slept fitfully. A dark sky enclosed the palace in its fist containing within it the sleep of restless dreams and midnight stirrings. I took a nameless dread to bed that night. And the dogs barked at the surrounding blackness for a very long time.

Five

I now knew for certain that Nana Sahib was eating with all the other children only so he could be with Baby Uncle. The next day we were back, having breakfast with him again. Full of omelettes and marmalade, we trooped out to while away the rest of the morning skirting the edges of the zenani bagh pond; letting the adrenalin of the previous day run its course by playing hide and seek in the mango orchard and waiting for the settled ennui of daily routine to claim us.

We played King and Loyal Subject in the pillared pavilion of the summer house. Filthy local abuse learnt in the servant quarters was jettisoned at the basement walls of the pavilion in squeaky voices so we could hear the volley of echoes ricocheting back at us like tennis balls. The waters of the pond were flooded in the basement in summer to keep the pavilion cool. We pretended we were drowning in a deluge and scrabbled for cover. Then Baby Uncle wanted to free the lovebirds in the kabutar khana, the bird house. 'I know you are Nana Sahib's current favourite, but don't stretch your luck,' I warned him. So we settled down to catching fishes from the pond. Baby Uncle's companions caught them in the cotton shawls they wore around their neck. We ran back with them in brass buckets to Kumud Mami Sahib's quarters to drop them in her aquarium. The bloated silvery fishes reminded me of her — trapped in Nana Sahib's net, thrashing their tails in a lelipeptic fit.

Soon we tired of the outside and took our horseplay to the halls and corridors. Baby Uncle and I were in a mood to vandalize. We studied the marble-eyed bust of a great-great-grandmother. She had been canonized for the asurya sparsha, a lifelong vow to never see the sun. I imagined she must have been quite like it in real life — un-pigmented, sunken-cheeked, marble-eyed — and wondered whether we should find a pencil to draw a moustache on her. The idea seemed novel to Baby Uncle who basking in paternal dotage was bold enough to do anything. The dhais were in the far end of the hall. I made Pushpa run for a pencil. A suppressed giggle of conspiratorial anticipation bubbled out of Vaishnavi's wide mouth. She was given the glare.

Baby Uncle stretched up to put a pencil line on great-great-grandmother's upper lip while her long face looked on in helpless and pallid disapproval. There was a sharp knock on the wall behind the bust. Baby Uncle fell back on the balls of his feet and dropped the pencil. Hearts stopped beating. Eye-whites became frozen pools of milk. Realization dawned on Baby Uncle first.

'It's coming from the corridor!' he shouted in triumph, much as if he was saying 'checkmate' to me at chess. He explained excitedly, 'It's the mehtar!'

In tacit understanding of a new game we pressed our ears to the wall. I knocked on the plaster. The clattering behind stopped.

'Did you find any gold in the shit?' Baby Uncle yelled so that the mysterious clatterer in the dark tunnel before him could hear.

There was no reply. What was the mehtar doing? Staring at the darkness around him in incomprehension? His muscles bunched, his ears straining more than his eyes, his ragged white dhoti offsetting the twenty-seven shades of dark around him?

'Did you find any gold in the shit?' Baby Uncle repeated and laughed, repositioning his ear so as not to miss his reply.

The reply came in a low voice but loud enough to carry, thick
like the bark of a teak tree, dark as the tunnel made for men to
carry the night-soil of rajas: 'No gold. Just the blood of poor
people.'

~

Kumud Mami Sahib was preparing to visit Nana Sahib to pay
her respects and was annoyed because her vas gharianis insisted
she wear the latest chiffons. An English photographer had come
to click pictures of the royal family.

'How many pictures is he going to take?' Kumud Mami
Sahib pouted, her pinched nostrils flaring in irritation as she
shook insistent hands off her braid, clattering away the gold hair
ornaments. The English photographer had just emptied his reel
on the royal family a few days ago. I still remember the clap of
the bulb, the shower of light, the sharp smell of sodium. The
royal family had stood in the light, puffed with pride, bodies
weighed down by gems and gold. Unbent, unbowed, Masters of
All, Emperors and Empresses of Smaller Lives, paying homage
only to the blood that ran thick and viscous in their veins.

Kumud Mami Sahib had been the most unobstrusive, the
most modest, the youngest daughter-in-law. She had stood
gracefully outside the velvet carpet, as per custom, precluding
the remotest physical contact with Yuvraj Mama Sahib. Now the
photographer wanted some exclusive pictures of her.

'Enough!' she snapped suddenly. 'I'm not dressing up again
for that old lecher.' Baby Uncle sucked in his breath; she hadn't
even noticed him. Though technically her devar, her younger
brother-in-law, he was too young to merit a serious glance. Then
a runner flashed in, her nose-rings flapping: 'Raja Sahib's dogs
are tied. He is ready to receive you.'

I joined Kumud Mami Sahib's retinue as it moved to the
Chandramahala. Across the courtyard the new summer sun hit
her and she reeled with the shock. 'Bahurani has had a swoon,'

the vas gharianis panicked, hurriedly producing her smelling salts. Finally, with a quick repositioning of the caparisoned umbrella and supported heavily by strong ghariani hands, Kumud Mami Sahib, squinting bravely against the sunshine, continued her journey to the Chandramahala.

Nana Sahib was finishing his photo session and did not look up when we arrived. Kumud Mami Sahib had no time to give pranams because the Englishman had not finished his obsequious fawning over Nana Sahib. He was from Calcutta. I found his pink face and hair the colour of sand attractive. He was different.

He asked Kumud Mami Sahib to take her place behind Nana Sahib's silver throne. She looked shocked. He insisted. She swayed and spoke with a strength in her voice I did not know her body contained: 'I cannot stand beside my father-in-law.' She stood bare headed, open, her angry expression a naked flaunt of immodesty. Her pallu had slipped off her head. From the corner of my eyes I saw a vas ghariani look at her as if she were itching to put her purdah back in place. I was the only child there, standing next to Kumud Mami Sahib. I could smell her, the way dogs smelt people. She smelt of stale winter roses and primeval fear.

'It's all right,' Nana Sahib soothed, worry creasing the corners of his eyes. 'We can accommodate a little of the changing times.'

Lightning clapped in my aunt's flashing eyes. 'This is what you have done, Englishman, be proud! You have turned this country on its head. Spoiling us rotten, like little children; making us fight like dogs over scraps of meat, while you rule. What wile, what deceit goes in the name of policy! Tell me do you feel no shame? Do you not know that a father-in-law and daughter-in-law in genteel societies are not seen together in the same photograph? This old debauched man whom I have been cursed to call father allows it. What a pet pony of the British he has become ...'

The words spewed out unchecked; Kumud Mami Sahib spoke them with a look of helpless bewilderment, almost as if she was wondering why she could not control the words that tumbled from her mouth. She frothed, she bubbled, she blustered. Her acid sentences singed the air and seemed to corrode her jewellery. The Englishman turned ruddy with embarrassment; Nana Sahib's breath stopped.

'This man, this debauch, do you even know of all his activities? Do you know that he murders his patidars? That he beats brahmins to death in granaries? That he sleeps with his Yuvranis and produces sons by the name of Uday? No wonder the child never gets off his lap...'

At last Nana Sahib shouted, 'Stop!' and at that simultaneous moment Kumud Mami Sahib's hand clapped over her mouth as if to stop the unspeakable words that issued from it. Had she not fled from the room knowing she had inadvertently let out a state secret her incoherent words would have been dismissed as the ramblings of a disturbed mind.

Nana Sahib slouched in his throne, his hand on his forehead, his sapphire rings winking disconsolately. The Englishman dangled his camera haplessly and averted his eyes. I stood there as if I had been hit on the head by something hard, like a brass bathing mug.

I do not know how many heard of Kumud Mami Sahib's outburst. News travelled fast through the network of attendants, servants and vas gharianis. Like a fire in an electrical circuit. But nobody would speak about it. The event disappeared into the great womb of zenana secrets, erased from conversation as if it had never happened. I thought of talking to Kumud Mami Sahib directly, to ask her if what she had said about Baby Uncle was true, but I baulked at the idea. The marshy swamp of grown-up wrongdoing was strictly forbidden to children.

My mother knew. I'm sure of it. I could make out from the skin stretched white around her tight lips as she and Nani spoke in low voices, as if collaborating on a confidential mission. My mind tried to reason out the issue. Who could be filling Kumud Mami Sahib's ears with midwife calumny? Dhaima? Santoma?

Pitamber? Shanti? I knew Shanti revelled in our misery. I was sure she spat in my milk. Kumud Mami Sahib was vulnerable, easily moldable. But she was no fool. She would have demanded evidence from the person who had poured poison down her ears.

Kumud Mami Sahib had come to Sirikot in marriage a year after Yogendra was born. Raghavendra was eleven. Yogendra was eight, or maybe nine. If he was nine it was impossible for Baby Uncle to be Yuvrani Mami Sahib's son. How could she have been pregnant with both Baby Uncle and Yogendra at the same time? There was no way of finding out, since dates were never clear in our days; there were no birth certificates. The only proof of one's birth were astrological horoscopes, highly confidential documents that only the rajpurohit and parents were privy to.

Most times, when horoscopes were exchanged during the arrangement of matrimonial alliances the dates were doctored to align the stars in favourable constellations and to conceal the candidate's age. Mothers kept an obsessive vigil on their daughter's beauty. 'You should be so fair that when you swallow paan the red juice trickling down your throat should be visible. You should be so fragile, that the weight of a rose in your hair should make you wilt.' Skin, hair and figure were stressed on because they were the first shameless exhibits of age.

The only clear proof and frequent giveaways of age were photographs. Like animals marking their territory, most men had a dangerous habit of penning captions below a photograph in neat legible handwriting. With typical patriarchal indifference to the fate of their daughters, they never forgot to mention the date.

I wondered whether to tell Baby Uncle what I had heard. But what would I say? 'You are not only my uncle, you are also my cousin?' What suffix is given to the product of a man and his daughter-in-law? I was consumed with revulsion for Nana Sahib. Did he not have enough women to piss on? Could he not spare his son? What would Baby Uncle do when he knew? What would his poor beaked nose and wide intelligent eyes do? And Nani, dull and stagnant green like the bathwater Nana Sahib rose out from, did she know? Old enough to be Baby Uncle's grandmother? What a laugh. She really was his grandmother.

In letters that Baby Uncle wrote me later, in middle age, he said he always remembered Nani in one recurrent image — sitting on the floor with him on her lap and mixing with her fingers a platter of meat curry, rice and ghee. He would never forget how she rolled the food into little balls and fed him with her hands. It was an image I know that never left him, because, unlike other Indian mothers, so few royal mothers fed their children with their own hands. I could feel the tears in the words he wrote; I can still feel them.

I rushed out of the Chandramahala to the nursery and lay on my bed in the children's dormitory. Baby Uncle stirred beside me. Let him sleep one more night, I thought. Let me always be awake so he can sleep, I prayed.

But I fell asleep.

And awoke to the sound of Baby Uncle's heart-rending screams.

~

I sprang up from bed as if a giant hand had jolted me awake. I thought it was the middle of the night but it was early morning. My burning eyes saw the sky outside stained a lecherous pink, the colour of Holi. Baby Uncle was being carried out into the corridors, kicking and lowing like a colic calf. Four vas gharianis struggled to hold him.

I sat on my haunches on the bed and matched him scream for scream, my throat throbbing like an animal trying to run from a predator. Even when my mind and body stopped screaming out of tiredness my throat couldn't. It would never have stopped if a hand did not clap itself around my mouth. I thrashed against the other hands that held me down. The main door of the dormitory shut with a bang. My younger cousins whimpered in their beds. The frosted white panes of the door stared back at me like the sightless gaze of prison guards. I peeled the hand from my face and could sense the dry epithelium of my throat rip and tear against the sound rolling out of my mouth.

'Stop them! Oh, somebody stop them! They are going to kill him!'

Bitter acrid liquid was forced down my mouth, hot smoke burning my hoarse lungs. I fell back on my bed, released from the grip of my captors. My younger cousins were all around me. Those eyes, I had seen them before, frozen milk.

My last glimpse of him was of his tousled head and his kurta which had ridden up to expose the clean midriff of a young boy or a woman. His bony toes were stiff and pointing straight out, tendons and muscles straining against his captors.

He was carried off in a supine position, like a still alive body being taken for cremation.

~

The green wooden beams on the ceiling; the pigeons cooing outside; the velvet softness of my monogrammed pillow; the exquisitely carved lamp blackened by the soot of midnight oil and my dark fears; soothing hands on my hair; worried frown on a woman's forehead. *Ma, where are you?*

When I came to, she was there, by my side, ready with the truth. It was a truth I did not care for. It had no wisdom to it.

'Don't cry, Leela. Nothing has happened to him. Stop this melodrama, please. He's fine. He's just gone for adoption.'

'The way they took him away, I thought they were going to kill him!' I said, after absorbing this.

'You've always had a wild imagination,' Nani said handing me a glass of herbal tea spiced with honey and tulsi. I looked at her closely. Did she not care? Of course she didn't. He was not her child. 'Why, Ma? Why has he gone for adoption?'

'Because,' Ma said in that singsong voice grown-ups have for brainless children, 'that's the best that can happen to him. What life does he have here? As the fourth son he'll end up as one of the santos. In Hanskinda, where he has gone, he will be Yuvraj. The raja there has no sons. It's a big state, they have many mines. One day he has a chance to be raja. It is the best thing to happen to him. He'll be grateful for it. One day.'

'But why now, Ma? He's only a child.'

'Baba was supposed to have sent him a year ago. We had delayed it for too long. The Raja of Hanskinda agreed to wait till Holi. Not a day more.' Ma feverishly folded the Nepali khoshti into small folds. I had never seen her fold clothes before.

I longed to put my arms around her waist and my head on her stomach. But I restrained from a physical demonstration as it was considered cheap and ill bred. My pent up anguish released itself in the quivering of my lower lip. 'I'll be good, Ma. Don't send me away for adoption.'

'Don't be silly, child. Girls don't get sent away for adoption. They get sent away for marriage. So save your tears for yourself.' Nani squinted as she spoke; I think she was fighting back tears herself.

'Be grateful for the time you had with him,' Ma said, pragmatic as ever.

Nine years. It was enough. And it was too little. Enough to be remembered by for a lifetime, but not enough for my childhood. I wrote him passionate letters and bad poetry on 'gilded cages'. I whiled away the next few days revisiting our favourite haunts. The fairy grass patch, the palace pond, the bathing kunjs. I let hot tears fall unattended onto the blades of grass under me, the sweetness of my pain hypnotic. I sank into the roiling pleasure of pity for him and me. The slow transformation had begun. Sorrow contented me. I could feel myself metamorphosing into an adult. New convoluted grooves inscribed my brain.

Many years later, I met Baby Uncle while driving through Hanskinda to a neighbouring state to broker a marriage for Dakshyayani's daughter. On the way the car broke down. We chugged our way to Hanskinda palace hoping to find him and maybe some comfort for the night. Over the years our correspondence had petered out. I couldn't attend the wedding of his son because my father-in-law had died that year. Custom forbade any celebrations within the year of a funeral.

He was there. In the still intact bone-white palace, under a naked bulb, sitting behind a table with a broken leg supported with bricks. His chair was the kind usually used by government clerks. He was obese. His beaked nose was buried under long years of steady flab. His eyebrows overran his forehead like creepers in a palace ruin. He wore a white vest and a cotton dhoti thin with overuse, darkened by cheap detergents. The hair on his chest had greyed. From a hairless chest to a grey one, somewhere along the way I had lost my closest childhood friend. He was not Baby Uncle. He was not even Uday Mama Sahib. He was a forgotten thing, decaying in obscurity.

Upstairs in the ballroom, his son, daughter-in-law and half-a-dozen grandchildren slept on mattresses spread on the floor, covered like shrouds in white bedsheets. There was no furniture. I could see only an earthen pot for drinking water, a shaving mirror and a comb.

He showed no sign of recognition when he saw me, save a slight upturn of shapeless lips; the slightest of confused smiles.

I understood why.

He probably did not recognize me either.

He did not see Leela. He saw an overweight woman whose teeth had rotted with tobacco abuse.

I do not remember much of what he said, except one line which he repeated many times, like a child learning a lesson: 'This system cannot continue. Monarchy will come back.'

I was struck not by how helpless he looked, but how useless.

Six

was tired of hanging on Yuvraj Mama Sahib's balcony railing. Ma and I had been waiting for him in his chambers for at least an hour but he was nowhere in sight. Ma needed to invite him for a family dinner in the zenana that night. She ordered his servant to start packing the venison pickle Yuvrani Mama Sahib had promised but forgotten about and sat in his chambers with the jars opened out on the floor in front of her, clucking disapprovingly at Yuvraj Mama Sahib's servant for spilling some mustard oil in his attempt to fill the jars to the brim.

Except for a few Chippendale pieces the furniture in the room was dark and spare, without the ubiquitous opulent tapestries, the ornate ottomans and enamel washbasins of the other rooms. The air in the rooms was stuffy and old and I sensed shadowy monsters flourishing in its unlit corners. The odour of stale incense and the night sweat of a sanctimonious insomniac overpowered the smell of the raat-ki-rani flowers burdening the balconies. A lunatic's moon hung over the crenellated arches. It lurked just outside the edge of the palace, like danger. Pushpa stood immobile near a curtain holding a lamp like an inanimate corner stool.

I moved to Yuvraj Mama Sahib's showcase of the *Encyclopaedia Britannica*. I picked out 'U'. For Uday. 'U' in silent homage to the constant absence of beaked nose and sheepish smile.

Between Uranus and Unicorn a letter slipped out and fell on my lap. It was freshly folded and signed 'Yuvraj', it was written in the local dialect. Without thinking, I handed it to my mother. She had no qualms about reading it. As her eyes skimmed the single monogrammed page, pearls of sweat sprang up on her upper lip.

Yuvraj Mama Sahib walked in just at that moment wearing vermilion marks on his forehead from the evening arti at the palace temple. He was chewing paan.

Ma didn't have time to compose her thoughts. Her confrontation was brash and undiplomatic. 'What is this?' she demanded of Yuvraj Mama Sahib, the letter a shivering premonition in her hand. I retreated in the shadows of the bookcase.

'Leave,' he told the servant still busy wiping the oil slick off the floor. The servant salaamed and fled. Yuvraj Mama Sahib did not notice Pushpa, probably mistaking her for a vase or a stool. 'Apa!' he countered, cracking a betel-nut between his teeth. 'Going through my personal things. Is this what Mrs Wood taught you?'

Ma's posture did not change, only her chest heaved, her mouth worked. 'Shame on you, Rajraj! Shame!'

My uncle sat down on the only other armchair in the room and looked around for his attendants before he remembered he had dismissed them. He had nobody to fetch him his silver spittoon. 'What shame?' he asked, resorting to swallowing his paan. 'When King Dashratha spotted one grey hair on his head, he handed over his throne to his son Lord Ram. This old man, my father, his whole head is white. And what does he do?' — his red mouth opened for a laugh — 'He uses henna dye.'

'So you plot to kill him.' My mother was still calm; her fury not yet unleashed.

'I'm not trying to kill him,' her brother trivialized, getting up to neatly pluck the letter from his sister's outstretched hand

and pocket it in his kurta. 'I'm just helping him along his way ...'

'*Help?*' Hysteria rose in my mother's throat, trying to find a breach. 'You got the most powerful tantrik in Sirikot to practise black magic on Baba! You call that help? What kind of help is that? Rajraj, you are the most religious, most pious of all of us. Why this craving for an earthly title? How can it possibly help you in your search for god?' My mother fought for control, and not succeeding, surrendered to a blustering incoherence.

Yuvraj Mama Sahib bowed his head to stave off her onslaught, like he must have done when they were children. 'It's my right,' he said without looking up. His self-righteousness made him vehement, hungry for vindication. 'Even Lord Krishna in the Bhagvad Gita says you must fight for your right. Destiny demands that I be raja. It wants me to fulfil my duty to Sirikot and its people.'

The rigidity of Ma's taut limbs was in total conflict with her slack trembling mouth, 'Don't do it.' She looked as if she was ready to cry and fought to regain control of her voice. 'I beg you, don't do it.'

'Sometimes, I wonder,' my uncle's head snapped back as if for a hiss and a strike, 'what would it be like if you were not the Rajkumari, the First Princess.'

'It's too late for that,' Ma snarled.

'Do you know,' he said, their eyes locked in mortal combat, 'Ma had a girl before you? They killed her, you know, because Baba's case was in the Court of Wards for annexation and he desperately needed a male heir.'

Pushpa dropped her lamp in a splintering crash. In the shifting light of the taper the red dye of her sari seemed to spread like a stain. Both their heads turned towards her like two predators who had suddenly caught scent of their prey.

'Leave!' They shouted in unison. Then Ma remembered me. 'Leela!' she screamed. I stepped out of the shadows. 'Go to the zenana! Get ready for dinner. Take Pushpa with you.'

'And send Shanti,' Yuvraj Mama Sahib ordered Pushpa.

We fled. Outside, I gave my own orders to Pushpa. She was to summon Shanti and proceed to the zenana and wait for me there. If she was questioned about where I was, she was to say that I was in the library, the most secluded area of the palace and one of my favourite haunts.

'If you ever sneak to anybody that I was here, overhearing their conversation, I shall personally drown you in the pond,' I threatened in my fiercest whisper.

~

I tiptoed in the shadows through the narrow galleries of Yuvraj Mama Sahib's kitchen to reappear on the opposite balcony of the room and sat under an open window pretending to be loitering there in case any servants passed by. From my position I could hear very little, catching only the words that rose in a swell and carried over the windows.

Long pauses punctuated the steady flow of Yuvraj Mama Sahib's speech. For once my mother seemed to have nothing to say. Shanti's voice was low and deferential but her tone held the authority of some secret information she was imparting. My mother spoke haltingly, after a lot of thought. Hauteur sometimes informed her speech but mostly her repartee sounded defensive. Twice her words carried their high plaintive note through the window to me. 'What is the proof?' I heard her say. 'What is the proof?'

Frustrated that even a sinful act like eavesdropping was not simple I decided to make a detour to the library before returning to the zenana. Located between the billiards room and the Chandramahala, it was a bit of a walk. Infused as always by fresh consternation at the sight of the librarian, because he was the spitting image of Nana Sahib, I read a story by Hans Christian Anderson and ruminated a little on the laws of chance that governed heredity.

When I returned from the library, taking a leisurely zigzag track back to Nani's quarters in the zenana, Ma and Nani were talking in hushed whispers. I entered casually and was a bit surprised that they didn't notice me. Pushpa was sitting so close to the bed she seemed to be hiding under it, every facial muscle straining under the pressure of unobtrusiveness. Shanti sat next to her, cutting off the straps of Ma's imported brassieres, and sewing the jagged edges. Ma was fond of foreign brassieres. But unaccustomed to their design, she wore them only after the elastic straps had been cut off and replaced by strings to be tied across her back. Nobody noticed that Shanti was crying. I wondered whether Ma had upbraided her when I left.

'It was a hasty decision on Baba's part,' Nani, tearless but tortured, placated Ma. She had the hardened air of a woman who has borne too many children, seen too much. Her long braid moved with every shake of her head. 'What could I do, Munna Ma? Your father made a cruel, hasty decision when I was unconscious from the pain of childbirth. The decision was not mine. He was very tense those days. You know what the Court of Wards is like. The state could have been annexed. People were saying that he should get married again. Could you believe that?' Nani searched Ma's averted face, and it was all she could do to stop from shaking her shoulders. 'I know that it was a sin. I know that Baba and I will be punished one day, but there is no point remembering a past we cannot change. But who told the Yuvraj?' Nani demanded, her voice strident now, angry. 'This is something only Baba and I know.'

Ma looked pointedly at Shanti and turned away, changing her tack. 'What about me? Why did you spare me? I was a girl too.'

'The situation was defused by then. Baba had already made plans for adoption from Devnangar. Luckily, Yuvraj was born within the next year, before the adoption was finalized. Yuvraj is the saviour of Sirikot, child. His stars are inextricably linked to ours.' My mother's lips curled in an ironic smile, as she nodded. Irony, I always remember as the curl of a woman's lips.

The sewing needle pricked Shanti's fingers and blood started oozing out of her finger, the colour of a precious ruby.

The turuhi sounded. We heard the high calls of the runners. 'Chalantu Vishnu!' — Long Live the Walking Lord Vishnu — and 'Vijay Karo!' they cried. Nana Sahib was here for dinner. The women wiped their tears and hurried out.

~

The family gathered around the dining chowkis and sat down cross-legged, one by one, according to seniority. The silver chowkis and cushions were laid along the borders of a hand-made alpana design on the floor. The courtyard had been scented and swept. The mridang players sat apart from the gharianis on the daphlis, their music soothing the frayed nerves of that night.

Brahmin women served up food-laden plates for the 'nazrana'. Nana Sahib directed his gaze on the food items. His look would dispel all the karmic and immaterial impurities of the food and the nazrana would be later fed to beggars outside the palace.

Nobody spoke. They were collecting their thoughts, allowing the music to give them respite.

My Mama Sahibs sat on Nana Sahib's left. Nani and then Ma sat on his right. The Mami Sahibs sat furthest away from the men. I sat between them, the only half-child, half-person in the gathering. There was no Baby Uncle, his absence a purposeful stab, a recognition of what was not, of what could never be.

From where I sat I could see that Nana Sahib had the largest helping of the three-tiered dish of saffron rice. He had already demolished half a kilo of wild boar. He must have been eating to fill some gaping hole in his body, because when he spoke his voice was devoid of emotion.

'It is good we are all here,' he said wiping his greasy hand on the towelled shoulder of his attendant. 'I want to speak and put to rest a lot of speculation and intrigue that has beset this palace. A family that does not communicate is a family doomed to disaster. Bahurani,' his hawk eyes swooped down on Kumud Mami Sahib at the end of the chowki. 'Are you taking the medication of the vaidya?'

The question was not only an enquiry. It was an accusation. She quailed, not taking her eyes or fingers off the partridge she was eating. 'Yes, I am.' Her voice was as small as remorse would allow.

'Good. Then let me redress some of the damage you have done. If you are not able to take the strain of what I am going to say, let me know beforehand, so your attendants can take you away.'

Kumud Mami Sahib squirmed under his withering sarcasm, her face a delicate pink; Kumar Mama Sahib continued relishing the wild boar curry, oblivious of his wife's discomfort.

'What you said, and the time and place in which you said it, could not have been worse.' Nana Sahib's voice was rising but controlled. His eyes grew round, theatrically contrived, as if he was trying to scare her and easily achieving his desired effect. Kumud Mami Sahib looked at her partridge as if it would grow wings and fly off her plate. Everyone else at the table ate slowly, their eyes on their platters, glad that they were not at the receiving end of Raja Sahib's scathing words.

'They call you a well-bred girl from the Nepalese royal family. Your grandfather in Himachal is considered a past-master in the niceties of English diplomacy. You are an erudite girl. They say you read books and write poetry. So, from whence such crudity in the presence of your elders? That too, in the full gaze of the public? Before a Britisher? And the things you said...' Nana Sahib slowed his rising torrent for effect.

'Bahurani, the damage you have done not only to me, but Sirikot is irreparable' — Kumud Mami Sahib's fingers mauled her food beyond recognition — 'still, in spite of the fact that I have the misfortune of marrying my son to a mentally challenged woman who publicly regurgitates filthy servant-quarter gossip on her father-in-law's face,' he paused and lightly ran his hand over his brow, as if to erase a troubling memory, 'I shall address your allegations one by one.'

My grandfather suddenly looked very old, an aged bull tired of servicing the demanding cows of his herd. The hennaed ringlets behind his ear were lank and unperfumed. His be-ringed fingers seemed bloated, puffed by water retention and anxiety.

'You said I have killed a black brahmin in the granary. I am told the evidence is a dream you saw. Bahurani,' he raised his voice though his eyes were deadening over some strange defeat, 'I suggest you do not overeat before you sleep. Bad digestion is usually the cause of troubled dreams. And please, for god's sake, if you do suffer nightmares, do not, repeat, do not subject me to them. I am not responsible for the morbid content of your monochromatic fantasies resulting from gastric upsets.'

Kumud Mami Sahib was inured to some extent by now. Her eyes glazed as she focused on the intricate engravings on the border of her platter. Her fingertips, caked with congealed rice and gravy, rested limply in her food.

'As for your second allegation. You think I killed the patidar. I don't blame you. Everybody thinks I killed the patidar. Your outburst was an even better advertisement than the fiasco in the court. It was a great fuel to the simmering fire. It will reach the ears of the English agents and the Indian government. Sirikot will be annexed for bad management and hopefully, if all goes according to your wishes, Russian and Chinese style Communism will take over Sirikot and the royal family will be executed, like Czar Nicholas. Wah! Wouldn't that be lovely?'

His words were beginning to have an effect on the rest of the diners. We bowed our heads over our food and shifted uneasily on our velvet cushions, embarrassed spectators to a public flogging.

'But your *third* allegation,' — from an inflamed ruler Nana Sahib again became the exhausted bull of the herd — 'your third allegation was the unkindest cut of all. It was the most indelicate, the most embarrassing'— Yuvrani Mami Sahib took a sip of

water and stifled a titter, then tried not to look at anybody in
particular. Nana Sahib studiously ignored her — 'A bahu is a
daughter. Shame on any man who allows a remotely lustful
thought to cross his mind, however fleetingly. Have I ever, and
you must speak now in front of everybody, given you cause to
even imagine such filth about you? Then why should it be any
different for the Yuvrani? Bahurani, you are a literate woman.
Tell me, does the traditional system of concubinage deprive a
man of decency and virtue? Do you think I am a man without
a conscience? A man without values? Do you think I could ever
entertain even in my wildest dreams unsaintly thoughts about
my own daughter-in-law? What filth churns in your brain! You
have made me a tired and broken man today. But still a question
has come up, and however odious it may be it must be resolved.
I have searched in my mind for conclusive proof against your
allegations, and I have found it.' Nana Sahib raised his voice
and addressed his attendant standing behind him without turning
his head, knowing he was there, 'Bring the photograph!'

Nani Sahib did the honours. She wiped her hands on a
ghariani's napkin and held the gold-edged frame presented to
her with both hands. A tight nod and a short gesture that the
frame should be passed on to Kumud Mami Sahib left her
holding the frame as if it were a written indictment of her
crimes. I tried to peek. It was easy because I had a pretty clear
view of the image. It was a zenana photograph. Nani, Yuvrani
Mami Sahib, Ma and her younger sister sat laughing on the
zenani bagh steps with Raghavendra. They looked so young.
Ma's unlined face, Yuvrani Mami Sahib's wide eyes laughing as
if at a naughty village joke. Nani, in better days, looking thrilled
to be sharing time with her married daughters. Yuvrani Sahib
smiling in the strained way women do in the presence of their
in-laws. Both mother- and daughter-in-law were unmistakably
pregnant. Nani with Baby Uncle and Yuvrani Mami Sahib with
Yogendra, obviously. The photograph though uncaptioned was
irrefutably dated by the presence of Raghavendra's idiotic toddler

face between the women. Two children were born immediately after Raghavendra and before Kumud Mami Sahib's wedding. Yogendra and Baby Uncle. If both Nani and Yuvrani Sahib were pregnant at the same time the point of contention was immediately resolved.

Kumud Mami Sahib couldn't take her eyes off the black and white images of an indelible past. The young, blurred black and white faces of the Sirikot royal family laughed at her inane allegations. Her brow clouded in conflict, mesmerized by the laughing women, till Nani Sahib snapped her out of it.

'Enough,' my grandmother said between clenched teeth. 'Raja Sahib has had the grace to justify himself. Let us not stretch this. You shall watch your mouth from now on, Bahurani, and think before you speak. There should be some difference in the behaviour of Raja Sahib's bahu and a common vas ghariani.'

~

Nana Sahib came to Nani's quarters after dinner and sat down in pensive silence blowing a thick pall of cigar smoke before a brooding audience of Nani and Ma. A bitter aftertaste of the meal remained. 'Munna Ma,' he said finally, exhaling so hard I knew he was at the point of some terrible confession, 'I do not know whether in the eyes of god I have sinned.'

Nani and Ma held their breath. Stop, I could feel them think. We do not want to know what you are going to say. But Nana Sahib did not seem to notice their presence. He was spitting out the venom he had held within for so long. He was seeking salvation by confessing a terrible secret, making me realize that rajas were human after all.

'The security chief showed me the correspondence between the patidar and an insider in the palace. The insider has to be a member of the royal family, my family, because the letters were written in Hindi and English. Only the royal family reads and writes these two languages.' He sighed, 'It was an assassination plot. I did bring him in for questioning. He was in the dungeons as Pitamber claimed he was. Yes, he was tortured. If only ...'

And I knew he would say it then and depart forever from my childlike image of grandfathers into the realm of blue-horned toads and centaurs and other fantastical creatures.

I did not wait. I ran out of the room all the way to the palace pond only wishing that they had stopped me from hearing what I thought I heard. But they hadn't.

They hadn't even noticed I was there.

Seven

The next morning was the second time that week I woke in an unrecognizable place. I was not in the nursery but in the zenana. Morning had killed sleep, shaking out night like loose change from my pocket. I did not so much see Ma rush past my bed as feel her panic-stricken energy. Beside me, Nani still lay peacefully asleep, her head resting on her crooked elbow. The giant four-poster hovered over us like an ancient banyan tree giving shelter to wayfarers.

My eyes focused on a blurry image of Ma as she sped past, disappearing down the hallway in her English night suit and slipperless feet. I looked around for Pushpa to find my slippers but she wasn't in the room so I sped barefoot after Ma, my body on high alert, my mind the vigilant maw of a hungry baby in the middle of the night. Catching up with her I realized it was not early morning, it was at least eight o'clock.

The kitchens in the corridors were already thrumming with activity and bent-backed sweepers swished centipede-like in the courtyards. My mother was heading towards the Chandramahala. Nana Sahib was in trouble! Oh god, what will happen now? The bringer of the news, a vas ghariani, ran alongside us, her face darkened by discreetly withheld thoughts.

As we rushed up the narrow wooden stairs to my grandfather's quarters I could hear confused voices in frantic consultation. When we entered, I saw Nana Sahib lying on his bed like a fallen tree. His face was unnaturally yellow. His eyes watched us helplessly, as if entreating us to stop his body from shaking in its final delirium. Instinctively, I knew death was in the room. Non-negotiable, a tax-collector unwilling to be talked out of his dues, watching the frothy saliva dribbing down Nana Sahib's chin with clinical satisfaction. He was dying. A pigeon lay at the foot of his bed, ceremonially dead, as if in preparation of some occult death ritual.

Nana Sahib's attendant Ganesh stood by the washbasin, his hands clasped in front of him, his head bowed. A monogrammed towel still hung from his shoulder, a wet patch imprinted where Nana Sahib's hand must have been. The washbasin was half full of murky water with gobs of spit and long threads of saliva. Between his fingers Ganesh clutched a small red can of tooth powder that Nana Sahib would not ever need again.

In a corner stood Potol, a small one-eyed servant whose livelihood came from shooing away pigeons while Nana Sahib slept. I suspect that this livelihood was entrusted to him just so people could avoid seeing his one eye, considered inauspicious, early in the morning. He was being interrogated by the vaidya whose long serious face looked longer in distress. There were no vas gharianis around. A silver tumbler of thickened milk by his bedside was the only evidence that he had been visited by a feminine presence. A bead-edged lace doily covered the tumbler.

'I do not know how long huzur has been like this,' Potol was saying. 'I was only told to send away the musicians today because Raja Sahib was not in the mood.' He sank down on his haunches and grasped his head between his hands. The vaidya looked at Ma as if seeking succor – the only clean-shaven man I had ever seen in the mardana.

'And him?' Ma pointed a long accusing finger at the dumbstruck Ganesh. More than attending to Nana Sahib she was looking for culprits, needing somebody to blame.

'I came in the morning, as usual.' His nervous muttering betrayed the terror of certain retribution. 'Raja Sahib brushed his teeth. I brought him his usual warm water in a brass utensil,' Ganesh stammered. 'Raja Sahib was constipated. He always drank warm water before his morning movement. But today he said he didn't need it. He brushed his teeth and went to the latrine.'

'Where is the brass tumbler?' Ma narrowed her eyes.

'The vas ghariani who brought Raja Sahib's morning milk took it away.' Then he crossed himself and touched his ears, 'He didn't drink it, Most Illustrious Jemma, he didn't drink it...'

Ma cut short his whining with unnecessary violence. 'How long was he inside the latrine?'

'Around half an hour,' Ganesh said abjectly. Ma entered the latrine and looked around. Three thunder-boxes were open, the chamber pots clean. The spouted silver cans on the left side of the thunder-boxes were full of water, ready for avdust. By the white enamel washbasin embossed in the blue dyes of Chinese pottery was a new bar of soap. The matching enamel jug was full of water. A monogrammed, fawn-coloured hand towel was folded and ready for use. It was evident that Nana Sahib had not used the bathroom. The mehtars were on four-hourly shifts. They would not have cleaned Nana Sahib's night-soil so soon.

Outside the latrine I could almost hear my mother's mind snap with a sharp metallic click. Nana Sahib groaned. She did not hear him. She was busy controlling a long suppressed hysteria fighting to find the light of day.

'Which vas ghariani was with him last night?'

'Phulwati,' Ganesh replied brokenly from the floor. 'She left in the morning when I came.'

'Call her!' Ma lost control of her senses. Her cry was not an order. It was a wild-eyed scream for blood. She was conducting a trial before her father was dead.

With Ma engrossed in the details of the crime and finding evidence, I moved unnoticed towards Nana Sahib. He lay twitching on his bed, a helpless witness to his own death investigation. He had the stricken look of a hunter shocked to discover that he had become the hunted. His eyes were staring out of his sockets. He was trying to speak. I moved closer to his mouth. It smelt of hot winds sweeping over dank forests. Of death, tobacco, and final reconciliation. Wasp wings fluttered in his mouth as he rasped for breath.

'Black' I caught a distinct word, then, 'blood' – the rest was lost in flapping insects drowning in a saliva bubble.

'Ma!' I cried out, urgent, forceful.

My tone must have registered in her deranged state. She did not look at Nana Sahib but grabbed the vaidya by the collar of his kurta. Her hair broke loose from its knot and cascaded down her back. She reached her face up to him as if supplicating for a kiss. 'Save him,' she begged. 'O lord Vaidyaji, save him! The wealth of Sirikot is yours, Vaidyaji, do something.'

The vaidya's embarrassed silence spurred her on. She rent his kurta from collar to hem. It ripped with a sweet sound and exposed a hairless chest. Kurta buttons sprinkled on the floor in surprised tinkles. His body swung limply as she shook him with manic energy.

'Ma, stop Ma, please stop.' I was weeping at her violence; at too many unfamiliar sights for a thirteen-year-old's morning.

'Munna Ma,' Nana Sahib's thin voice brought Ma's half-crazed force to his side. His voice was suddenly clear and frictionless. 'Draw the curtains, Munna Ma, why is it so dark?'

Ma was a sobbing mess of hair and tears. 'It's not dark, Baba, the curtains are drawn.'

'Munna Ma, a thousand pins are pricking me. Munna Ma, now I'm losing sensation in my legs.' His eyes were wide, watching an open dream, his face showing no pain.

Phulwati appeared at the door, frightened but surly. She looked fresh and dewy compared to the old age and death in the room.

Ma fell upon her with Nana Sahib's ivory-handled cane. Phulwati warded off Ma's feral power with dextrous ease. 'You will rot in hell, Phulwati! What guts, Vaidyaji. Do you see the guts of this snake that my father cradled in his bosom? You wretch, you shall die for this! Poison in his milk, that's what she did. Evil ingrate!'

The swish of the cane was powerless against Phulwati's sinewy arms. My mother concentrated her energies on the soundless rhythm of her beating. The people in the room stood silent, waiting with Phulwati for Ma's animal energy to tire. I thought she would never stop.

When Nani entered, the first thing she saw was a fruit-fly's cautious forays on Nana Sahib's staring left eyeball. It was so strange, I thought dreamily. Why does he not blink to make it fly away? When I followed the direction of Nani's gaze back to her face I knew that she was looking at the thousandth death of her nightmares. This was the one she could not prevent. It had stepped out of her fears and had become a reality.

Nani Sahib sat down on the teak rattan chair beside Nana Sahib's bed with impeccable composure. The teak in the chair shone from the deepest of its ebony depths, as if eager to rise to the occasion. Her eyes didn't leave Nana Sahib's face. 'It's all over, Munna Ma,' was all Nani's still breath would allow. Nani, who could not face a summer sun without her smelling salts, confronted her husband's death with the fortitude of a true queen.

Ma fell on the floor next to Potol. Her legs sprawled out in front of her, her wild eyes staring, her hair in disarray.

Like any other grief-stricken vas ghariani.

~

Time follows a different pace in a house of death. Events move at frenzied speed yet are experienced like the surreal underwater movements of the deep sea.

I don't know who arranged for the lotuses. Kilos and kilos of them. A hundred kilos of lavender-pink, slender-stemmed lotuses were brought in in baskets. They were poured on Nana Sahib like water and he disappeared under them. Stainless, blameless, lotuses, the symbol of purity, of god himself. I thought Nana Sahib would groan under their suffocating weight. But he lay under them quietly, like the rotten core of a fresh apple. Uncomplaining at last, his heart cold as ice. The pristine smell of the lotuses brought us some respite. It sanctifed our grief.

A wail rose up from the heart of the palace and spread outwards towards its ramparts, and upwards towards the sky. It was a giant cry moving up and beyond; as if all of humanity had joined to weep for mortality. The rajpurohits filed into Nana Sahib's rooms and pierced the air with Vedic mantras. All eyes were lowered. All heads were bowed. The kettledrums had stopped their rolling. The music had fallen silent. The raja was dead; Sirikot was in mourning.

The rajpurohits rummaged for Nana Sahib under the lotuses and placed him on the floor. Live fingers closed dead eyes. Tulsi leaves and water from the Ganges were placed on his tongue from little silver thuribles. The chanting was a constant litany. So we live and so we die. Mortality begged for reprieve.

I wondered where Nana Sahib was. Had his ancestors come to receive him? Or had the patidar stared at him with bloodied eyes and barred his way? Was he lifted on a golden chariot to the clouds? Or was he staring at the end of a mehtar's tunnel, smelling of night-soil? He was alone now. Only the intentions of his earthly actions would keep him company. Their merits would bind him or liberate him. His performance in the afterworld would reflect on us. We reap the fruits of our ancestors. The chanting swelled and ebbed like a lunar tide, aiding Nana Sahib's soul to the beyond. Its power made me dizzy.

Everywhere, men and women beat their chests and tore their hair. They fell on the ground and smeared their faces with dirt. They rolled and ranted and shrieked, letting the phlegm of their bodies run its course.

Suddenly Ma stood up and started walking towards Yuvraj Mama Sahib's quarters. She had walked that path many times before but never had she staggered across it with such intensity of purpose. Ma cut right through the throng of mourners, swaying not because she was moved by their grief but because she was overwhelmed by the single-mindedness of her intent. I ran after her.

~

In his chambers, Yuvraj Mama Sahib sat alone on a chair, clutching at the folds of his dhoti, his face slack and bewildered. He looked lost; an orphaned child. He raised his face to Ma as she strode up to him to make it easier for her to strike him across it with a resounding slap.

'Congratulations!' she said as quiet as Nana Sahib's death. 'The raja is dead.'

Yuvraj Mama Sahib turned his face away, tears starting from his eyes. He waited a few seconds for an elusive calm before saying, 'I didn't kill him, Apa, I really didn't.'

'Of course, you didn't.' Ma's face twisted into the exaggerated grimace of a Kathakali dancer. 'You have been conducting the pujas for his *health*, for his *long life*.'

'Listen, Apa, listen to me. The tantrik I was corresponding with, the letter you had found – it was a very old letter. If you had read our latest correspondence you would know that I am blameless.'

My mother opened her mouth to speak and then closed it again, squinting in confusion.

'Yes, I had ordered black magic on my father. I even gave an ounce of my blood and seminal fluid each day for six months, but it never worked. Anyway, all that happened a year ago. None of the pujas worked. You know what the tantrik said? And I have his letter to prove it. He said that any tantrik puja on Baba was useless. His spiritual armour was too strong. You see, he has

been giving tarpan to his ancestors everyday, since I can remember.
He has their blessings, they protect him.'

'You do know the immutable principle of tantra, don't you,
Rajraj? To gain that which is not yours you will lose something
precious of your own. The heavens only know what you might
need to sacrifice for this most criminal act of usurpation.' Ma
spoke the words like a casual curse; slant-eyed, her head cocked
to one side. 'I have seen many ambitious yuvrajas. But patricide?
I had only read of it in books on Roman history. And their
stakes were so much bigger. You did it for Sirikot? A mere
afterthought in the list of the big princely states of India? A
pimple on the butt of history? What are we but seventeen
generations of zamindari of a few hundred villages? If you were
the Nizam of Hyderabad's son you would still be a criminal in
the eyes of the law and god. But for Sirikot? Such a big crime
for such a small state?'

Yuvraj Mama Sahib drank in my mother's sarcasm. He
seemed to need her chastisement, almost revelling in it. And
when he argued it seemed to me he was arguing not with her,
but with himself: 'We had the same tutor for Roman history,
Apa. Remember, how I used to weep for all the unfortunate
princes who assassinated their fathers? We are all victims of
birth, but who can be worse victims of biology than us? What
other qualification do we have besides the legitimate hour of our
birth and the names of our parents? We are puppets of Chance,
cows tied to the stake. What do we do with our lives besides
twiddle our thumbs and wait for destiny to hand out our crumbs?
The lowliest untouchable is freer than us. He is a victim of
poverty, not of the blood running in his veins. He is a slave of
the raja not the whims of his parents. If it is ties of blood that
allow us life and earthly prosperity is it unfair that those same
ties should take it away? Our father ordered the death of his
first-born, a helpless infant who could have had a whole life to
live. Was that not a crime? What is wrong about conducting a
few pujas? He had lived his life. His time was up. And I did not

assassinate him. I just prayed that Fate would intervene. You can
be emotional about Baba, Apa, because you have nothing to
lose. You are too overpowered by the nostalgia you suffer when
you pine for your childhood home, your maike, in your husband's
palace. In my position you might have done just the same.'

'So this is how you justify things to yourself when you can't
sleep at night,' Ma mocked. 'These are the twisted ravings of a
power-hungry man of god. A man trying to be Nero, imagining
that Sirikot is the Roman Empire. What a sick mind you have.
What a false prophet you are. What a horrible afterlife awaits
you, brother. Your karmas will hound you wherever you go!'

'Don't you think your daughter is a little young to be listening
to all this?' Yuvraj Mama Sahib tried to deflect my mother's
rage without looking at me.

'My daughter must learn sooner or later what a rare
commodity goodness is. The sooner, the better.'

'You do know he died of a heart attack? It could have
happened to anybody at his age.'

'I got to the vaidya before you twisted the official statement
of a heart attack out of him. He had already told me that all the
symptoms indicated poisoning. Whether it was a slow acting
poison or a quick one, who did it and why, I promise you, Rajraj
I shall soon find out.' Then, like a woman possessed, my mother
tore out a lock of her hair and threw it on the floor. 'On her
father's deathbed, his daughter takes an oath. She shall not rest
till she finds out who murdered him!'

'Baba had many enemies,' Yuvraj Mama Sahib taunted, his
eyes turning to roasted stones. 'There are many secrets in the
zenana.'

'I know,' Ma parried. 'Most of his enemies were in the
palace. Only yesterday he confessed that the patidar was receiving
orders of assassination from within its ramparts.'

'So you presume it was I? If you are looking for clues about
the correspondence with the patidar, perhaps you would do
well to investigate your beloved sister-in-law. Did you know it

was Kumud who wrote to him?' Yuvraj Mama Sahib spat out
at her.

Before Ma could speak there was a knock at the door.
Outside, in the courtyard, the silk-clad pandits, who had sprouted
like seasonal flowers after the rain, went about their business,
consulting and confabulating, discussing the delicate issue of
royal death and succession. It was one of them. He coughed
timidly and enquired of Yuvraj Mama Sahib whether he was
free to discuss the purchase of puja items for the coronation.

'Oh, yes, he is free,' Ma said over-brightly. 'More than free.
He has been looking forward to this moment all his life.'

She bowed low, and when she raised her head her eyes were
wild though her lips were smiling. 'You do your duty, Raja
Sahib, and I shall do mine.'

Eight

alking back with my mother to my newly widowed grandmother's quarters I was dreading what I would see. My· apprehensions were well founded. Nani sat on an elevated marble platform in the courtyard surrounded by the elderly grandaunts who lived in the northeast wing of the zenana. Like scavengers who had first rights on the carcass, they had swooped down on her to conduct the rituals of widowhood. They were sincere, well meaning and very wrinkled; two of them were widows themselves and showed Nani the sort of empathy lepers give to new entrants in their colony. Further away sat a crowd of village women with hooded heads belting out their tired requiems in coarse voices.

Nani Sahib had already been divested of her gold karghani and her diamond kundan necklace. Her much favoured emerald earrings were gone, revealing misshapen earlobes — the heavy jewellery she habitually wore had cut her ear-holes into vertical slits. I watched Nani carefully take off her diamond nose-stud and hand it to a weeping Dhaima. Then she removed her thick jadau meenakari gold bangles followed by her glass bangles, which she slipped off one by one. She was careful, measured, as if disrobing for a luxurious bath. Her diamond anklets came off next. Then her numerous gold toe-rings, her navlakha epaulettes and her finger-rings and, finally, the ornaments of her hair.

Freed from its jewelled clasps her thick black hair tumbled onto the marble floor on which she sat, black dye staining white. Her bare arms, bare wrists, and bare neck were discoloured, a lighter shade where the ornaments had been. The furrows between her brows and her sagging mouth were an anomaly. She was actually a young bride getting ready for a wedding ritual.

Nani Sahib gave a small smile which burned a hole in my memory for ever. It was the coquettish smile of a temptress conjuring a prank on her lover. 'Is Raja Sahib ready?' she asked Shanti in a sweetly maternal voice. A mother asking her daughter whether she had eaten.

'It should take another hour,' Shanti stammered as she usually did when she was paid attention. 'The army has surrounded the cremation grounds and some guards have taken position around the Lion Gate of the palace. They say it's the Collector's orders. They don't want any ugly incidents.'

Since I didn't know what 'ugly incident' she meant I whispered an inquiry to my mother. 'Shh,' she whispered back. 'Not in front of Ma.'

'What happens next, Bua Sahib?' Nani was asking her aunt-in-law. My grandmother did not know much about the complicated rituals of widowhood simply because she had never wanted to. Nani had always been very arrogant of her suhag, her married status. I know that she had ignored and mistreated her own younger sister, her closest childhood confidante, because of the early demise of her brother-in-law and her sister's inauspicious widow status. She had not allowed Nana Sahib or her sons to visit her sister's province even in her time of grief, as if widowhood was a contagious disease. She had sent the estate manager to convey her condolences, a brutal insult in any circumstance. When her widowed sister visited she would not let her touch her vanity case or use her dressing room. Though her sister was invited to all her children's weddings she was not allowed to sit in the puja mandap or give her blessings. Her sister bore these insults with great dignity and never failed to be at Nani's side when she needed her. I wondered how she would feel when she heard of Nani's widowhood. I knew Nani would be deeply offended if she didn't visit.

'We have to take you for your ritual bath now.' The gentleness in my mother's great-aunt's voice was a clue to the extent of the misery that awaited her. With that bath she would wash off all memories of her previous existence and step into the austere life of the unsexed.

'You know what, Bua Sahib?' My grandmother smiled sweetly at her aunt. 'Maybe we should wait. I would like to postpone the ritual till after the cremation. Raja Sahib has still not left the palace, you know.' And with that Nani started to slip her bangles back on.

The confused vas gharianis looked at the elderly aunts for direction; an aunt's hand gesture commanded restraint: 'Stay, she is still in shock.' Smiling, unaided, Nani put her jewellery back on as slowly and carefully as she had taken it off. Savouring her last hours as a married woman, buying time even though her husband was a corpse being dressed for its funeral. Like the black-faced female langur I had once studiously watched in the zenani bagh guava orchard who had carried the carcass of her child around for days until the other female langurs snatched it away and buried it.

Then Phulwati appeared, breathless with running, and absolutely unfazed by the glowering women. If I had been her, I would have shied away from the zenana at a time like this. But she could not hold back the wonder of her news: 'It is true!' she exclaimed. 'What the holy man had said long ago. That when the birthmark descends on his Esteemed Rear he would die. The purohit priests who have been dressing up Raja Sahib for his last procession said it was true. Raja Sahib's birthmark has descended to his royal backside.'

'And what were you doing there, Phulwati?' Dhaima started a coarse dialogue in the local dialect. 'Did you think that Raja Sahib still needed your services?'

'What do you mean birthmark? What did you see?' Ma questioned, unable to restrain herself.

Phulwati gesticulated excitedly, no longer an arrogant concubine but a young girl made artless by wonder. 'I saw it. A black birthmark right up to his nether parts. Spreading around like a fan, just like the holy man said.'

A few vas gharainis started muttering the names of their gods. Others more sceptical of divine providence taunted her: 'And how do you know how the holy man described it? He died before you were born.'

'I know,' Phulwati made a self-righteous moue, 'because Raja Sahib told me.'

'Where was his birthmark when you last saw him?' Ma asked after an awkward silence.

'Last I saw him, that is last night, it was in the small of his back, I think.'

'Really!' Nani Sahib said as she put on her nose-stud, her lips twisting. Irony. The twisted curl of a woman's lip. 'Last time I saw him his entire back was full of birthmarks. But then that was a long long time ago,' Nani laughed. 'I haven't had much time or opportunity to track travelling birthmarks.'

'Ma,' Ma suddenly said. 'I should go and investigate.'

'No,' Nani admonished. 'You shall not disturb your father on his final journey. He had bleeding piles. What this stupid girl is talking about is haemorrhoids. Let it go. Don't subject your father to any more indignities.'

'The priests and vaidyas were astounded by the amount of blood that came out from his rectum,' Phulwati made a face, as if she could still smell the stench. 'Buckets and buckets of it. They say he ruptured his liver.'

'Ma,' my mother insisted, 'I should go and see for myself. I need to find out as much as I can about the effects of the poison. It will throw light on how it was administered.'

'If poison was administered,' Nani said quietly.

'If poison was administered,' Ma conceded, glaring at Phulwati. 'After Baba's body is cremated there will be no way of finding out.' I was surprised at the ease with which Ma said 'Baba's body'; how easily Nana Sahib had become a 'thing'.

'No,' Nani was firm. 'You stay with me. I need you more.'

Torn between two parents, one dead and one alive, Ma relented. She favoured the one still breathing, I thought bitterly.

I did not get time to brood over my mother's callousness however as I was drawn to a whispering huddle of vas gharianis who had separated from the group. They were walking off towards the edge of the courtyard. When they saw me sidling up to them they quickly shut up.

'Tell me,' I ordered snatching at the words I'd heard, 'which boy? And what taste? You were saying?' I cocked my eyebrow and added some bass to my voice.

An older vas ghariani who had as many wrinkles as the years in my life was amused. 'What do you want to know about these adult things? Lovely Jemma Who Makes Lotuses Blossom When She Walks, enjoy your childhood.'

'I want to know, and I want to know now.' I kept up the thickened voice and frowned for effect. But I ended badly, almost pleading with them, 'You can tell me. Promise, I won't tell anybody.'

The wrinkled vas ghariani considered me with a bemused expression and relented after a raucous but indulgent laugh. 'What I was telling my friends is that in my time rajas were more virtuous. They were like gods. They still are, but of late their taste in sex has started changing. They say that Raja Sahib was extremely virile, a true Breeding Bull, the "Mardand Sand", but younger vas gharianis have been saying that of late he had developed a taste for boy flesh.'

I imitated my grandmother's composure. 'Boy flesh?' I studied my nails. 'Nana Sahib ate boy flesh?'

That provoked guttural guffaws. The wrinkled vas ghariani cracked her knuckles on my forehead in a fond gesture to ward off the evil eye. 'He didn't eat them, my Lotus Petal Huzur, he screwed them.'

More ungainly guffaws. I decided to give them the full brunt of my superior intellectual knowledge and made a face of manifest disgust. 'You ignorant crones. You don't know anything. You old wrinkled onions, illiterate buffoons. Don't you know that sex happens when a man and a woman spend the night together in the same bed?'

Unhumbled by the piercing insight of my knowledge they exploded with laughter and continued on their way. The wrinkled vas ghariani hung back a while and cupped my chin in her gnarled hands, her face a bas-relief of longing. 'I'd give the rest of my teeth to be a child again,' she said.

~

While Nana Sahib was being festooned in all his death regalia by severe and focused pandits, Yuvraj Mama Sahib sat on the gold throne in the durbar hall for the 'interim coronation'. In attendance were the royal family and some patidars. The throne could not stay empty during the long cremation rites of a dead raja. After the prescribed thirteen days of funeral rituals a date would be fixed for the formal Rajabhishek. Invitations would go out to important relatives and states and the gem-studded coronation would be attended and conducted amid much fanfare. State guests would fill the mardana and the outhouses. Relations from the immediate and extended family would overflow the zenana. Resplendent in Nana Sahib's jewellery the newly appointed raja would bow his grave head before an elder while a nine-yard-long safa was tied around his head. A turban ornament due to the king, the sarpench, an aigrette usually of great value, would be pinned on it. The raja's weight in silver would be donated to the poor. He would conduct pujas in various temples and receive the gods' choicest blessings. Brahmins would be fed endlessly. When he led his first royal procession, seated atop his caparisoned elephant, through his numerous villages, he would throw silver guineas to his adoring public while they showered rose petals at his feet.

But Yuvraj Mama Sahib would have to wait for all that, at least for another two weeks. The cremation was not yet over. It would be many days before Nana Sahib's ashes would reach the family mausoleum. There, in the memorial samadhi of rajas situated near the western gates of the palace, Nana Sahib's remains, mostly some pieces of skull, some finger bones and ashes, would lie under a marble cenotaph beside the detritus of six preceding rajas of Sirikot.

My woebegone mother sat among the attending audience carefully watching the rajpurohit's every move during the interim coronation. Chanting his never-ending mantras he tied the state sword around Yuvraj Mama Sahib's cummerbund and anointed his forehead with the rajtilak, using ten different items three times. There was vermilion, turmeric, rice, milk, honey, petals of a red flower, cowdung, curd, camphor and sandalwood. After the rajtilak ceremony was over and the ceremonial Sirikot sword had been handed over to Yuvraj Mama Sahib, faithful to the scriptures, the rajpurohit enquired of the newly appointed raja the following question: 'There is a rotting cadaver lying in the opposite room. What should I do with it?'

Yuvraj Mama Sahib, unfamiliar with this ritual, looked around him and twitched in embarrassment.

'It is custom to say,' the rajpurohit said to the raja and his audience, '"Take him away and burn him."' When Yuvraj Mama Sahib hesitated, the rajpurohit added in a fierce whisper loud enough for us to hear: 'Kingship is eternal and unimpeded by human death. You too are just a vessel.'

The ritual admonition over, the rajpurohit proceeded with the worship of Yuvraj Mama Sahib, much like that of the gods in our temples. When the ceremony finished the rajpurohit turned to the court. 'Does anyone have anything to say?'

Ma got up from her cushioned chair and walked towards the elevated throne, the tears streaming down her face dripping off her chin and ending as dark blotches on her blouse. She spread out the anchal of her sari in the gesture of petition beggars in the street use. When I heard her thin quavering voice I burst into tears.

'I beg this raja with all the humbleness of my spirit that he look after the welfare of his widowed mother. I beg him with folded hands to drop his alms on my lap. Please do your duty as a son.'

Weeping broke out among the women. Yuvraj Mama Sahib's brimming eyes threatened to overflow. From a constricted throat he squeaked out his promise, 'I vow to do my duty, as raja, as son, as brother.'

While the women were wiping their noses noisily into their saris, deliberately unmindful of handkerchiefs, a visibly shaken Kumar Mama Sahib prepared for the funeral procession. Indian custom behooves the eldest son to perform the last rites of his father. But among royal Rajputs this is forbidden, the duty falling on the son second in line to the throne. Kumar Mama Sahib had just been called back from the shikar party in a hunting camp. I have never seen him as sombre as when he prepared to ride alongside his father for the last time. All the laughter lines had vanished from his face.

When the royal procession went out it was already getting towards dusk. Nana Sahib left the palace accompanied by the pomp and show he had been accustomed to. Beaters kicked up dust in rhythm to the drumbeats of daphlis. Women ululated the way they usually did when the raja was passing by. Young contortionists danced all the way to the cremation ground to the cacophony of musical instruments. Shehnai fought mridang and both overrode the trumpet. Seventeen generations of rajas were praised in song. A cortege of caparisoned elephants and horses followed the richly decorated bier in which Nana lay, never to open his eyes again.

Kumar Mama Sahib led the other pallbearers from the front and on foot. He did what is so important in any Indian rite of passage, he 'gave shoulder'.

The turuhi player led the procession. Turuhi, the royal instrument played to herald the raja's arrival. The player was Nana Sahib's childhood friend and I had heard that they were both born at the same hour and on the same day. From the highest ramparts of the zenana we women could still catch the strains of his plaintive music, a snake charmer leading the serpentine queue to its destination. Women are forbidden to participate in cremation rites. I don't know why. Maybe it is to spare our delicate temperaments from the brutal rituals of real life.

I listened to the tears in the turuhi player's music, imagining him mourning for his childhood friend the way I had mourned for Baby Uncle. I had heard that Nana Sahib and he had often whiled away the time composing tunes on the turuhi, Nana Sahib uncaring that the instrument was contaminated by his friend's spit. Surely, he was crying. Not only with the innocent sincerity of the subjugated but also because he had lost his livelihood, like the hundred vas gharianis in the palace. Would Yuvraj Mama Sahib retain them?

I looked at Ma. She was standing on the pedestal of a statue for a closer look, shielding her brow with the palm of her hand, her eyes burning the distance, her mouth open.

Nana Sahib had been carried through a bristling cordon of cavalry to the cremation site. Since he was royalty a canopy covered his funeral pyre. From our distance we could see it, a tiny bed.

Soon Kumar Mama Sahib would circle the pyre and let the earthen pot of water balanced on his shoulder fall to the ground. It would splinter into smithereens and release the astral body from its mortal coils. Then he would take a lit torch and ignite the pyre. When, unlike the softer parts of his body, the skull would refuse to burn in the engulfing flames, Kumar Mama

Sahib would conduct the 'kapal kriya', the smashing of the skull with a bamboo rod.

When the first lick of flame lit up the tiny dot in the horizon, like a crimson worm devouring an ant, the zenana ramparts were still, as if we were not even there, the puny conflagration only a soundless flower blooming in our third eye. We sensed the heat of the poisonous fire, and the warmth of a new summer Nana Sahib would never experience. It was over. We went back inside.

Sitting in the zenana prayer hall for two hours, I was staring anxiously at Ma. While the other women took refuge in the incessant supply of zenana tears my mother sat motionless, in a trancelike state. Suddenly Dhaima appeared like a madwoman amidst us. Ma gazed at her blankly, as if nothing could break her contemplative mood. Dhaima's kohl had streaked down her cheeks mixing with her sweat and tears and making her look grotesque, a caricature of terror. She looked as if she had walked out of a cyclone. Her wheezing was so terrible that nobody could understand what she was saying.

'Rani Sahib, Rani Sahib — ' she sucked in air and fell on her knees, her head hanging as if ready for decapitation.

Ma pulled her up by the shoulders and shook her violently, 'Rani Sahib, what? Rani Sahib *what*?'

Dhaima's head rattled brokenly with every shake. Her eyes rolled, as if she were ready to faint. 'Rani Sahib has committed sati,' she said.

~

The stone concrete felt strange under my bare feet. My ribs constricted my heart. My lungs rasped for air. All that running and still the palace temple was so far away, our bodies so slow. Was the palace really silent, or had my eardrums burst? Steps, steps, more steps, tennis court, stone, concrete, walls around me, grass, pebbles, stones, walls everywhere, will we ever reach on time? A feverish thought insisted, kept insisting, *She did not say 'she might commit sati,' or 'she was going to commit sati,' she said, 'she has committed sati.'* Past tense.

Two squirrels chased each other in the temple courtyard. I could see the Govinda idol playing his flute in the sanctum sanctorum, his balmy smile of cosmic indifference increasing my impotency. In the pleasantly worshipful setting to the west of the temple courtyard was the scene of morbid nightmares. A circle of blackened stones. A rudimentary human shape, like a burnt effigy. Only the charred roundness of a hairless skull decipherable under the debris of human soot. Maybe the faintest shadow of a facial expression. That, and the image of stick-like legs blowtorched into my future memory, even though I looked away that very instant.

The smell of burnt human flesh is an odour so sharp it can cut you and make you bleed. It fills the nasal cavities and sticks to the brain in black particles. I think those particles entered my womb and I passed them on to my children.

Shanti knelt next to a rectangular tin of paraffin. Beside her lay a misshapen log of smouldered sandalwood. In her hands, neatly folded, was the embroidered extremity of Nani's sari, the anchal. She and Ma looked at each other in stupefied awe. Beside me, Pushpa yawned and in a sharp reflex I slapped her for her temerity, realizing only later that her reaction was from hysteria. Shanti handed over the creaseless anchal and gave her account in a surprisingly coherent voice. Each word she spoke mortified me with its extreme finality. It made me grope inwards and remember my scriptures.

Like Nani's great-grandmother-in-law who died never letting the sun touch her, Nani, on that balmy evening paid the highest tribute to purdah, the 'system' as she called it, and the traditions her mother had taught her. I doubt that in her mind she was committing suicide. She was simply erasing the possibility of life without her husband. I also doubt that it sprang from an abiding love for Nana Sahib; it sprang from the conviction of her beliefs.

Nani had meticulously prepared for her sati. The English, wary from previous experiences, had cordoned off the cremation grounds because sati was usually performed with the wife sitting on her husband's pyre, his head in her lap. Nani Sahib had waited in the palace temple. She had taken care to dress in her wedding finery; she would not meet her husband looking plain and unadorned. She had sent Dhaima on the mission to procure a smouldering log from her husband's pyre after everyone had left. Then, in the courtyard, in full view of Dhaima, Shanti and a few prostrate villagers, with the rajpurohit chanting his eternal hymns, she doused herself in paraffin and lit up like a torch.

It is said that a true sati does not burn by self-immolation but by self-combustion, as the primeval sati, the wife of Lord Shiva, had done. Though the villagers who had witnessed the sati ran through Sirikot proclaiming that Nani was indeed a Devi, a goddess incarnate, because she had self-combusted, I did not need the rajpurohit to tell me that this was not true. Nani had used the burning log. This did not prevent her deification in the eyes of everybody. I am sure if Nana Sahib were alive he would have been very proud.

In the years that followed Nani Sahib was brought closer to godhood. In fact, the sati temple built on her remains became even bigger than the Govinda temple, because the anchal of her sari remained intact. The anchal is that extremity of a garment that covers a woman's bosom, her face and her modesty. It was this that was viewed as a manifest sign of Nani's purity. 'My anchal will not burn,' Nani had told Dhaima. The fact that it had remained intact was likened to Sita's unscathed walk through Lord Rama's flames. It proved that her modesty was intact, pure as driven snow.

God forgive my cynicism, because my mind has been sullied by the clinical objectivity of the books I have read in European literature, of Charles Dickens and Alexandre Dumas. But I could not help thinking that the anchal did not burn simply for the reason that its heavy silver embroidery rendered it less combustible.

If Nani was really so pure, she would have either self-combusted or walked out of the fire unscathed like Sita did in Lord Rama's test of fire.

Every event has two causes, a material cause and an immaterial cause. Somebody has said, 'We only know one hundredth of the reasons why things happen.'

I did not know then, at the age of thirteen, as I do not know now, at the age of seventy-two, the laws that govern life and death.

I have no doubt that Nana Sahib loved his wife. But I doubt whether his love influenced her decision to commit sati. I think Nana Sahib had nothing to do with her sati. She did what she believed in. She was only doing her time-honoured duty. What is death but a brief slumber before you wake again?

That day in the palace temple, when I looked at Ma, I felt I was the mother and she my child; she looked about her numbly, sightlessly, blinded by infernal thoughts. In one day, she had been orphaned.

In her hands was the sealed letter that the rajpurohit had handed Dhaima. The last letter Ma's mother would ever write to her. Nani's last words to Ma, conveyed by Dhaima were, 'Try and understand, this is what I believe in.'

My mother had mourned for her father. But she did not know how to mourn for her mother. How do you mourn for someone who hasn't died but has joined the pantheon of gods?

❧ PART II ❧

Nine

Over us summer was a steaming blanket; heat waves in the distance were like splintered glass through which we watched the landscape reel in shock. The baking stone walls of the zenana forced the women to take refuge in open courtyards and the cool shades of the orchards and mango groves. The punkah swingers worked overtime, and maintained their rhythm even as they dozed off. Yuvraj Mama Sahib issued an order that though he would not be practising concubinage all the old vas gharianis and their children would be retained. In fact, he made very little changes in the staff. Even the turuhi player got to stay.

Baby Uncle was unable to attend Nana Sahib's funeral because his adopted father said that it might upset the boy's 'delicate balance'. Baby Uncle wrote me increasingly piteous letters on his homelessness, and asked me how many times god would orphan him. My own father and paternal grandfather attended the funeral and left soon after paying their condolences. They had urgent matters to settle before the coming Independence. In fact, Independence and the almost certain annexation of the Indian princely states were more discussed than Nana Sahib's death and Nani's sati. I couldn't help thinking that Nani's sati was a complete waste and she should have chosen a better time.

The last of the state guests and relatives had left and only Choti Nani, Nani's widowed younger sister, tarried. Ma's tenacity in keeping her was an overwhelming need for surrogacy. Choti Nani was forced to keep postponing her departure.

Yuvraj Mama Sahib had shifted to the Chandramahala, and had proposed many reforms in the course of his durbars. He immediately founded a college and ordered two new temples to be built. He sanctioned the construction of roads, bridges and homes for doctors who were migrating to Sirikot from Calcutta. He organized a committee of pandits to collect all the scriptures written in the local dialect. He was contemplating selling off the elephants and turning the stables into an Ayurvedic dispensary. He kept saying that we had to plan for the accession to the new dominion status of India once the English left.

Ma was being treated for symptoms of a nervous breakdown. She took tablets at night to sleep and lay in bed throughout the day, continuously reciting the Gayatri Mantra.

The vas gharianis whispered that my younger uncle had started drinking heavily. Once he was so inebriated that he almost threw a vas ghariani's baby, who had crawled into the room, off the window. He mistook the baby for a cat.

Kumar Mama Sahib had reached his nadir grappling existential causality during his father's last rites. For thirteen days he had slept on the floor. Obeying custom, he abstained from sexual intercourse and focused on singing the Lord's name and reading the scriptures. As decreed, he wore his father's dressing gown, ate his favourite foods and smoked his Havana cigars. After endless brahmins had been fed, he prostrated before them just as the mehtar had prostrated before Nana Sahib and Nana Sahib before the temple gods. The brahmins raised their sandals over his head and shook the dust of their feet over him. After the transmogrifying last rites were over, Kumar Mama Sahib surrendered to the study of fatalism in Phulwati's bewitching arms and the alcoholic trance.

Kumud Mami Sahib, her hair open and tangled, took to practising the veena in the rose garden, while her husband, deep

in the throes of carnal gratification, registered mild surprise that
the larger truths still eluded him.

Yuvrani Mami Sahib moved into Nani's quarters, adjoining
Ma's, making her constant bickering over the lack of respect
meted out to her too close for comfort. Yuvrani Mami Sahib had
decided to sit for a portrait and hang it next to Nani's in the
Banquet Hall. She played rani to the hilt but during private
durbars in her courtyard her body language betrayed that she
was trying too hard. The more insufferable she became, the
more besotted her husband, the new raja, grew of her: 'Look
how lightly she walks,' Yuvraj Mama Sahib nudged me. 'The
softest batashas wouldn't crumble under her feet.'

'My mother is a nymphomaniac,' their son, Raghavendra,
informed me.

'And what does that mean?' I grudgingly enquired.

'Isn't it obvious, silly?' said a contemptuous Raghavendra
continuing his unerring ability to grasp the wrong meaning of
words. 'It's a maniacal nymph.'

In a new way, the palace regained its fulcrum of normalcy.
After a paralytic period of anxiety about their future, the vas
gharianis were relieved to get back their old status. The children
of the royal family stuck to their immutable routine of play,
meals, sleep and subdued mayhem. Shanti and Dhaima shuttled
between Ma and Yuvraj Mama Sahib in frenetic consultation.

As for me, in the absence of Baby Uncle, I had drawn
closer to Pushpa. Her weak shadowy presence calmed me. She
helped me ward off the innumerable hauntings that troubled
my nights. Not only did I hear Nana Sahib's shuffling feet on
the wooden staircase and Nani's absent hookah rumbling in
her courtyard, I felt the dead patidar's bloodied eyes watching
the kitchen corridors. Outside Kumar Mama Sahib's chambers
I thought I heard the ludbudiya ghost's shrieking laughter
joining Kumar Mama Sahib's ribald merry-making. I wished
the lamps and torches wouldn't create so many shadows at
night.

Pushpa's philosophy was simple and reassuring, thank her dear heart. 'Ghosts can't hurt you, Jemma Sahib,' she said. 'They are only air.'

~

In the blessed daylight of one morning, a few days later, Ma returned from Nani's sati mandir looking firmly resolved. She sent a runner to Yuvraj Mama Sahib. Sensing that some new and interesting development was afoot I followed her to the Chandramahala.

My uncle put his pen down and stood up from his desk when I offered him my first pranam of the day on entering his room. 'Juhar, Yuvraj Mama Sahib,' I said folding my hands and bowing low.

'I've been promoted from yuvraj to raja,' he reminded me. 'Don't you think you should change the way you address me now?' His indulgent smile couldn't soften the crushing reprimand in his words and blood rushed to my face. I was upset by my faux pas and embarrassed by his pettiness. I decided that henceforth I would simply call him 'Mama Sahib'. I did not mean him any discourtesy. In my mind I was deleting the offending prefix.

Ma slumped into an overstuffed armchair. The anchal of her sari had slid off her shoulders; it looked sloppy and quite unlike her. 'I have been going over Shanti's demands,' she said raising her chin, as though trying to rise above her crumpled clothes. 'I think we should give her three rooms in one of the outhouses. That will improve her status from the vas ghariani's quarters. But at least she will be out of the palace.'

Yuvraj Mama Sahib compulsively twisted the cap of his fat gold-tipped Parker pen. 'And how will you explain it?'

Ma shrugged. 'She was instrumental in Ma's sati. Ma had a soft spot for her. The reason is hardly an issue.'

Yuvraj Mama Sahib's eyes shifted about in contemplation. 'Send for her.'

When Shanti came in she looked about the room. Yuvraj Mama Sahib had brought his Spartan tastes to the Chandramahala. The rooms had been shorn of Nana Sahib's heavy tapestries. The paintings of English bugle boys and obese European women in see-through garments had been removed. So had his ostentatious Edwardian furniture. Still a love seat remained, and for a moment Shanti considered it. But she remained standing.

When the proposal was presented to her she turned it down. 'Either you give me my status, my haq, by divine right or nothing at all. I am quite happy in Dhaima's quarters. For thirty-two years I have lived like that. I can continue for thirty more.'

Ma casually flicked at a nonexistent fly. 'If you were really so used to your lifestyle you wouldn't be creating so much trouble for us.'

Shanti's ramrod posture straightened further. The scar from her left chin to her left ear throbbed for attention. Her impertinent tone made me gasp but left Ma and Mama Sahib unruffled.

'Don't even try to judge my thoughts, my words or my actions. You have no idea what life I have led for thirty-two years. Either you give me my right or you don't. I am' — her eyes flicked towards me and she chose her words carefully — 'I am not going to settle for half measures, not now.'

They had been conversing in the local dialect. Ma, inexplicably, turned to Hindi. 'If our parents didn't give you your right, why should we?'

'They didn't know.' Shanti's voice was small. Her smile was slow.

'My father knew,' Yuvraj Mama Sahib confronted her. I wondered whether it was a bluff, whether he was testing her.

'He knew,' she conceded after a pause.

'Ma didn't know.' Ma's statement betrayed the slightest hint of a question. I somehow got the impression that Ma and Yuvraj Mama Sahib had asked her these questions several times. 'Why didn't you tell her?'

Shanti was contemptuous, holding down Ma and Yuvraj Mama Sahib like pieces of toast under a fork. 'What if I told you that she always knew? That before she committed sati the rajpurohit witnessed her declaration that she wished I got my right?'

'The rajpurohit will say anything for a few gold coins —' Ma didn't raise her voice but when she finished the steel was beginning to show.

Shanti's laughter had an edge of an elusive sadness. 'Why don't you just say you don't believe me because you don't want to believe me? You are a very greedy woman, Jemma Sahib. You want everything for yourself.'

Ma's brow darkened. 'What is this right you keep bargaining for, as if it were vegetables you are buying in the market? You can't demand your right, Shanti. You have to earn it. We can't give an audience to every vas ghariani's daughter who carries fantastic tales.'

Shanti stood her ground. 'If you don't believe me why are you offering me the outhouse?'

Ma's eyes were opaque and cruel. She scared me. 'To give you the benefit of doubt. Out of the goodness of our hearts. You can take it or leave it.'

'I leave it. And I curse you, and the blood that runs in your veins. It's either my right, the right of god, or nothing at all.' Shanti stormed out of the room and Yuvraj Mama Sahib looked at Ma in exasperation. Ma was breathing heavily as if she had just run a mile.

~

That night I went to sleep terribly disturbed. Beside me, Ma snored heavily from the effect of the drugs. I tossed and turned and couldn't help envying Ma her sleep of forgetfulness. I couldn't get Ma's conversation with Shanti out of my mind. That, and the horrific events of the last few weeks, burdened my imagination

the way no haunting could. I couldn't shake off the treacherous
idea that Ma was in cahoots with Mama Sahib about something.
They had conspired together, hatched some heinous plot. They
had tried to bribe Shanti, attempted to buy her with an outhouse.
Why was Shanti's silence so necessary? What did she know that
they were trying to hide? Did the secret lead to Nana Sahib's
murder and Nani's unfortunate sati? Did Nani carry some terrible
secret to the funeral-pyre? I remembered how brooding and
withdrawn Nani had lately become, how different from her
normal ebullient self. I felt that the patidar was also responsible
in some way. Ma had sworn to find the killer. Her vehemence
could not have been faked. It could be that Nana Sahib was an
innocent victim of her conspiracy, that she had not really intended
for him to die, but the risk had always existed. Maybe that was
why she was so overwrought. Her hands and feet would go cold.
She sweated profusely and sometimes muttered aloud, which
made me scared for her and myself. It was not grief, but guilt
that made her toss and turn at night and take refuge in drugs
and mantras.

I was at the age when adolescents discover that the parents
whom they have worshipped as children have clay feet after all.
I have read that psychologists call it identity realignment. But
that night, lying with her on our silver bed, looking at the cracks
on the wooden beams in the ceiling, I did not experience identity
realignment. It was more like identity amputation. My mother
was not a goddess whose feet were made of clay. She was a
taloned monster.

I tried to console myself thinking I was not the only child
doomed to a family of sinful parents. Raghavendra was condemned
to a mother rumoured to have produced a child from her father-
in-law. His father harboured patricidal thoughts. Malini's mother
was thought insane. Her father was a drunken debauch. Baby
Uncle's father had murdered dark-skinned brahmins in cold
blood. Why should my mother be any different? Why should I
be so lucky?

Suddenly I could not bear to sleep on the same bed as my mother and went out into the corridor to shake Pushpa awake. She was sleeping on a floor mattress. A ladybird with ridiculously large spots swelled up and fluttered off her hair. I usually enjoyed collecting the myriad-hued insect species that comprised the nightlife of the zenana, putting them in little boxes pierced for air holes and pretending I was Charles Darwin the scientist. But tonight my mind was hungry for different answers.

As I waited for Pushpa to wake, I heard the low sound of Yuvrani Mami Sahib's laughter floating down from what used to be Nani Sahib's terrace. She was giggling. I heard the clash of bangles and the sound of bodies in muffled agitation, then a dull thud like the sound of a falling tree. When my eyes focused in the dark I saw from where I stood the filmy curtains of her canopied mosquito net. She was sleeping on the terrace and somebody was with her.

Pushpa's eyes and mouth opened simultaneously. I clamped my palm over her mouth and she reacted by widening her eyes in a comical mask of horror. I had woken her up to escort me to the toilet, but now I changed my mind. 'Shut up,' I said, 'and follow me.'

I did not look back to see whether Pushpa was behind me as I climbed the crenellations of a trellised arch and hoisted myself quietly behind the overgrowth of bougainvillaea on Nani Sahib's terrace. I knew she would be there, my faithful shadow. I thrilled at my intrepid and pioneering sense of adventure and had already started framing the words of the letter I would write Baby Uncle about my exploits.

Now I could clearly see the silhouettes of two, barely clothed, supine bodies under the mosquito netting. They were motionless. From where I crouched I could see the back of their heads. The ends of their cigarettes glowed in the dark like two amber eyes watching us. They were talking in whispers and I heard Yuvrani Mami Sahib say, 'It would be safer downstairs.'

I motioned to Pushpa and like two little monkeys we slid down the wall of the terrace using the cement cornice and the window lattice for footholds. Instinct told me that the vas gharianis would have been excused from duty that night and I was right. We fled to Nani's dressing room, and turned down the lamp that rested on a corner stool. Then I opened the door just a crack so that I could could see and hear the illicit activities that were to take place. My heart throbbed with a treacherous excitement; I couldn't believe what an incredibly intrepid sleuth I was.

Yuvrani Mami Sahib entered, dragging Kumar Mama Sahib by the hand. Without his tunic he looked like a vulnerable lamb being led to slaughter. I thanked my stars I had not involved any of his children or hers in my nefarious expedition. The anchal of the new queen's sari trailed the floor, her bosom exposed in a wanton display of her sex. Her lower lip was in the grip of her teeth and her hooded eyes spoke such brazen sensuality that I was embarrassed about spying into this most intimate and secret aspect of her shame.

They tumbled onto Nani's silver four-poster in a fashion that suggested an advanced state of inebriation. I turned away from the crack in the door and shut my ears to their salacious sounds. I do not know whether my body trembled out of guilt or fear or voyeuristic pleasure. I was overwhelmed by an image of my mother and the humiliation I would feel if she ever knew what I had done. Pushpa, unperturbed by the forbidden act, as if she had witnessed it many times before, watched them without blinking.

Huddled between Yuvrani Mami Sahib's vanity case and a dressing table stool, I heard snatches of conversation between inexplicably vulgar noises that I am in no mood to elucidate, even for the sake of reportage. Their laughter was suggestive of the baseness of copulating animals. She teased him about Kumud Mami Sahib, and he called her a cow and said, 'Whenever I see her I am reminded of my toothless, sexless, widowed aunt.' He proclaimed Yuvrani Mami Sahib 'the wife fate denied him'. He said he would willingly kiss the dust of her feet. She called him the real 'Mardand Sand', the true Breeding Bull. Their love talk was punctuated by the shudder of glass bangles and the careful quietness of clandestine movement. Their gossip of the royal family was shameless and scurrilous. They called Yuvraj Mama Sahib 'the false prophet' and Ma 'that vicious meddling nosy parker who thinks she owns Sirikot'.

'I believe my demented cow of a wife is investigating the death of some black brahmin.'

'We should be careful of that wife of yours, if she can even pick up the skin tone of the people in her dreams. Do you think she can see us in her dreams?'

'If she suddenly runs out of her quarters screaming and tearing her hair out, you can be sure of it. But don't be fooled by Kumud's docile appearance. She's a little Communist pig. She tried her radical political ideologies on me once and I swear I almost hit her. I wouldn't be surprised if one day she murders all of us in our sleep.'

'My Mardand Sand, you credit her with too much guts. And as for the black brahmin, I know she's been snooping around.'

'Really?'

'She talked to the rajpurohit, didn't she? Smart woman. The incident happened during his father's time. Around the time the Yuvraj was born. So only the old retainers really know.'

'How do you know?'

'I know much more than poor Kumud will ever find out. You see, I know the rajpurohit likes me. He's young, and the way he looks at me I know I can make him eat out of my hand if I want.'

'You don't need feminine wiles. You are Rani Sahib now.'

'Anyway, he knows because of his father. He told me, even though he has been sworn to secrecy, and this is a state secret.'

'Oh, forget it. Take off your jewellery, it hurts.'

'No, listen. Around the time the Yuvraj was born Raja Sahib spotted a young brahmin girl bathing in the river during one of his hunting parties. So he propositioned her.'

'What has that got to do with the black brahmin?'

'Patience, my bull, patience...so she folded her hands and begged pardon. Apparently, Raja Sahib said in front of witnesses that he pardoned her and would not force her because she was a brahmin woman and he respected her decision. You do know that was the time when the old raja had become so notorious for carrying off young brides on their wedding night that weddings in the village took place in secret, without the telltale music of the shehnai?'

'What rubbish. The villagers welcomed the raja's touch. *Droit de signor* was considered rajprasad, a royal blessing.'

'Not for everyone. You know what a pervert your father was and...'

'Well, okay. Get to the point.'

'The woman was pardoned. She had a husband and a child. Now do you get it?'

'I'm sorry, I don't. Please get to the point.'

'The black brahmin was her husband, you dunce. He was beaten to death in the granary. The rajpurohit's father was told to have him cremated quickly and tell the villagers he had died suddenly of snakebite.'

'What happened to the child?'

'The child was abandoned in an untouchable village.'

'And the wife?'

'Apparently, Raja Sahib maintained her in a house away from the palace. She died during childbirth.'

'And the rajpurohit risked his neck by telling you all this?'

'I told you. I can make him eat out of my hand.'

'You sorceress!'

My mind was becoming a confused collage of snakes, screams, cremations and the pain of childbirth. I saw Nana Sahib enter the collage on a horse, while Kumud Mami Sahib played the veena and Ma walked the palace at night like Lady Macbeth.

I was dizzy. The closed air of Yuvrani Mami Sahib's dressing room was stifling me. I was claustrophobic and succumbing to hallucinations. I was desperate to run out of the room, back to the safe haven of my mother's bed.

But it was a long time before Pushpa and I could get out.

Ten

During the course of the funeral rituals of both my grandparents, Kumud Mami Sahib's family had visited Sirikot. Her niece had been left behind to provide solace to a wistful Kumud Mami Sahib. The niece, Lalita, turned out to be a very westernized girl, a couple of years older than I, and utterly annoying. Providing entertainment to her and 'showing her around' became my onerous task. Her condescension to our 'primitive ways' put my teeth on edge. In spite of my graciousness, she kept on about how we were not really royalty at all because Sirikot did not get the Ruling Chief title from the British, unlike her own grand state of Purankot in Gujarat, which had three gun-salutes.

That was too much. I told her we were a four-hundred-year-old kingdom enjoying the hereditary title of raja given to us by divine right and the people of Sirikot. I said I knew a lot about Purankot. The Purankot lineage led back to a string of tribal chieftains, unlike Sirikot whose illustrious pedigree came from the most aristocratic and blue-blooded of Rajput stock. I let her know that Purankot had never fought a war, had practised the diplomacy of treachery and that the old raja, her grandfather, was not even the Yuvraj, but the second son. He received the Ruling Chief title by licking the boots of the British and betraying the true and deserving Yuvraj who was a freedom fighter and a staunch believer of liberation for the motherland.

I said I knew that their palace was not even an old one but a nouveau riche eyesore built on the barbaric sacrifice of a poor brahmin whose last wish was that the kingdom be named after him. His name was Puran, and the sacrifice was conducted to propitiate the gods who kept obstructing the construction of a palace based on trickery.

Kumud Mami Sahib's niece told me, quite shrilly, that for my kind information her brothers were smart and handsome unlike the 'socially backward men' here. They went to Eton and Harrow and were the best polo players in the world. The men here didn't even play polo properly, all they were good at was some amateur pig-sticking, on those rare occasions when they were not lolling in the arms of the ugly ghariani tribals. My grandfather had a mistress who was an American film actress, she said. You people hardly go abroad. You have probably never seen Harrods in your life. And you women never get out of the zenana. You are so backward. You have never worn hunting breeches. You can't ride, and I'm sure you don't know the difference between an eight bore and a twelve bore rifle. You don't even have any ADC's. You only have attendants. My grandfather shot six hundred tigers. Your grandfather shot only sixty. My grandfather has a house in Surrey. Does your grandfather have a house in Surrey? Oh, and by the way, where was your grandfather during King George's coronation in Delhi? I am sure he was standing at the back somewhere holding my grandfather's spittoon.

I got up from my cushioned seat in the elephant howdah and threatened to push her off the elephant. Puriya, the mahout, glanced back at us worriedly. For him the routine afternoon elephant ride was heading towards disaster. Pushpa sat cross-legged between us, watching us as if she were watching a film. Durga the elephant was the only one unconcerned. She stopped to take a blithe shit and eat some bamboo.

Lalita was half a head taller than I. She was horse-faced (or so I thought) and had big teeth. I told her that just because I didn't wear western clothes and was not as shameless and badly bred as her to go riding in full view of the public, it did not make me less smart. I was a crack shot, played good tennis and had visited, with the family, all the nightclubs in Calcutta.

Unlike Purankot people, Sirikot people were not the pet ponies of the English. That is why we did not sweat over polo or ape the British. We were a proud traditional race of the bluest blood, uncontaminated by the bloodline of second sons. My grandfather didn't have a house in England because it rained all the time there, and they don't take avdust, but use only toilet paper. We do not trust people who do not have clean backsides. So there!

I did not mean to push her, in fact I hadn't. I only took a step toward her but Durga intervened by suddenly stepping up her ambling pace. The next thing I knew, Lalita was hanging from the howdah railing. Puriya was torn between helping Lalita and controlling Durga. Pushpa stared at me in silent reproach. Lalita hung on for dear life, wearing an expression of mild surprise. I debated what to do. If word of this altercation got out and if Lalita was mean enough to tell the elders that I had pushed her, as I was sure she might, I would have hell to pay. I would be severely upbraided for ill-treating a Sirikot guest. Nobody would appreciate my valiant efforts to defend Sirikot.

So, profusely apologetic, I made a big show of rescuing her from the jaws of death, and hauled her back into the howdah. In my dutiful ministrations, I hoped that the twinkle in my eye would convey to her my high moral ground. Providence had punished her. I had won my argument.

Reaching the raised platform where the elephant halted so we could get off at a little gate that opened into the balcony, I waited for Lalita and Pushpa to alight. Then I ordered Puriya to make Durga kneel. Puriya drove his ankush into Durga's skin and she sank to her knees. In a cavalier display of arrogant fearlessness, I climbed off Durga between her thickly lashed eyes, using the leathery wrinkles of her proboscis as footholds and casually looked down at Lalita to see whether she was impressed. She was. Unlike her, I had no fear of climbing down an elephant's front. I enjoyed sliding off an elephant's trunk flanked on either side by its placid eyes, imagining I could feel its mammoth thoughts throb under me. Durga coiled her proboscis around me and gave me the gentle spin she knew I enjoyed before placing me safely on the ground. What pettifogging hustlers children are!

Lalita and I avoided each other over the next few days. She became an ambiguous smudge on the other side of the zenana, an unknowable minotaur hidden behind mists of exclusion. She stuck to her side. I restricted myself to mine.

All along, the summer blazed. Sirikot disappeared behind blinds made of khus grass, dampened to keep at bay the unrelenting sun. The cremation fires singed the green of the Sirikot forests to a combustible brown. The flames of Nani's devout gaze scorched the birds and dropped them dead from the sky. Centipedes curled up in desiccated knots. The flowers in the pleasure gardens wept from thirst. Lawns receded like a middle-aged man's hairline. Ponds and lakes languished in the open like parched mouths. Punkah swingers fell asleep even as their hands continued to move. Servants became slack and irritable. Women appeared outside their heavily curtained apartments only in the evenings when temperatures were cooler, like animals searching for a waterhole. Only the children were unconcerned, indifferent to the baking stone and cement of the courtyards and the fiery breath of the winds blowing through the pleasure gardens.

Village and palace suffered the heat of a troubled conscience.

~

But like a short temper, the summer was brief, it did not seethe for long.

In June, a changing warmth and the sound of kettledrums in the clouds announced my thirteenth monsoon.

The vault of the sky became a leaky roof that finally caved in. The downpour pelted Sirikot with the urgency of a long promised fulfilment. Sometimes the rain fell with military regimentation in straight lines. Sometimes it zigzagged, pelting any which way, and I imagined naiads dancing in mischief. Life sprang wherever the stinging drops fell. I watched in a fascination still not jaded by years the communion between earth and sky.

The night silence of the palace was drowned by the cacophony of scurrying lives calling out to their mates. Flies shed their wings near storm lanterns and writhed on the floor like lewd naked dancers. Insects outdid each other in ceremonial shapes and colours and presented themselves at our feet for appreciation of the latest fashion. Fireflies staggered in orgasmic saturnalia till the wee hours. Moths died in mounds on our courtyards and balconies, as if tired of abundance. Peacocks pulled out squirming snakes from the wet earth like noodles stuck to the bottom of a plate.

Unlike the cornucopia of tiny lives around us that were living and dying briefly and gloriously, I soon tired of the insistent rain. Its noise and wetness wedged into the holes of my body and seeped into my brain. The monsoons became an itchy rash, a parasitic condition. Underneath the façade of etiquette and the decorum of formality secrets festered like unmentionable sores.

I spent most of my time tending to Ma in her quarters. She lay on her bed sedated or sleeping, muttering in delirium. I answered my father's politely concerned letters and kept a strict watch on Ma's medicines, in case they were poisoned. Ma's illness and Sirikot hospitality prevented Yuvraj Mama Sahib and Yuvrani Mami Sahib to enquire even discreetly about our plans for departure. I knew our continued presence was beginning to irritate them. We were, after all, guests. In spite of Ma's proprietorial hold over Sirikot this was only her maike, her parental home, a relation made more tenuous by the death of her parents. She was in no condition to keep her promise of finding the murderer and bringing him to justice.

I longed to return to our own palace, away from Sirikot's debauched mysteries, the absence of Baby Uncle and the hostile presence of horse-faced antagonists. I heard from some vas gharianis that on clear days Lalita was seen riding through Nana Sahib's fields in breeches. I gasped at the scandalous news. Lalita was fifteen years old, old enough to strictly maintain all the norms of purdah. How could Kumud Mami Sahib, her ward and aunt, permit such a blatant thwarting of the Sirikot code of conduct?

When Ma heard of the incident she roused herself enough to forbid me to associate with Lalita or any of Kumud Mami Sahib's ilk. Beside herself with disgust, Ma's anger, for a brief incendiary moment, breathed back some life into her. Her display of venom was an inspired one. I had seen the Tongue's attack on many previous hapless victims, but Lalita's fall from grace gave me a particularly wicked pleasure.

'What's wrong with Kumud?' Ma started a virulent attack on my absent Mami Sahib. 'Has she no sense, not a modicum of decency? She must be a faisha woman herself, to send off her niece in the open without jurisdiction.' Faisha was a Persio-Hindi word commonly used in the zenana. It stood for women who were not yet prostitutes but showed all the inclination and aptitude to become one.

I tired of Ma's tongue. Her malicious outburst strengthened my desire to leave Sirikot as soon as possible. But it would be a long time before my wish would be fulfilled, because India stood poised to become a free country, to gain its much-fought-for independence from foreign yoke.

And, even before that, I was to become a woman.

~

It happened one rained-out Sirikot morning. Baby Uncle's Santoma and Dhaima dragged me weeping from the toilet. I surrendered to their consoling arms and bemoaned my fate. Unfortunately, it was the only day Ma was not lying in bed hallucinating about cremation fires. Her hair was untied and uncombed. She asked the two stroking, cajoling women what the fuss was about. When they, in sympathetic deference to my self pity, informed her that I had begun to menstruate, she asked everybody to stop the racket.

But what would she know about my misery, I retaliated.

After a long time in many months I could see that Ma was amused. 'Yes, what would I know about your misery. I'm only a woman and your mother.'

'What do you know about motherhood other than that it's a damn good excuse for everything?' I was in my element, plumbing my anguished depths.

I had joined the army of pariah women, 'untouchable on certain days'. On days that I was menstruating I was not allowed to enter the temple and would have to maintain a two-foot distance from the brahmins when they came up with the prasad of the evening arti. I would have to stay out of the mardana and for four days not touch any male who might be wearing the sacred thread. In case I kept my malaise to myself those who knew would loudly warn male members of my condition. In this way every male in the palace, from the Mama Sahibs to the attendants to Raghavendra would know of my shameful disease. I could not go to a kitchen and watch food being cooked. I could not go near fasting women. I could not worship or take the name of god. I could not go out of the house during this time. And there was more. My soiled clothes would be thrown in a bin that would be washed by the rajdhobis. Muscled, but emasculated young men would wash my innermost secretions and participate in my disgrace.

Oh god, if only the earth would part and accept me the way it had accepted Sita!

But the worst thing was I would never sleep in the nursery again. I would only wear saris. Ma would now start thinking about my marriage.

'Stop your whining,' Ma ordered, tired and irritable. 'What has happened to you happens to half the people in this world. It is part of growing up. A very natural phenomenon.'

'Then why the untouchability, Ma? *Why?*'

Ma cut through my angst brutally. 'No more drama! If this happened at any other time a mandap would have been erected in the courtyard and you would have had to sit through a puja three hours long. All the men and women in the palace would not only have known about your new status, they would have been present through the puja. All the brahmins would have been there. Lucky for you we are in the mourning period, so there won't be any pujas. Nobody will know. At least not everybody. So shut up like a good girl and do what the vas gharianis tell you.'

Then Ma left to take her medication and I was left all alone to deal with my anguish.

In the afternoon, while I sat still consumed with self pity reading Rider Haggard's *She*, Lalita came to visit me, flopping down easily onto the corner of my bed. I envied her her carefree mobility. I did not look up from my book.

'It's not so bad, you know. You'll get used to it.'

'Absolutely super. So you know too.'

'If it's any consolation,' she said, 'it's quite as bad in Purankot as well.'

Actually that little nugget of information did console me. I put the book down and faced her open smile. She had brought me a present. When I opened it, I was amazed at the wonders of disposable technology. I warmed to her. She was a kindred spirit, fit for collaboration.

'So now can we stop avoiding each other?' Lalita was amiable and I was more than happy to make peace.

'I thought you were avoiding me,' I said.

'I avoided you because you acted as if I had stabbed you in the back. I thought we were just having a difference of opinion. But you refused to go to Kumud Masi's picnic. And you didn't come when we called you for a game of canasta.'

'I didn't know whether to trust you. I didn't know whether you would tell Kumud Mami Sahib. After all, I was extremely rude to a Sirikot guest.'

'Don't be a donkey, Leela. She's too broad-minded to ever think ill of you. Anyway, she steers clear of what she calls idle gossip.' I remembered the havoc Kumud Mami Sahib's vulnerable ear to idle gossip had caused earlier but held my tongue.

'Pushpa tells me you are trying to solve a murder mystery.' I raised my eyebrows at Pushpa, surprised at her perspicacity and she opened and shut her mouth in quick succession. 'I'd love to solve a murder mystery. I love Agatha Christie. And I must be trusting you more than you trust me, because I know you haven't said a word to your mother about our fight.'

I thought of Ma's criticism of Lalita and my guilt forged a trust towards her that I didn't actually feel. Suddenly, Lalita seemed my only hope of getting through a lonely monsoon and this season of murderous intent. I looked at her hard and long and decided to tell her everything.

~

From then on, Lalita and I held our trysts daily in the summer house, safe from adult visitors for whom it was too wet and squelchy. They would, anyway, not have cared to be spotted there, airing themselves during the mourning period. Discussing 'the case' was the only game we had that provided a reprieve from the incessant rain. The problem was that both of us insisted on being Sherlock Holmes and there were no takers for Dr Watson.

'So who are the suspects and what are their motives?' Lalita asked, her choice of terminology, indicative of her familiarity with detective fiction, impressing me.

'All of them,' I said enigmatically, happy at having defused the potentially damaging political situation the elephant ride had created. 'Yuvraj Mama Sahib because he wants the throne, Yuvrani Mami Sahib because she wishes to be rani, and Kumar Mama Sahib because Yuvrani Mami Sahib wanted Nana Sahib dead. He is her emotional slave because she is having an affair with him.'

'Why should your Yuvrani Mami Sahib bother to tell Kumar Mama Sahib of her plot when Yuvraj Mama Sahib was already plotting to kill the raja?'

'Because,' — and I hoped the careful intonation of my consonants created the necessary professorial impact — 'Yuvraj Mama Sahib doesn't know about Yuvrani Mami Sahib's plot.'

Lalita chewed her fingernails. 'Isn't it strange that both husband and wife are planning the same murder without informing each other?' she said.

'If you were a good detective, Lalita, you would have known the minute I gave you the first clue, why this is possible. Yuvrani Mami Sahib is having an affair with Kumar Mama Sahib. Obviously, not only are husband and wife not close, they keep a lot of secrets from each other.' I saw the first glimmer of respect in Lalita's eyes. Today was indeed a good day. 'Okay, now let's move on. Kumud Mami Sahib — ' I hesitated. I was on thin ice here. Any rash conjectures would not only tip off Kumud Mami Sahib, if she was not already alerted, they could also get me into serious trouble. 'She wanted Nana Sahib dead, because she is a good and virtuous woman, she would not suffer debauchery.' At least, I thought, Lalita could not fault me for holding Kumud Mami Sahib in low regard.

She looked at me as if I had grown a horn between my eyebrows. 'Virtuous people don't kill,' she pointed out.

'True,' I conceded, wanting to bite my tongue, knowing that I had taken the cause of objectivity too far. 'Without a doubt, all these four people are the most likely to be guilty because all of them had access to the patidar, who had already tried to kill

Nana Sahib before. As you remember the patidar was corresponding with somebody within the palace.'

'Wait a minute, why should the patidar be corresponding only with the royal family? He could be plotting with anybody.'

I hoped my sigh of exaggerated patience proved to her what a recalcitrant student she was. 'Lalita,' I drawled, 'I did mention to you that though the patidar was not part of the immediate royal family he was still nobility. Who else do you think he would be corresponding with besides the royal family or their relations? He would surely not design assassination plots with the servants? Besides, the rest of the palace is mostly illiterate, they hardly read and write Hindi and English, the languages the letters were written in.'

Lalita was chewing her lower lip, her big teeth gnawing and demolishing tremulous flesh. I regarded her fearlessly. My previous self-consciousness before her presumed smartness had evaporated. What was there to fear about her? She looked as if she would suddenly neigh and buck and bolt out of the room like a polo pony. 'What about your mother? She could also be corresponding with the patidar,' she asked.

We had finally come to Ma. I squared my shoulders against parochialism and the pull of family. 'She could, but she didn't. She wasn't present in the palace on the dates the correspondence took place. But she could be responsible for her father's death indirectly. Because both Ma and Yuvraj Mama Sahib are bribing Shanti for a secret she knows and they want to hush up.'

'What secret?' Lalita's commitment to autophagy showed no visible sign of ceasing.

'That is for you to find out and me to know,' I said, hoping my words were cryptic enough; my eyes suitably hooded. Pushpa watched me perform in that silent and blank way of hers, like the class dunce.

'Shanti is Nana Sahib's daughter,' Lalita brightened.

'Everyone is Nana Sahib's child.'

'She knows where the buried treasures are? She has seen Yuvraj Mama Sahib do something terrible that would compromise his position as raja?'

I thought of Yuvraj Mama Sahib's letters to the tantrik and laughed in disdain. 'There are very few things that can compromise a raja.'

'She has evidence that your Nana Sahib killed the patidar,' Lalita said setting in motion images of the last unfinished words I had heard Nana Sahib speak and my desperate run to the palace pond.

'No, no, no. Let's move on to our next and last suspect.'

'But, we haven't even considered Shanti's motives.'

'Okay,' I said. 'Let's consider Shanti.'

'She was having an affair with the patidar. Your Nana Sahib killed the patidar so she took revenge.'

'If Shanti had had an affair with the patidar she would also know whom he was corresponding with. If she knew whom he was corresponding with there is obviously somebody else who was plotting the murder. Ergo, she is not the murderer.'

'Unless there are two murderers.' Lalita was thoughtful, her lower lip bloodless in the grip of her teeth. 'Why could she not be the one corresponding with the patidar?'

'Lalita, you duffer,' our game had made me more familiar, 'if she was corresponding with the patidar they couldn't have been more than love letters. If they were plotting to kill Nana Sahib, surely they would have planned it during a more private rendezvous.'

'You may be right,' she allowed.

'Moreover, Shanti doesn't speak Hindi. And don't you think any correspondence with the patidar would take place only with those members of the royal family who didn't have free access or mobility outside the palace? Like, for example —'

'The women of the zenana.'

I waved my wrist at her. 'Elementary, my dear Watson.'

'Watson, yourself.' Lalita glowered. I wished for a less wilful subordinate, like Pushpa. But Pushpa could never be a subordinate. She was tabula rasa, a blank slate, accepting whatever you wrote on it.

'What do we do about Shanti's secret?' My unwilling Watson glumly asked.

'Exactly,' I said, feeling the aged wrinkles of experience in my voice. 'Don't you think Shanti's secret is a key clue to the murder? It ties everybody together —' and makes Ma an indirect suspect because of her desire to keep the secret quiet, I finished the thought in my head.

Pushpa made her first and only contribution to our masterful enterprise of puzzle solving. 'Jemma Sahib, can I please go home and take a piss?'

I pulled out a wet branch lying about and waved it sternly at her: 'You are not going anywhere. You can pee later, behind a shrub. Now sit down and listen to us talk.'

~

'Let us consider our last, but not least, contender.' We were back in the summer house the next day. 'Phulwati is more interested in Kumar Mama Sahib. She is vindictive and spiteful. She once publicly expressed her desire to see Nana Sahib dead when he insulted her,' I said.

'The least likely culprit,' Lalita countered. 'She has nothing to gain from the raja's death. She's from a humble family, as most mistresses are, and she would not give up a king's riches for an insult. Mistresses are used to insults. The very status of mistress is insulting.'

'Yes,' I parried. 'But, remember, she is having an affair with Kumar Mama Sahib. Maybe, to a lesser degree, but he is as capable of supporting her as Nana Sahib. Plus, he is younger and handsomer. With the raja she was the current favourite. With Kumar Mama Sahib she has a long-term career. Also, if Kumar Mama Sahib has a motive for murder and knows of her hatred for Nana Sahib she is his best tool.'

'Wait a minute,' Lalita frowned. 'Would a son want the death of his father over his love of another woman, especially one as feckless as Yuvrani Mami Sahib?'

This was my turn to show off. '*Crime passionnel*,' I said, Mrs Wood's French lessons finally coming to use. 'Crimes of passion, dear one, crimes of passion. The cruellest acts are committed in the name of love. It is a strange beast, this love.'

'Be that as it may,' Lalita spoke with the fearfully rhetorical tone of someone about to launch into a speech of her own, 'I still think Kumar Mama Sahib does not have motive enough to kill. He is not even motivated enough for passion, how could he commit a crime in its name, a crime *de la creme* or whatever. If he is truly passionate about Yuvrani Mami Sahib, how come he is also carrying on with Phulwati? You can't commit one crime of passion for two separate people you love exclusively, and who both also simultaneously wish the same crime.'

'But Nana Sahib was old. He would have died soon!' I defended Phulwati with some warmth.

'Who knows about matters of life and death? If people died soon because they were old why would they need to be murdered? Just as we are certain we may not be alive tomorrow, we can also be certain we may not die.' My horse-face was spouting philosophy. I was getting to like her. 'And you know what I think about revenge? It is a strong motive for murder, but it should be equal to the reason. I think your real suspects are Yuvraj Mama Sahib, he's such a false prophet, and his wife, Yuvrani Mami Sahib.'

After some more heated debate we progressed to the glass of milk on Nana Sahib's bedside. I told her about how Ma had immediately checked it for poison but the milk had been clean. Not that this meant a great deal. Nana Sahib could have consumed a slow-acting poison the night before, or even in the morning, and the offending glass could easily have been replaced by Phulwati. On the other hand, Nana Sahib could have died of the effects of slow poison administered over days, even months. I had found a book of poisons in the library. They were of three

types. Injected poisons like snakebites and poison-tipped darts
were mostly neurotoxins and acted on the subcutaneous tissue
and the bloodstream. Ingested poisons travelled through the
digestive tract. Contact poison was rare to find and spread through
the subcutaneous tissue and the bloodstream. All of them ranged
from slow acting to fast. The fastest a poison could show its effect
was in one or two minutes.

No royal family member could have as deep a knowledge of
poisons as the palace servants and vas gharianis did. They lived
close to nature and understood its basic rhythms in a way we
royalty could never fathom. We were an indolent lot, our use
mostly ornamental. We were not of much use besides marrying
and breeding. Phulwati, like the rest of the serving class, possessed
talents more fundamental than our embroidering or painting.
She would know which foods were dangerous. She would know
which tasteless powders could poison the body without showing
any symptoms. She would know which herbs could provide the
fatal dose. I remembered Nana Sahib's saliva foaming at his
chin. The red tin of tooth powder could have been tampered
with. Phulwati practised black magic. That itself threw light on
the kind of person she was. I told Lalita that even if Phulwati
was not the murderer she was definitely an accomplice.

'To solve this mystery,' Lalita wrote on the wet mud at our
feet with a twig, 'we need to find out two things: Who the
patidar was corresponding with, and Shanti's secret.'

All three of us stared at the wet mud. Pushpa, with the
exasperation of a bewildered maths student, Lalita with a smudge
on her chin and I, as if staring at it long enough might sketch
the killer's face at our feet.

~

That evening, Kumud Mami Sahib summoned us both to her
chambers and lying wan and pale on her bed with her arm
thrown limply across her forehead warned us about our meetings.

'Children, do not discuss sensitive issues like the death of the old Raja Sahib in front of the servants, even if they are your companions,' she sighed. 'It will only get you into trouble.'

Lalita and I frowned at each other. At the first opportunity we grabbed Pushpa by the hair and pushed her into a secluded corridor where on pain of death we made her confess that it was she who had tattled to Kumud Mami Sahib.

She did so, whimpering and pleading, folding her hands and falling at our feet. 'Please, Jemma Sahib,' she wept. 'Don't hurt me. I am even more scared of your mother than I am of you. She forced me to tell her what you two talk about. She then ordered me to disclose this to your Kumud Mami Sahib so she could stop you.'

'You fool,' I hissed at her. 'Don't you know that what we discuss is important? It is not just idle zenana chatter!'

'Please, please, don't tell your mother I told you,' she begged. 'She'll flay the skin off my back.'

'And you think I won't?' I roared at her, wondering why my mother had not directly upbraided me, uncharacteristically resorting to the sneaky tactic of inciting Kumud Mami Sahib to tell me off. Did she know that I had lost faith in her?

Pushpa had to be punished, so we pushed her off into the deepest edge of the pond; it was a good thing she could swim, or she would have surely drowned that day.

~

As our discussions became deeper and more earnest, Lalita and I decided to meet without attendants, not even Pushpa. We repaired to the summer house and pondered Nana Sahib's last words for several long, rain-drenched hours while the bullfrogs croaked their opinions in the palace pond.

'Blood', we thought hard about the word, reducing Nana Sahib to a cryptic crossword clue.

'Means family ties,' I said. 'Since he had said it in Hindi, the word also means murder. What else can it mean?'

'It also means that the poison was a blood poison. It travelled through his bloodstream.'

'But he used the adjective "black". Black makes a coherent sentence only when it is used in conjunction with the first two meanings of blood, that is family ties and murder.'

'Yes,' I said. 'So we have two meanings. The first is black blood, meaning a family relationship evil in nature, and the other is black murder, meaning an evil murder. Wait, Lalita, I just remembered. Kumud Mami Sahib,' — Lalita tensed at the mention of her aunt but I continued nevertheless — 'she had mentioned a certain black brahmin during her famous accusation.'

I told her what I had overheard in Yuvrani Mami Sahib's quarters. We digressed a bit from the subject as I related the incident with a few girlish embellishments that I shall not disclose here for the sake of propriety. When we meandered back to the essential point, after much giggling and many breathless enquiries on Lalita's part, I told Lalita about the black brahmin's wife who had died at childbirth, how an older child had been thrown into an untouchable colony and how her husband, the black brahmin, had been savagely killed by Nana Sahib's men in the granary.

'I'm sure his entire family is haunting the palace as we speak,' Lalita shivered. 'Did your Nana Sahib maintain her in a house somewhere in Sirikot? Is her son still alive somewhere? Does he know? If he did, then he would surely have a motive for revenge. Did her second child really die at childbirth? We have to know.'

'There is nobody I can talk to within the palace whom I can trust enough.'

'Why don't you send Pushpa on a few errands to find out from the rajpurohits? They know everything.'

'Not Pushpa, she's too much of an idiot.'

Lalita darted an assessing look towards me. 'Oh, don't be so sure. I've seen her make faces at you and your mother.'

'But, Leela, I still don't understand how you are connecting your Nana Sahib's "black" to the black brahmin. The black brahmin died much before your grandfather did. And he may not even have been called the black brahmin, like you keep calling him.'

'I know because Dhaima told me.'

We sat silently on the stone steps of the pavilion, letting the horrors of the tragedy seep into us afresh. From where we sat on the steps we could see the basement. It was in spate, flooded by the murky waters of the pond. Under a ledge a white owl's large shocked eyes looked at us in accusation. 'What if,' I said.

'What if —' she prompted.

'What if the woman's child was starved at the stake near a treasure site? What if the child was the jokho ghost?'

'No, Leela, no!' Lalita gave a little scream.

She was right. That would be too much tragedy. We would not permit it. We reined in our imaginations, blocking off the thought. I shivered. 'Her son must still be in an untouchable colony, if that's what really happened to him.'

'Leela, don't you see, that is worse than becoming a jokho ghost? The child of brahmin parents, living as an untouchable, sweeping the streets, washing clothes when he should be studying the scriptures and teaching us about god?'

'Do you know, I have never seen an untouchable colony.'

'I've heard that they live like animals. They are filthy and eat anything that flies, crawls or walks.'

'Let's go and see one,' I said with an air of decision.

'Please, Leela don't go crazy on me.'

I stared at Lalita's ladylike simpering in disbelief. I told her we were going and that was final.

Yuvraj Mama Sahib had done a lot of travelling in Sirikot after Nana Sahib's death. Palace whispers said the reason was not only fear of the coming Independence; the people of Sirikot didn't like the new raja and blamed him for Nana Sahib's death. Nana Sahib's ruthlessness had always been a state secret; his ignorant people had worshipped him, falling at his feet, prostrating themselves and ululating every time he passed by. Yuvraj Mama Sahib, they considered an overachieving upstart. Strangely, they distrusted him because he had tried to eradicate the age-old vas ghariani system. His welfare projects and socialist plans of development for Sirikot did not mitigate their hatred. While Nana Sahib was 'the father of the people', Mama Sahib was 'raja only by accident or premeditated murder'. While Nana Sahib was the 'Breeding Bull' Yuvraj Mama Sahib was the 'Two-Headed Snake.'

A few days ago, when Yuvraj Mama Sahib had been preparing to go to pay his condolences to the grieving relations of the dead in an untouchable village, I had asked to go along.

'Do your pestering in your own home, child.' Yuvraj Mama Sahib's words had stung me to the quick. In the summer house I planned our little expedition almost like an act of revenge.

Yuvraj Mama Sahib had planned a picnic outing to Nana Sahib's Bardela farmhouse the next day. It was agreed that Lalita and I would slip out from there and visit the colony.

'But how will we slip out? We can't go there escorted in palanquins. We don't even know where the colony is,' I said, suddenly thinking rationally.

'I know one person who could help us,' Lalita said.

'Who?'

'Syce, a stable boy. Quite handsome, actually. I don't know whether you know him. But he also tends the gardens sometimes and is very eager to please.'

A snake coiled three times in my breast. 'Really. How do you know him?'

'Very casually. He seemed loyal to your Nana Sahib, I think we can trust him. I'll speak to him tomorrow.'

'Okay,' I said, my thoughts in tumult.

'I shall get the stable boy to arrange for two horses. He will show us the way.'

'What if our family misses us? What if they find out?'

'You blame it on me. Tell them I took you for a ride. I have heard so many snide remarks about my riding, one more won't hurt.'

Humbled, I agreed. I did not dare tell her that I barely knew how to ride.

Eleven

It was a clear day.

Sun-dried clouds spread their wispy old woman's hair and basked in the drowsy light. Sparrows and mynahs and crows and monkeys chattered like noisy brokers on Wall Street, as if it were a good day for business. A retinue of servants had gone on ahead to Bardela to prepare for the afternoon meal.

Almost everybody in the family had agreed to come, including some elderly aunts who emerged from their apartments like old leviathans surfacing for air. I must confess for a long time I did not know how I was related to them. I knew them only as the ubiquitous Aunt, minor but necessary fixtures of the zenana. I guess, like me, they also needed to get away from the oppressiveness of their thoughts

I went with Ma in Nana Sahib's Chrysler Windsor. Ma looked well for a change, the colour back in her cheeks. Lalita followed in Kumar Mama Sahib's Bentley and, when I looked behind, she and Kumud Mami Sahib were deep in animated conversation. Momentarily, I regretted baring my secrets to Lalita. In consternation, I realized that she knew all my secrets; I didn't know any of hers.

The cars ploughed through roads that had turned to mud syrup. In the distance, coconut trees standing sentinel, seemed to be nodding off on duty, their dreadlocks waving in dreamy confusion. It was true, I felt it too, the anticipation of romance in the air.

The rich tropical winds blowing over the Sirikot fields lifted everybody's spirits. Bardela was a pretty farm situated on the banks of the Bardela lake and surrounded by coconut groves. Beyond Bardela were miles and miles of mustard fields. I still maintain that the balm for a tortured soul is the sight of sun-kissed mustard fields all the way till the eye can see. The gouged-out colour of Van Gogh's richest yellow is enough to stuff the holes of one's heart with more sunshine than one can bear.

When we got off the car I stood aside for a moment and took in a deep lungful of icy pollinated air. Its healing touch never failed to bring tears to my eyes. Villagers in the Bardela area had been warned that the ruling family would be spending their day in the area. They had been cleared off and asked to stay away, outside a radius of ten miles of the fields, so the girls and women could venture out far with their attendants.

Tables spread with monogrammed white tablecloths tucked in neatly at the sides were set up in the clearing by the lake. The flower decorations set in the centre of the tables were superfluous in such a natural setting. Bearers bustled behind a canvas partition where the food was kept ready for serving but outside our view. I recognized the exquisitely carved washbasin stand and matching enamel jug. It was Nana Sahib's. So Yuvraj Mama Sahib was already appropriating his father's possessions, I thought bitterly. My mother must have noticed too, but none of us were in the mood to spoil the harmony of the perfect morning.

I have always wondered how, in those days, such elaborate arrangements for large groups of people were accomplished without any visible sign of effort. Work was completed unobstrusively and I had never seen incidents of servants not arriving or the food not being prepared on time, or, as now, a harried woman behind it all, huffing out orders. When I became a housewife, I sometimes wondered who had decided the colour of the tablecloth, and whether the roses should go on top of the flower decoration or at the bottom, and when dessert should be served, because I never saw a zenana ruling lady watch over these things. The towels were never dirty, the silver and gold cutlery was never stolen, and somebody would place Nana Sahib's washbasin back in exactly the same position in the lavatory, without breakage.

After a heavy meal of succulent mutton curries and pilaus full of cloves and dry fruit all I wanted to do was curl up on the makeshift beds prepared under the all-embracing shade of a banyan and go to sleep. The women had already retired to their apportioned area of shade. Some to play a game of whist, others to sleep.

The cottage cheese had been softer than butter. The shahi toast of fried bread soaked in sugar syrup and served with pistachios had had the right consistency of sweetness. No, my stomach sagged under the weight of too much food. I didn't want to see any untouchable colony today. Today was a day for sleep.

But Lalita was from the western frontier. She did not suffer from the indolence we easterners did. She marched me a mile in the wet noonday sun across the mustard fields till I spotted three horses tied to an acacia tree. Blood dammed up in my cheeks, my knees were suddenly out of joint. Was it he?

It was.

My heart threatened to jump out of my body and make a run across Van Gogh's yellow. How many times had I thought of him as I'd lain awake at night, tortured by the stillness of the zenana? How many times had I seen him briefly, all too briefly, a vision, just off the hibiscus tree, or passing by in the courtyard? How many times had I held my hand to my cheek where he had touched me?

Here he was, standing taller than I had last seen him, his curls shining and his mouth ripe as a plum, holding the reins of three horses, smiling sardonically at me, ready to serve her. I felt cold and stricken. Lalita, in enviable composure, ferreted out two riding habits from a folded muslin cloth and handed one to me. 'Quickly, go behind a tree and change.'

It was then that I realized the foolhardiness of my decision and the cold unfamiliarity of the situation. Utterly miserable, I confessed that not only had I never worn a riding habit before, but that I barely knew how to ride.

I explained to Lalita that Ma and Baba had strongly disapproved of my enthusiasm for riding lessons. The only riding I had learnt was in secret during Ma's afternoon siesta time when the Dhairwar stable boys had taught me the mount and other basic commands. I had taken a few rounds of the field on a horse with a rope tied to his bit led by the stable boy. I could handle the trot but had never experienced the canter. I would never manage without the lifeline of a rope and definitely not in a riding habit.

'So you want to travel ten miles to a village in a sari sitting side-saddle on a horse while this fellow leads you by the bit?' Lalita exclaimed in disbelief.

'What else do you want me to do?'

He stood aside, away from our feminine bickering, and nuzzled the horses with his cheek. Even though I didn't look at him I sensed he was looking at me, his presence boring needles into my heightening agony. It was that gesture, of easy camaraderie between magnificent man and magnificent animal, that made me throw caution to the winds. 'What the hell,' I said to her. 'If I fall or get killed at least it'll be your fault. Let's go.'

When I stepped out from behind a tree in Lalita's riding habit I felt as if I had broken all the rules that bound me to virtue. For all purposes I stood before them as good as naked, divested of the last inhibition that had hitherto guarded my moral life. I hesitated before them. Lalita didn't give me a second look and mounted her steed. But the expression on his face was worth my shame, my descent into the disgrace of a faisha woman.

He helped me mount. There was that brief touch again, of his dry hard hands. Some nascent learned skill in my primeval memory came to me kindly, giving me the gift of freedom. I leaned forward and whispered the horse's name in its ear. Fear fell off me like the other garments I had shed. I kicked into the horse's flanks and we moved off effortlessly in a single file. When my horse broke into a canter fear came back momentarily, like a pincer at my throat, but my body unconsciously adjusted its seat on the mount and my mind broke away from its shackles again.

I concentrated on keeping rhythm with the pulsating animal I'd straddled and lost count of time. I was riding the crest of a musical note of a wild flute. I was atop the wings of an eagle gliding over fields of trapped sunshine. Beneath me was the rippling synchronicity of shimmering horseflesh and foaming bit. I rode and I rode and I rode, focusing on becoming a singular beat of Nature's pulse, in harmony with the rest of her.

Below me, my animal moved like a repeating stanza. Speed shook my long hair to its roots and I became a female zephyr teasing the fluid skin of a yellow ocean. From time to time, he, my mate, my male partner, cast anxious glances at me that thrilled me to goosebumps; I spurred on to find newer speeds and higher levels of freedom.

～

We came upon the untouchable colony unexpectedly, in a small clearing. Thatched roofs of mud huts huddled together like old men in straw hats who had sat out in the rain for too long. Bleached goat tracks made dirty inroads into puddles of muck, giving the impression that the huts were dissolving in the rain. Half naked men and scantily clad women sat or walked around their huts, their faces deeply lined by base living. Blank clay waiting to be molded, eyes seeking and seeing a type of wisdom I would never understand. I was assailed by the overpowering stench of rotting vegetables and human waste.

The untouchables walked towards us when we dismounted, their expressionless faces blank, moving like one organism with a single mind. For the first time since we'd left the picnic I experienced real fear. This was obviously not a good idea. We had wandered too far from home. We had put ourselves at too much risk. But at the same time I was fascinated, watching the untouchables in their natural habitat for the first time, as if they were Darwin's in-between species. The difference between this and all that I had previously known showed me a social landscape that would stay with me. It would come up when I took the name of god; when I introspected into my life and the vagaries of fate.

Quietly obedient, they stood in a row, waiting for us to speak. I looked askance at Lalita. She was at a loss. I could tell that her wild rides into the Sirikot countryside had never taken her this far. I realized that it would be difficult to hide our identity; many of them had surely worked in the palace and recognized us. Though my mind said that the Sirikot people were too worshipful and devout to cause bodily harm to Sirikot royalty, the fact remained that we were two young girls without official chaperones and without purdah, far from home, in very unfamiliar territory. Our riding breeches did not help one bit. Only the heavens knew what trauma our clothes must have inflicted on those poor people.

'We heard that a few people had died of poisoning here,' I took the initiative, my dry mouth surprising me. 'We have come to personally pay our condolences.'

Faces cleared. They whispered among each other and prostrated themselves on the ground. When they got up their clothes were soiled with mud. 'Agya' and 'huzur,' they called us and outdid each other in a litany of flattery. My nostrils prickled. Again, that strange smell of boiling animal hide or decomposing carcass, I could not tell which. I wanted to get away from these people and their smell, fly over the fields with my handsome rescuer by my side. But before I left I had to do my duty.

'I would like to meet the families of the deceased.'

Fighting broke out between them. Mercifully, I could not quite follow the vicious growls and snaps in the coarsest slang of the local dialect. I was alarmed by the increased intensity of their altercation, as if they were ready to tear each other out with their teeth. Finally, a straggly group appeared, led by a woman who, much to my mortification, was suckling a baby on her naked breast. Two urchins stood behind her, their hair stiff and golden with dirt. Their bare feet were full of sores. Beside them stood two stocky, broad-shouldered youths and an old blind man whose eyes were dipped in ice. Lice stood out sharply in his white beard. They stood in front of us and stared expectantly.

Oh, I thought, in a sudden revelation, they want money. But I didn't have any. So I took off a thick gold chain around my neck and let it fall in the palm of my hand. Lalita took off her pearl drop earrings. We didn't know how to hand them over without touching the untouchables.

'Put out your palm, old man,' our handsome escort told the blind white beard. 'And distribute the proceeds of the sale to the families of the deceased.'

Hosannas and ululations by the women standing by rang out as we dropped our jewellery into the old man's scaly palms. He trembled as the gold touched his skin. I must confess I was moved by the magnanimity of my pity. I was young. I did not know that showy gestures of giving alms smacked of insincerity and a pompous sense of superiority.

I declared my desire to visit their homes. I said I was thirsty and could somebody give me a glass of water? My statement was like the launch of some lethal weapon. They all dropped to the floor, prostrating themselves in one fell swoop; the sightless old man prostrated in the opposite direction and addressed a gulmohur tree by accident: 'O Illustrious lords, descendants of kings and gods, do not slight us. Do not force us to commit sin. We are poor, unfortunate people. We will not be able to bear the force of your touch. It will strike us dead.'

Lalita's fight to suppress her helpless giggling threatened to make me start too, and I struggled hard to prevent such a lack of propriety. It did not help that the villagers thought we were boys because we wore riding breeches. I thought that my face would split open and only laughter would spill out when, all of a sudden, one of the men flexed his broad shoulders. He looked me in the face. His cold brown eyes seemed familiar but I could not place him. His voice was strong and even, cold water dousing me into sobriety: 'Our esteemed Rajkumari,' his voice was darkly sardonic. 'Do not burden us with your touch.'

I smiled at the irony. How mutual the condition of untouchability was! You cannot practise it, without becoming an untouchable yourself. Do not burden us with your touch, the brown-eyed man said. I was as much an untouchable to them as they were to me.

But I have always been stubborn in the face of opposition and that day was no exception. I moved towards one of the mud huts. Lalita followed me. The crowd, smelling rankly of unwashed sweat and compost, parted to avoid my touch.

My handsome escort (I address him as such because I cannot bear to call him Syce the stable boy) stopped me at the door of a hut by grabbing my elbow in a vice. 'You've finished what you came here for,' his intimate whisper was unwarranted; too bold. 'Don't make matters worse. Let's go.'

'You keep your hands off me!' I flashed at him. I tried to peel his fingers off but he was too strong for me. His eyes wandered steadily over the contours of my face before he shrugged and turned away.

The hut was cool and dark inside. Only a small window tampered with the clean symmetry of mud lines. There were no furnishings. No utensils except an earthen pot and a mud stove. A few clothes hung from a rope tied across a corner of the room. There was no place to sit. I realized guiltily that I had wanted to visit a mud hut more out of tourist curiosity. These people were

too poor to extend hospitality. Chastened, I waited for somebody
to offer me a glass of water or some food. Nobody obliged.

'Will nobody give me a glass of water?' I enquired of the
staring crowd. Realizing nobody would, I walked into the mud
hut and lifted the lid of the earthen pot. It contained coarse
unpolished rice soaked in water. I dipped my hand into it and
ate a fistful. My act of defiance sent a shiver through the
crowd. When I walked out of the mud hut my Adonis's eyes
were tearing me apart. Lalita waited for me by the horses. They
snorted and worried the ground, impatient to leave. I walked
through the parting crowd and tried to alleviate their horror of
the sacrilege I had committed. 'How were the people poisoned?'
I asked the woman suckling her child.

She mumbled incoherently in the local dialect. The brown-
eyed man took over, and I was surprised by his language, which
was quite polished. 'We had a feast some time after the raja's
death.'

'So you were feasting because the raja was dead?'

'No, Rajkumari Sahiba,' his tone was neutral and controlled.
'It was a wedding. The black lotus was used by accident in the
meat. You see, the black lotus, when it gets overripe, bleaches,
and looks like a normal lotus. It is extremely poisonous. More
poisonous than the king cobra.'

A cry rose from the crowd, 'The raja's passing is a bad sign.
Evil times are upon us!' The women started their ululations.
'The gods are sacrificing us for the death of the good and just
raja!' they wailed. Some women burst into tears, and some into
song. The overpowering stench hung over the air, like a miasma.

~

I couldn't mount my horse on my own. My escort bent and
locked his hands, bowing his head so as not to look at me. A
stray lock fell on his forehead. I used his cupped palms as a step
to hoist myself up. He did not flinch under my weight.

A few yards from the village, near an embankment of long grassy weeds, my steed suddenly reared, raising itself on its hind legs and belting out a frightful neigh. My reflexes were not sharp enough to register how and why it bucked; all I remember is the sensation of flying and the salty taste of blood and earth in my mouth and a searing pain in my shoulder. When I opened my eyes, a shiny black gecko with a white stripe painted on its back averted its eyes and skimmed off into the grass past the nodding leaves of a galgal tree and the printed edge of a red sari disappeared into a copse beyond the embankment. I passed out again.

I thought I saw the brown-eyed man standing far but clear in the blurred periphery of my vision, his face contorted in some legendary bitterness. He picked up a handful of dirt and facing me, let it fly from his fist. He was taking an oath, or pronouncing a curse. I could read his lips and gestures. I thought he said, 'Die, Sirikot, die!' The magnitude of his hatred, etched in every line of his face, was such that I felt singed. And I knew then that the venom pouring out of his mouth would reach out and destroy every succeeding generation of my family.

I have a vivid recollection of Lalita's cool hands wiping my face with a wet handkerchief. Even clearer and not without some emotion is the memory of my stable boy running a finger under my collar to examine my collarbone. 'It's not serious.' It gave me immense pleasure to notice that his face looked pale and drawn. His fingers lingered on my throat. 'There's nothing broken, but you have to be careful. Somebody frightened the horse on purpose, Rajkumari Sahiba. And I'm sure it was a woman.'

'Let's get out of here.' Lalita was scared. The sun would be setting in an hour. Our girlish adventure had taken a serious turn. But I was giddy-headed from our exploits and the stable boy's close physical proximity — the smell of his sweat, like fresh-cut grass, the inky blue mountains in his eyes. He fashioned a sling from his turban and I rested my arm in it. The delicate problem of transportation was solved by my sitting side-saddle in front of him while he rode cradling my shoulder and holding the reins with one hand and leading my riderless horse with the other. My shoulder ached where it touched his arm, my body stiff not from pain but from his closeness.

We made slow progress. I made distracted contributions to the debate about whether Lalita should move on ahead and tell the elders in the picnic spot that I had gone with Pushpa for a walk and was lagging behind. Pushpa, of course, would have to be told to keep her mouth shut. But the stable boy was loath to be alone with me. It was then that I realized the grave risk he had put himself to, to satisfy my passing fancy to 'see an untouchable village'. If word of our audacious trip ever got out he was in danger of a terrible whipping, or even banishment. If he was found alone with me, riding in the wild hills of Sirikot, he was justified in fearing for his life. But cradled in the manly forbearance and concern of his arms, I shut out these thoughts and listened to the steady thud of his heart. His mouth was grim, his cheekbones chiselled in stone.

This time it was I who made the first move.

'Hey, stable boy,' I said in my haughtiest tone. 'What's your father's name?'

He gave a short laugh. I saw stretched skin and teeth. 'That worries you, doesn't it? I would worry if I were you.'

I flushed to a slow boil. 'And what, pray tell, does that mean?'

He ignored my anger. 'My father and his ancestors are Afghans who have been in the service of your family's armies for centuries. Most of my restless forefathers moved on when the peace and prosperity of Sirikot saw little fighting. But my grandfather suffered a hip injury so he stayed back to tend Raja Sahib's horses. We are poor, we lead modest lives, many of my relations are farmers, but we are also warriors, like you.'

His answer satisfied me. His Afghan ancestry explained his stunning looks. 'Are you trying to compare yourself with me?' I enquired lazily, wishing that the ride would never end, that the sunset would never come.

'No, Rajkumari Sahiba.' He looked down at me and his smile was slow trickling honey. 'I have no illusions about the difference between us. We are separated by a distance that cannot be covered on foot.'

'On a horse, then?' I asked in what I thought was sweet insouciance. For the first time in my life I was flirting. And I believed I was doing a good job. 'Or a motorcar?'

'Maybe,' he said. 'In another time and place.'

Was that his voice or the wind whispering in my ear? The rhythm of his breathing lulled me into a dreamlike trance. The reeds rustled in friendly conspiracy. That day, I could have ridden with him to the farthest corner of the earth, if only he had wished it. 'Why did you risk your neck today, to take us to the village?' I asked, daring to settle back on his wiry shoulder. It was, after all, a long ride.

'To make you happy.'

'Me, or Lalita?' I tensed for his reply.

Lalita rode ahead, outside earshot.

'You.'

I closed my eyes and let the sun shower her gold on me.

'What if you get into trouble?' I asked, selfishly satisfied by his answer.

'Whatever happens,' he said looking at me in that lingering way that can be more intimate than the most physical of touches, 'You must remember I did it not out of respect or fear, or to obey your command, I did it because —'

'Because?' I prompted.

'Because, for a few fleeting moments, I wanted to be with you.' I was more cowardly than he was. I did not dare tell him I felt the same way he did.

'Why did you stop me from touching the villagers?'

'Because I am older and wiser than you are. My grandfather used to say, "You cannot hold the ocean in a sieve."'

'What rubbish!' I argued. 'Haven't you heard that every drop counts?'

'I don't know about all this, Rajkumari Sahiba. All I know is that you have been impulsive and I have been stupid. But thank you anyway. At night when I sleep, there will be much more to dream about.'

The rest of the day is hazy. We reached the picnic spot and found all our relations and Ma waiting anxiously for us. The severe berating Lalita and I received on our return and our forced isolation from each other for the next few days did not really bother me. Lalita and I received our share of sarcasm, scolding and verbal whiplashes from everybody, from Ma to all the Mama Sahibs and Mami Sahibs. I even received a mouthful from the rajvaidya who treated me.

~

I never saw him again. I never found out who leaked the details of our secret trip, or when the stable boy was beaten, or how much; nor whether only he was exiled or his entire family was banished along with him. I realized afresh the capacity for tight-lipped secrecy the serving class was capable of.

They took him away, wiped out his existence. But they could not erase the contours of his face or the curve of his arm from my memory. It was not as if I would have run away with him and married him. I wouldn't have. We were separated by too many worlds, too many distances that could not be crossed on foot. I did not want to cross those distances, cover those worlds.

The empirical reasons that caused me to rest my injured shoulder against his chest while we flew over a seamless sea of ochre were many. I was enraptured by my few hours of freedom from the zenana. He was young and so was I. We were physically attracted to each other. We must have been. It was a day for poetry and madness. Even today I feel no shame or guilt.

In the days of the state, we had absolute power over people's minds and lives. But this was the first time I had complete power over someone's heart. He was the only person of the opposite sex I have known beside my husband. The love my husband and I shared contained the maturity of age and tradition. What that youth and I shared was the essence of love in its most reckless form. It was love from another country. A country where love was the pain of separation. Where love was an unkept promise.

And I am grateful to him. He showed me the difference between happiness and ecstasy. He left me a memory of a fleeting moment of such intensity, the like of which I have never been able to recapture in all my living years.

He taught me the greatness of innocence.

May god protect him and keep him well.

Twelve

In a few days Sirikot's honour staggered back into place. My quarantine from Lalita was lifted when our guardians tired of their vigilance.

Yuvrani Mami Sahib brooded over her hookah and watched me from under thick eyelashes when I crossed her courtyard. 'Thank god, I'm not cursed with daughters,' I'd heard her say.

Kumud Mami Sahib had chided us more gently: 'You've reached an age when you must start learning to control your passions. The trick is to obey your elders blindly, whatever your heart may say. To be a Rajput woman is to be in an army, Leela. Your elders are your generals.' Her speech had been more slurred than usual and the blue-webbed bags under her sloping eyes contrasted with her pale mountain skin. Her epileptic fits had increased in frequency, in mock disregard of the rajvaidya's potions. I'd listened to her strictures on well-bred Rajput girls quietly without wondering too much at the lack of irony with which she spoke. Lalita was her niece after all. Looking back, I think my influence on Lalita was more pernicious than hers on me. In spite of all her exposure outside the palace she did not push to radical extremes the way I did once I was spurred to action.

Thankfully, the Mama Sahibs were too embroiled in the much-talked-of Independence to worry too long about our misdemeanours. We heard that in England Sir Conrad Corfield was pleading the case of the Indian princely states with the viceroy. Yuvraj Mama Sahib and other local rulers hoped that they would be able to continue their autonomous status after Independence, though most princely states were resigned to acceding to the Indian dominion in such an eventuality.

~

'They are drugging her,' Lalita said.

We were lounging about in Kumud Mami Sahib's rooms after several days of lying low.

'Who is drugging whom?' I enquired, helping myself to a mango from a bucketful of mangoes, submerged in water to keep them cool. I inhaled the green scent of the fruit then squeezed the mango with my hands in a fatal embrace before putting my lips to its spout and sucking out its flesh in a kiss.

'Kumud Masi Sahib.' Lalita was playing *The Blue Danube* on the piano. Through the iron bars of the window we could see Kumud Mami Sahib attending to her coterie of women in the courtyard. They sat at her feet, their heads covered, their hands waving in eloquent expression, their midriffs squashed into dark chocolate rolls by their sitting positions.

'Those are not drugs, Lalita, those are the rajvaidya's potions.' Mango pulp dripped from my palms in fat orange gobs.

'Don't be such a philistine, Leela, why don't you cut your mangoes and then eat them?' Lalita said in disgust.

'Because this is the Indian way. The less British we are the better.'

'Wipe that mango off your chin. No, they are not giving her the rajvaidya's potions. They are giving her opium.' Lalita wore solitaires on both her ring fingers. Her hands moved like pretty spiders over the white keys.

'Really? Who?' I moved to the washbasin. Pushpa poured me some water from a jug.

'The vas gharianis.'

'Why?' I asked, my hands now dry and clean.

'Your uncle, Kumar Mama Sahib's orders,' she said, so bitter that she didn't show a trace of it. 'He thinks she is crazy. If she is kept drugged then she is less trouble, isn't she?'

'Poor Kumud Mami Sahib. She is the kindest soul in the zenana.'

'There's a saying, "Lions are never sacrificed, only lambs".'

'Hmm,' I said, as if it were an interesting adage.

'See that plump woman talking to her, in the brown sari?' Lalita suddenly pointed to the women in the courtyard. 'The one wearing a medallion around her neck? She's the patidar's wife.'

'You sure?'

'She came yesterday too. She comes quite often to visit Kumud Masi Sa. She said she would bring all the notes the patidar received from the mysterious correspondent inside the palace.'

My eyes shone. 'Do you know what this means? We could be close to solving the mystery!'

'Leela! Look! She's handing them over.'

We watched with barely restrained excitement as Kumud Mami Sahib took the offered letters and moved her attention to the next woman.

'Follow her, Lalita, and see where she hides them,' I said in a furtive whisper, suddenly remembering Pushpa, and quickly glancing around; she was busy admiring her bony figure in Kumud Mami Sahib's full-length mirror.

~

Acquiring the letters was easy. Kumud Mami Sahib entered her chambers, visibly exhausted after listening to the petitions of the women, and in full view of our greedy eyes stuffed the letters into a pigeonhole in her writing desk. The very same desk on whose edge I had sat, sucking off with my tongue the last of the mango hairs still stuck between my teeth. We waited for her to stroll off in the direction of the palace temple, for her ritual hour-long worship, before snatching the letters from her desk. We ordered our attendants to play hopscotch in the corridor and promised a mango to the winner. Pushpa was getting roundly defeated as usual.

The letters were telegraphic; just short, one-line messages. All unsigned, written on scraps of paper, folded so many times that in some places the words were smudged. They were written in Hindi and English, languages both of us understood. We stared at them, re-reading them many times but unable to make any sense of them. The sentences were terse and gave away little, usually referencing a name to be visited or spoken to, or the time of a rendezvous. The names were always in initials, M and K and P.

'How does this work?' Lalita wondered. 'Why did our mysterious correspondent not simply send word through a trusted spy to fix the time of the appointment or to send a message?'

'Because Nana Sahib's espionage system is unbeatable. It is very difficult to break the system of spies the security-in-chief has established among the vas gharianis. Nani used to say that not even a leaf could tremble without her and Nana Sahib's knowledge. How else do you think Nana Sahib found out about the conspiracy? These letters were probably sealed in envelopes and dropped off in a secret location, under a stone, an owl's nest or something and picked up by the patidar and therefore in the possession of his wife. To answer your question, he did not send any oral messages because ears can talk.'

'Why is Kumud Masi Sa bothering with these?'

'For the same reasons that we are. She wants to know who is responsible for Nana Sahib's death. Besides, Kumud Mami Sahib was communicating with him, wasn't she?' I said, examining the letters under a lamp.

Lalita looked at me sharply. 'So you've been listening to ghariani gossip as well. Or maybe it's the wag wag wag of your mother's vicious tongue.' Hurt and bewilderment lengthened Lalita's face further, if that were possible.

I threw the letter on the table. 'Speaking of gharianis,' I ground out my words, 'has your aunt told you of the havoc she wreaks every time some evil hag feeds some juicy tidbit into her ears?'

We were back to the elephant howdah.

It was Lalita who gave in first, unwilling to jeopardize the only friendship she had in the zenana, and I was grateful for it. I knew then that after our wild adventure in the Sirikot countryside, our special bond could strain but never break.

'Don't take it that way,' she proffered. 'It's just that I feel so sorry for Kumud Masi Sa. Sirikot is so different from where she grew up, in the carefree environs of Nepal and Himachal. My aunt is not used to the intrigue and debauchery of this concubine-ridden palace. It suffocates her. She's wilting away.'

I thought of Kumud Mami Sahib's pale face and almond eyes, like a mountain Madonna. In a see-saw vacillation of my previous show of temper, tears filled my eyes. 'Look at her own husband,' I decried. 'Even he keeps her opiated so she won't be a nuisance to the palace. I agree with you, Lalita, some vas gharianis are given more respect in the palace than Kumud Mami Sahib. And that look her children have, of the perpetual fear of scolding.'

Lalita picked up the letter I had thrown on the table. 'I know people are saying horrible things about Kumud Masi Sa's correspondence with the patidar. Even her husband accused her of plotting against his father. He has asked her to leave Sirikot many times. He thinks she's crazy and that she plotted the murder, that she was inciting the patidar.'

'I know, Lalita,' I intervened, 'but it wasn't the patidar who killed Nana Sahib.'

'But he was plotting to,' Lalita agonized. 'And haven't we discussed that the killer is somebody who carried on his unfinished business?'

'And that that somebody could be Kumud Mami Sahib,' I said inadvertently, wincing when I realized that I had spoken aloud. But Lalita did not take offence.

'But, Leela, Kumud Masi Sa told me about the nature of her correspondence with the patidar. They shared some political ideology called Communism. Once, at a mushaira party, he had recited a couplet, much to the ire of Nana Sahib's sycophants. You know what an intellectual she is. They struck up a rapport and wrote to each other ever since.'

'What is this Communism I keep hearing about?' I wondered. 'Is it something dirty, like Yuvrani Mami Sahib's illustrated books?'

'Oh, much worse,' she assured me. 'It is a system in which they believe that the poor should destroy the rich and distribute their wealth among the needy. Communists are what you could call book-reading dacoits. They also wear brown uniforms, eat the same food and abuse god.'

'How funny. What did poor god ever do to them?'

'I know. It would be a pretty dull life without god.'

'And why kill the rich? It's not their fault they are rich. I don't understand these intellectuals. They've actually created a philosophy out of envy.'

'No, you see they feel the rich have become so by bleeding the poor. They want to return them their rightful wealth.'

'Like Robin Hood?'

'Yes, and the French Revolution.'

'Yes, but that was a revolution not a philosophy. I mean, isn't this ideology illegal?'

'It probably is. That's why Kumud Masi Sa and the patidar were so secretive about it.'

'Yes, but Lalita, it is a dangerous philosophy, isn't it, if it's like the French Revolution? Did you hear what they did to that cake lady, what's her name, Queen Antoinette?'

'Nothing like that, silly.' Lalita squinted at the letter. 'Kumud Masi Sa and the patidar just discussed books.'

I took a letter from her hands and read it. '*No*,' it said. '*Three a.m. tomorrow, after dinner.*'

'I know who the mysterious correspondent is,' I still remember my words and the chill I felt when the realization dawned. Read the letter. "Three a.m., tomorrow, after dinner."'

'That's what I find so confusing. It must be a mistake. The writer obviously meant lunch. Though even three is late for lunch. And it should be p.m. not a.m.'

'The writer made no mistake,' I said. 'Obviously this letter was written by somebody who wanted to change the patidar's previous hour of appointment. The letter is in English, so obviously it has to be somebody from the ruling family. And there is only one person in this palace who has his dinner at three o' clock in the night.'

'Who?' Lalita was clueless.

'Yuvraj Mama Sahib! The one and only Lord Ram who could not wait for King Dashrath to die! What a saintly man he turned out to be. Keeping a back-up plan for assassination, just in case his black magic did not work.'

Lalita looked around the room. Day was recoiling against the probing shadows of night. 'I'm scared, Leela,' she said crossing her arms around herself. 'I really really want to go home to Purankot. It's not like this there. It's nicer. Poor Kumud Masi Sa, to think even I had doubts about her. Oh, god Leela! Leela?' Lalita grabbed my shoulder suddenly and my heart leapt like a bullfrog into my mouth. 'Suppose his spies are listening to us right now? Suppose, Yuvraj Mama Sahib is listening?'

I looked around. The stone eyes of the tiger head trophy in the hallway looked more sinister than usual. I clutched Lalita and we embraced tightly, grasping flesh under nail, two girls standing in a landmine. 'I know what I'll do,' I said finally, regaining my composure.

'What?' It looked as if this would be the word she would repeat for a while.

'I'll tell Ma about this. She'll know what to do. She's taken an oath to search out the murderer. And she is the only one who knows how to handle Yuvraj Mama Sahib.'

'And the letters? We can't possibly leave them here.'

'Why?'

'Because Kumud Masi Sa will put two and two together, imbecile. You think you are the only genius who can see the connection? Maybe I should come with you when you speak to your mother.'

'Maybe not, Lalita. If she knows you are involved, she might, you know... react differently....You are family, but, I mean, not directly so...'

We put the letters back in the pigeonhole and then Lalita saw me off to the steps leading down the terrace and away from Kumud Mami Sahib's courtyard. She squeezed my hand and gave me a brief hug; sisterhood a warm glow encircling us.

Thirteen

Yuvraj Mama Sahib was conducting the chariot festival in Sirikot. I was present for the ceremony with the rest of the ruling family. Never, throughout the year, during any other festival, was there such a turnout of people. From the chariots we could see the throngs darkening the horizon — snaking down the roads, crowding the grandstands, overrunning balconies. Even we, the royal women, who came in palanquins in a tight cordon of screens, could not avoid the crush of body against body. Armpit odours mingled and hung heavy in the air. The sweat and devout tears of old and young, man and woman, flowed in helpless worship. People stared at the ruling family in open admiration. Rudimentary, almost formless, wooden statues of Lord Jagannath, his sister Subhadra and brother Balram were taken out of the temple to the beat of gongs and drums and put into three chariots. Yuvraj Mama Sahib and all the palace pandits helped to drag the idol of Lord Jagannath, tied with thick hemp ropes, to the auspicious spot. I took the opportunity to inform Lalita of the etymological roots of the word 'juggernaut'. It obviously came from Jagannath. She was impressed.

Watching Yuvraj Mama Sahib sweep the chariot that day, I observed how deeply he concentrated on every sweep of the golden broom. He had to be king and mortal, devout and regal, superior and subservient, at the same time. His jaw was set, his face dark, his movements as solemn as a tomb.

Later, in the temple, the citizenry of Sirikot and the neighbouring states came up and prostrated before the ruling family. They took turns, falling like ninepins, attracted to us like iron filings to a magnet. After Yuvraj Mama Sahib, Ma got the maximum prostrations, much to the chagrin of Yuvrani Mami Sahib, who stood sheepishly in a corner in the temple courtyard, unloved, unvenerated. Even I got some prostrations, maybe because I was Ma's daughter; Raghavendra got hardly any.

~

It was perhaps because of this evidence of the love that the people of Sirikot had for Ma, that Yuvraj Mama Sahib entrusted her with the responsibility of cataloguing the Lord's jewellery in the Temple Trust, and with dividing Nani's jewels among her daughters-in-law.

When I went up to my mother's room the heavy oak doors of her chambers were closed. I pushed them open and found her sitting cross-legged on the bed, alone, surrounded by jewellery. She asked me to shut the door and went back to writing in a long register. All around her were steel trunks, some open, some closed, with 'Rani Sahiba, Sirikot' written on a few and 'Temple Trust' on the others. Sapphires, rubies, emeralds and diamonds were strewn on the bed and on the floor and in heaps on the chairs, all gleaming like the malevolent multicoloured eyes of exotic sea animals. There were nose-rings, tunic brooches, aigrettes, necklaces, earrings, diadems — every conceivable ornament for extended limb and pierced body part.

I have always been uncomfortable around too much jewellery. In Sirikot as well as in our palace in Dhairwar, the palace jewellery was hauled out from the iron rooms of the ganta ghar once or twice a year and examined, for what purpose I am still unsure, though I suspect it was examined and looked at much for the same reason a miserly moneylender counts and touches his money before going to bed. To feel secure.

I have seen all the women in the zenana, my mother and Nani — and even Nana Sahib — eerily entranced by the inexorable power of precious stones, their eyes dilating as the reflections of the ethereal light from the gems held them captive, forcing them to surrender their will; as if to possess those gleaming stones was the sole happiness left in this world. I have seen my elders weakened with greed.

As a child I have sat through animated discussions on the science of gems. It is said that the stones can affect our health, our longevities, our fates, our lives. I believed it then. I still do.

I sat on Ma's bed and fingered the triple string of Ceylonese rubies, like congealed clots of pigeon's blood, and ran my fingers down the brittle translucent stones of a red riverbed. I held the 'Mughal Set' against my throat. An exquisitely crafted pearl and diamond choker that started from the larynx and trickled down to the cleavage, it was heavy and cold, like the tears of a vestal virgin solidified and cast on the melted gold of a gun or a pharoah's sceptre, or a scimitar used to assassinate emperors.

'Don't touch that,' Ma snapped suddenly and pointed her pen at me. 'It is not yours.' I dropped the necklace and it slipped soundlessly on to the bed like a poisonous flower wilting from the lack of touch. Ma had succumbed; she was already dazzled by the hypnotic sparkle of the jewels. They were all around her, like coiled serpents, ready to bare their fangs any minute. She would die willingly, a happy victim. 'Here, try this one.' Just as suddenly, Ma changed her tone and handed me a diamond brooch, its intricate rays forming a scintillating but frozen star. 'You like it?'

'No,' I said. 'You know I'm not interested in jewellery.'

'Don't be facetious, Leela. Everybody is interested in jewellery.'

Ma was so engrossed in sorting out the jewels that her brow was knitted with the immensity of her task. The only way to get her attention was to shock her. So I came straight to the point and told her I knew that Yuvraj Mama Sahib had killed his father.

'He didn't do it,' she said calmly. I was shattered by Ma's lack of surprise, especially since I was so sure. I had clear proof.

'Ma, he was the one corresponding with the patidar.'

'Like so many others,' she said, shutting her register and facing me. 'Like Kumud, for instance.'

'Yes, but he was also performing tantra puja on Nana Sahib. You won't deny that! I was there when you found the letters.'

'You were?' My mother studied my face thoughtfully. I am sure she was thinking about the depth of my involvement and my insatiable curiosity about Nana Sahib's death. Then I remembered Pushpa's admission — about Ma wanting to thwart our investigations — but decided now was not the time to bring it up.

'I know about Rajraj's correspondence with the patidar. He told me about it,' Ma said finally. 'They were planning to overthrow the government, not assassinate the raja. They were discussing a new, modern style of administration. They wanted to do away with redundant and traditional schools of thought.' Ma looked at me in keen appraisal, 'But, Baba, your Nana Sahib, didn't know that. He thought the correspondence was a dangerous assassination plot. So he had the patidar killed. But you probably know that by now, inquisitive little monkey that you are. He confessed it the night before he died, after that fateful Project Kumud dinner.'

'How was he killed?' I asked. Blankly; without feeling.

'He was beaten to death in the dungeons. Then his throat was slashed. Didn't you hear Baba's confession?'

I remembered my flight to the pond that night, not wanting to hear what I knew was about to be said. Something dreadful, something that would rip the last vestiges of innocence from me and leave me naked, grown-up. Nana Sahib sank a bit deeper under his marble cenotaph.

Beaten, they were always beaten, in the granary, in the dungeon. Some in the stables, or behind the hibiscus. Some quartered like the ludbudiya ghost, some starved, like the jokho. I stared at Ma, not seeing her. *Let me go or let me die.* The patidar was lucky. He had died while we were doomed to purgatory.

'Leela, you won't understand all this. You are too young to bother about court issues. Go play with Raghavendra. You know what, I'm thinking of presenting my doll collection to you.' Ma smiled at me brightly. She collected a handful of sarpeches — turban ornaments — and dropped them into an intricately carved casket of ivory and sandalwood. Ornaments within ornaments.

'I don't want your doll collection! You think I'm still a child! You think I don't know! I know that you are in cahoots with Yuvraj Mama Sahib!' My chest heaved at her insensitive disregard of my maturity. In mounting confusion and anger I blurted, 'The two of you planned this together! *The two of you murdered Nana Sahib!*'

I turned to flee from her, but she caught me with a bone-chilling, '*Wait!*'

I stopped. I had to face her now. 'Are you out of your mind?' She enunciated each word as if they were stones she was biting one by one.

There was no going back. I flung at Ma a month of suppressed, angst-ridden conflict and deepest suspicions about her dastardly role in Nana Sahib's death. His dying words had been 'black blood'. I knew what he meant: The blood that ran in my veins, the blood nurtured and irrigated from her womb, was black as the darkest caves of hell. I was born of a mother as evil as the Roman empresses. I must bear that cross as bravely as my tender shoulders would allow. The blemishes of our birth are tattooed on our foreheads for the world to see. But I would fight her, my mother, my birth, as long as my body would allow.

'I know everything, Ma! Everything! I know why you are suffering from a nervous breakdown. It is not because of grief. It is because of guilt. You have conspired with your brother. By letting him convince you of his innocence you have conspired with him. Otherwise, why are you not hunting down the killer as you swore you would? Why do you spend hours in the Chandramahala with him discussing matters of state? Why are you not going back to my father and your legally wedded husband? This is not your home. But you stay on, because your brother has blinded you with promises of power!'

My mother's eyes glazed over as if the truth of my statements were sending her into a trance. Encouraged by her deepening sense of guilt, I spurred on, 'I grant that you did not plot Nana Sahib's murder, but by collaborating with Yuvraj Mama Sahib, especially when you and I knew that he was practising tantra on Nana Sahib, you are guilty, Ma, you are, you are! Look at you. You ask me to play with your dolls. He asks you to play with his trinkets. What is the difference?'

'You will not speak to me like that, you hear me? I am your mother. I forbid it.' My mother sank down on the edge of the bed and pressed her knuckles against its hard edge. I thought she would make a lunge for me. I started shouting. Spittle sprang from my distorted mouth and suspended briefly in the air. 'What will you do, Ma? Kill me? Or beat me? Go ahead, beat me, let Yuvrani Mami Sahib in the adjoining quarters know what a cultured family we are. Don't deny it, Ma! You can't. That's the reason why you swallow all those potions and recite mantras all day. You are guilty, Ma, you are guilty. As guilty as Yuvraj Mama Sahib. That is why Shanti is blackmailing you and Yuvraj Mama Sahib. That is why you two are presenting her with houses and property. What happened, Ma? Did Yuvraj Mama Sahib brainwash you with the patidar's philosophies on new administration?'

Ma's limp palm brushed her brow, as if to remove the clutter. 'This is what happens when you don't notice that there are children in the room.'

'Tell me, Ma, please, you have to. You must.'

'These patidar's letters you say you found,' Ma suddenly got a grip on herself and countered my childish inquisition, turned it around. 'You say you found them in Kumud's desk? You really must stop snooping around people's rooms. What will she think when she finds out that my daughter has been raised to be a kleptomaniac?'

I was nonplussed for a moment, unable to rally forth a defense.

'And how did they get into Kumud's desk, anyway?'

'She is in touch with the patidar's widow.'

'Really, now. Her interest in the patidar is going too far. I must speak to Rajraj about this.'

I didn't want to get poor Kumud Mami Sahib into more trouble and I blabbered confusedly hoping to quickly change the subject. I confessed that I had heard a conversation between Kumar Mama Sahib and Yuvrani Mami Sahib about the black brahmin, the relationship his wife had with Nana Sahib and how she died at childbirth.

'And where did you hear this conversation between Bhavani and the rani?' Ma banged shut the jewellery caskets and snapped the little clasps; bands fastening on metal pimples.

I did not tell Ma that I had hidden in the rani's dressing room. I told her I had overheard them from the courtyard. That I had wandered there because I couldn't sleep.

'What time was it?' Ma asked, systematically putting the jewellery away, while I was held, pinned down, like a monsoon moth in my own collection.

'It was late,' I admitted, wondering how she had taken away my thunder and how this unexpected turnaround happened. 'Everybody was asleep.'

'And what were Bhavani and the rani doing?' Ma asked without blinking.

'I don't know. Talking, I guess.'

'What about?'

'Oh, this and that.'

'Specifically, what? Were they discussing something urgent or was it general gossip?'

I realized too late where my mother was going. She knew I was hiding the truth. But she was more interested in finding out the sordid details than the effect they might have had on my sensibilities. I was silent. Knowing that what I said next would incriminate them and me. If they were discussing matters of vital importance I should be able to tell Ma what they were and it could be cross-checked. At least a crisis would defuse the scandal, because nothing short of a crisis should bring a bhabhi and her devar together to her apartments in the middle of the night. The situation was even more serious since Yuvraj Mama Sahib had been away to Delhi at the time, consulting with the Chamber of Princes on matters of accession to the Indian union. I could not lie about the urgency of their discussion and not be caught out. On the other hand, if I said 'general gossip' it would be obvious that they were having an affair.

I resorted to anger, deciding to punish Ma for the difficult spot she had put me in. 'They were making love, Ma,' I said nastily.

Ma got up from the bed as if to hit me and then realized it was not my fault. She sat down on the bed and hung her head. Her shoulders sagged. 'Where are you, Ma?' she called out softly to her dead mother. 'Where are you? You would have known what to do. Sirikot has changed, Ma. The world has gone wrong.'

Poor, persecuted, disillusioned Ma. The world was going wrong for a thousand ruling families in India in a way she could not even begin to imagine. She got up and started to pace the room, muttering under her breath and reciting the Gayatri Mantra. I watched her like a predator and caught her at her most vulnerable. 'Why is Shanti blackmailing you?'

She did not reply. She quickened her pacing. Her steps were nervous, her gestures bird-like.

'Why is Shanti blackmailing you?' I didn't dare to breathe. I was close now, so very close.

She sat on the bed. She keened gently, remembering the pain she had been living with and could no longer tolerate. Her forehead was dotted with beads of sweat. 'Get me my medicines, Leela.' She pushed aside the caskets and lay down. I fetched the thick oily fluid from the mantelpiece. She put three spoons in a glass tumbler and raised herself on her elbows to drink it.

'Why is Shanti blackmailing you, Ma?'

My mother lay down and stared dully at the wall, her legs spread out stiffly, straight, oddly straight, in front of her.

And then she told me.

The bottle of medicine was suddenly too heavy for me. I set it down on the bedside table before it slipped from my fingers. The table was of Burmese teak, pigmented the colour of burnt sienna with paintings of the Bodhisattvas on it. I wanted to disappear into those paintings, to be absorbed into their serene faces, to rest petrified in that wood. Now that my mother had spoken, I wanted her to unspeak the words, so we could go back to a world where they didn't exist.

I knew then that there would be no redemption for Ma. She was doomed. If there was proof, she had sinned for not meting out justice. If there was no proof, she had still sinned for wanting proof about tragedy. I tried to bring some reason back into the lifeless room by asking her endless questions. For some reason my interrogations had held her captive. She had needed to talk. As her daughter I was the safest recipient of her tortured thoughts.

Ma sat on the edge of a trunk as if it was a boat, her eyes wild and staring as she tossed over a deep troubled ocean. 'We have to pay our dues,' she said. 'We must reap the fruits of our actions, our ancestor's actions. Baba lived his lies. Ma lived hers. And I shall live mine.'

'But, Ma... it's against the law.'

If Ma hadn't spoken with the cold deliberation of one arguing a case in court, I would have taken her wild eyes as a sign of insanity. 'My child, we are the law. The thoughts in our heads are the law. It is our thoughts that make the law, it is this law that breaks. When the law is broken it is the thoughts in your head that will make you act out your retribution. Remember what I tell you very carefully, Leela. You do your karma. Do not worry whether others are doing theirs.'

'That's not what you or Nana Sahib or a ruler does when there is a crime committed in his lands. People have been hanged for crimes.'

'That's administration,' Ma was airily dimissive.

'And Nana Sahib's murder?' I was incredulous, 'Doesn't that come under the jurisdiction of administration?'

'Your Nana Sahib's case,' my mother said with the aplomb of a prophet, 'was personal, it was fate, karma. Unlike other cases of administration, which are impersonal. Therefore, not karma.'

~

At bedtime, when each scrap of jewellery had been catalogued and removed to the ganta ghars, my mother, lightened by the burden we were now both sharing, drew me close. Her voice was gruff with maternal feelings held in check.

'I am not a perfect mother,' she said, kissing the numerous lockets of gods and saints that dangled from a gold chain around her neck; a nightly ritual. 'I cannot be a perfect mother, because I am not a perfect person. Parenting is flawed by nature, like the yellow sapphire. I have never fed you with my hands, or clothed you, or sung you lullabies the way the mothers of the world do. When you feel angry and upset with me, as I am sure you will many times in the future, I want you to be consoled. Because if I have truly done you wrong, then without a doubt, I shall be punished.'

With that Ma closed her eyes and turned her back to me. The mattress made a wave in her wake and I imagined I was floating on a sea, and the silver bedpost before me was the mast of my ship. I shut my eyes and tried to close out my thoughts. Deliberately, I played out my favourite fantasy. I had a stowaway

in my hold. He had curly hair and a chiselled nose. I would sail
to the end of the world and bring back treasures that would
dazzle my beloved ...

A small army of tinkling anklets rushed upto Ma's door.

'Huzur, Raja Sahib has called for you. Quick, Jemma Sahib,
Raja Sahib wishes all of you to proceed post-haste to the
Chandramahala. Please, Jemma Sahib, you must hurry.'

I was at the door. I looked behind to see my mother's
reaction. She had not moved from her sleeping position. Only
her eyes were open. 'I'm not in the mood to go to the
Chandramahala now,' my mother announced.

Baby Uncle's Santoma rushed in through the door. A crowd
of vas gharianis milled into the room with her, like garish
butterflies. 'But you must, Jemma Sahib,' Baby Uncle's nurse
said. 'You really must! India is free! They are coronating the new
raja!'

Ma's laugh was the short bark of a hysterical deer.

All the way down to the the Chandramahala Ma swayed as
she walked, drunk with giggles. 'What was it you said again?' Ma
burbled.

'They are coronating the new raja,' the bewildered vas ghariani
repeated.

And Ma, holding her sides, sat down on the stone steps of
a pavilion, unable to control her laughter.

Fourteen

We trained our ears to the radiogram's head — which was shaped like an awkward extra-terrestrial resting on four, thin, ungainly legs — and like Nana Sahib's Golden Retreivers listened with cocked heads to the high-pitched exultation in His Master's Voice. It was Jawaharlal Nehru, his voice crackling like starched linen.

I had met him once, three years ago in Calcutta. I remembered him vaguely and briefly, the way I remember the world-renowned Bismillah Khan play the shehnai at my wedding, briefly and vaguely. Nana Sahib, my father, and my paternal grandfather, all rather inactive members of the Congress party, had gathered at my paternal grandfather's house in Park Street for the Congress party meeting. A Kashmiri Pandit, Jawaharlal Nehru was a short man with a pink face and a permanent smile and he looked like a neatly-dressed schoolmaster. He smiled at me in that intimate but impersonal way people have when they meet too many strangers in a day. He told me I had an artist's face. My paternal grandfather turned an apoplectic purple at the statement. He thought Jawaharlal Nehru was trying to insult them by making obscene comparisons to cheap artists who peddled their talents to make a living. It took my father, a more worldly-wise man, some time to explain to his father that in most parts of the world comparisons to artists are taken as compliments.

~

Sirikot, unlike my father's state of Dhairwar, had never received the 'Ruling Chief' title from the British. The title of raja in Sirikot was hereditary, coming down four hundred years. For the last hundred years, our covert alliances through marriage and diplomacy had rested with the Marathas, the thorn in the British side. Eighty years ago, Sirikot had ruined its chances for the title of Ruling Chief when the Raja of Sirikot refused a British agent the use of a hundred elephants of the Sirikot army to quell an uprising in a neighbouring state. After Independence, Sirikot would not get the benefits of the privy purse, a compensatory package promised by the then home minister, Vallabhbhai Patel, to the princely ruling chiefs.

In 1950, the Abolition of the Zamindari Act would take away thousands of acres of Yuvraj Mama Sahib's arable fields. What remained would be contended by all the bastards of Sirikot and rot in files in land dispute courts. Unlike Sirikot, where the decay started early, almost immediately, my paternal home, Dhairwar, nominated with a minimal privy purse, would wait till 1970 for the axe to fall. That would be when Indira Gandhi, Jawaharlal Nehru's daughter, some would say herself dynastically acceding to India's prime-ministerial seat, drove in the last nail. She would abolish the privy purse. The rajas would be dead for good.

Today, after fifty-nine years of Nehruvian 'socialist republic' independence, in the sleepy hills of Sirikot, not much has changed for its people. There are no tarred roads and very little electricity. The only schools are the ones Nana Sahib had built. The only hospital stands over the stables of disbanded elephants. The only institution competing for modernity is the degree college Yuvraj Mama Sahib had founded. Artisans, potters, bugle-players, merchants, jewellers, dancers, musicians, painters, night-soil cleaners, pandits, sweepers, astrologers, Sanskrit scholars, temple pujaris and, of course, the turuhi player, still have no concrete means of feeding their families. They come to the Sirikot palace demanding justice like in the olden days. But the palace is empty.

The Sirikot royal family was reduced to penury. Independence must have been a source of severe disenchantment to Yuvraj Mama Sahib because he had entertained patricidal thoughts only a few months before the coming of it. Sirikot lost most of the artifacts and family heirlooms that lay about the palace like carefully strewn litter. The gold thrones and silver beds were taken during income-tax raids. In an effort to save some of Sirikot's artifacts, Mama Sahib donated elephant howdahs, jewel-encrusted daggers, ivory palanquins, and lapis lazuli and jade statues to the Calcutta museum. Showcased as the Sirikot collection, it was subsequently stolen. Sirikot lost fourteen houses on beaches, hill-resorts and cities to the government.

Over the years, I have read stories of the licentious excesses of maharajas. The quaint and quirky tales of jewellery and harems, elephants and eccentricities are all true. Rajas tended towards corpulence, were pickled in foreign liquor and were used to the permanent press of female flesh. My great-grandfather in Dhairwar had conducted a very expensive nuptial ceremony for the wedding of his favourite bitch with his neighbouring state's pedigreed Alsatian. Gold-embroidered invitations were sent out to his relations and he sulked for years because some of them didn't deign to attend. Every year he would go through nine months of pretended pregnancy and even attend court with a pillow strapped to his belly. He delivered the pillow in his harem after nine months amid much jubilation and the serious ministrations of palace doctors.

My mother's sister, married into a wealthy Ruling Chief family in Uttar Pradesh, was forbidden to ever stay in Sirikot because her parental home was not up to their standard. After great difficulty, she obtained permission to visit during Nana Sahib's funeral, but stayed in the outhouse as her in-laws had decreed. During the motor drive to Sirikot, she menstruated in the gold-plated and silk-upholstered Rolls-Royce. The chauffeur had received instructions that, in such an eventuality, he must detour to Benares and dip the Rolls-Royce in the holy Ganges and scrape the paint off the vehicle. He acted out his instructions and my aunt was never forgiven for the damage she caused the car.

And there are other stories.

The founder of Sirikot, Raja Uday Karan Singh from the Kachchawa clan of Amber in Jaipur, was a man so pious that when, during a hunt, his eyes fell on a disrobed woman bathing by a stream he returned to the palace to take a ritual cleansing bath to expiate the sin of 'looking at another man's wife'.

When the Raja of Kalapathar's palace was put up for auction by a British government infuriated by his revolutionary resistance, many spectators had turned up for the bidding. But not a single bid was made because he was believed to be a just king. His palace was saved. The Raja of Naunagar did not touch a single coin in his state treasury. He was the only raja I know who worked for his living. His livelihood came from the royalties he accrued from the children's stories he published. It was the Maharaja of Baroda who patronized and nurtured the great leader of the Harijans, Baba Ambedkar. My granduncle from Dhairwar gave away a lot of his land during the 'bhudan' movement, even though he was no longer the raja and didn't have much to his name. I know a lot of my relations who gave away their lands and many who opened up their palaces for saints and wandering fakirs.

Every villainy is redeemable.

My own grandmother from Dhairwar practised her dislike for material prosperity in an active manner. She formally renounced the world and only wore the orange colours of a renunciant. She slept on a thin orange mattress, kept a few orange saris in a plastic orange basket and wrote her spiritual experiences in a small orange diary.

I know for sure that both my grandparents, of Sirikot and Dhairwar, opened up their granaries during droughts and floods. Every festival marked in India's crowded lunar calendar was an occasion for charities, donations, food and clothes. Lagaan, or revenue, was exempted during years of crop failure. Not a day went by in the courts and harem courtyards when a discontented subject could not submit his petition, his fariyad. Complaints varied from the urgent to the ridiculous. It could be a water riot or an unfaithful wife. All petitions were heard and acted upon. How many times have I seen my grandparents hand over, on an impulse, a pearl necklace or a finger ring to reward the inspired offering of a cook or a bringer of glad tidings? How many weddings they conducted, how many births they blessed and funerals they paid for, how many orphans they incorporated in their complicated palace system. The wealth in the treasuries may well have come from the blood of the poor — as a night-soil carrier had once shouted from a dark palace tunnel — and my experience of Indian monarchy may be tinted by the naïve rosy colours of childhood, but I would still like to believe that some of the wealth of the princely states came from the god-given fertility of the soil of our country.

It has been argued that instances of royal largesse display dependence on the whims of an absolute ruler. There are no arguments against the truth of such an argument. But I cannot help but miss the grandness, the magnanimity and the hospitality of what is today dismissed as aristocratic whim. It is a manner of generosity learnt and fostered over centuries.

Where in this artificial new millennium is there valour? Where is the chivalry? Where is honour? Where are the colours of gold?

'Everything has vanished like burning camphor,' my mother said, eyes blinded by the smoke of her dream-like life.

~

In the Chandramahala that night, servant, dog, ruler and ruling family did not sleep 'while the world slept'. For us it was the beginning and it was the end. On that midnight of the fourteenth of August in 1947, man, woman and animal hardly moved, so spellbound were we by the talking radio. We were swept away by the romance of Jawaharlal Nehru's rhetoric. Lumps in our throats, wiping our eyes with the edge of our saris, we were happy to be totalled by the greatest leveller after death — democracy. We were willing to burn the bridges to our heritage; to remain anchored only in the irradiant future. Shoulder to shoulder, we wanted to walk with 350 million other new citizens and fashion a great nation. Let the drums roll, we thought, for we will walk as one.

'Long years ago, we made a tryst with destiny,' Nehru said, 'and now the time comes when we shall redeem our pledge.'

'A moment comes,' he said, 'which comes but rarely in history, when we step out from the old to the new, when an age ends, and when the soul of a nation long suppressed finds utterance.

'At the dawn of history, India started her unending quest, and the trackless centuries are filled with her striving and the grandeur of her successes and her failures. Through good and ill-fortunes alike, she has never lost sight of that quest or forgotten the ideal which gave her strength. We end today a period of ill-fortune and India discovers herself again.

'There is no time for petty and destructive criticism,' his thin voice vibrated over cosmic static, 'no time for ill-will or blaming others. We have to build the noble mansion of free India where all her children may dwell.'

His words had a profound effect on my young mind. Truly, this was the coronation of a raja. I knew that in new India, we, the Indian royalty, were the 'ill-fortune' he spoke of. It was we, who did not fight the British but collaborated with them to gag the 'soul of a nation long suppressed'. We, who harkened back to a long lineage of illustrious warriors. We had to 'step out from the old to the new', we had to let 'an age end', we must allow 'the noble mansion of free India' to be constructed over our archaic palaces. It was time for the hammer and sickle, for the steel giants to belch out industrial fumes, for the wondrous machine of modernity to crank its way to progress.

History teachers shall long debate the strength and truth of Nehru's rhetoric. Their opinions will vary. As for me, I am sure Nehru's extempore speech came from a troubled conscience but a clear heart. He made mistakes – the way we did. There was the blood of the poor on his hands – just as it was on ours. His descendants have paid the dues of their ancestors, in the same way that we have. The line turns round and comes full circle, there is no escaping it. You cannot hold the destinies of other lives in your hands and not suffer for it.

Freedom is an intoxicating drug. As children we partook of it freely, while our elders were more circumspect, worried as they were about an uncertain future. But even they did not want to seem peevish when India struggled with a crisis more horrific, more far-reaching, more inhumane, than ours could ever be. As Pakistan and India bifurcated, our country's amputed limbs bled. Punjab bled. Lahore bled. Pakistan bled. India bled. A fever of agony coursed through our country.

Already confused, we in Sirikot did not know what to do with our enthusiasm.

~

'How can we call ourselves free when our hands are cut off?' I asked Kumar Mama Sahib some days later. Ever since Independence had been declared, my uncle's movements had become very lethargic. Instead of hunts and trips to the city, he lay about the courtyard in a muslin kurta and dhoti, smoking his hookah and listening incessantly to the talking radio head. Kumud Mami Sahib lay on the easy chair next to him with a book of poems folded at its spine – Robert Frost, I think. They were a handsome couple, made more endearing by the strain of aloofness between them.

'Because Nehru believes it is better to cut off our hands than have them tied behind our back,' he replied.

I was not convinced. 'Why didn't Nehru allow Jinnah to be prime minister, as Gandhiji said he should? Then there would be no Partition, would there?'

Kumar Mama Sahib held a pinch of snuff to his nose and snorted. I didn't know whether he was sniffing at the snuff or at Jawaharlal Nehru. 'Then how would our great idealist Jawaharlal Nehru get his chance at power? And there is another problem,' Kumar Mama Sahib said. 'If Jinnah becomes prime minister then India runs the danger of becoming a Muslim state.'

'So what is wrong with that?' I retorted. 'Hindus and Muslims have been living together since the dawn of history. We Kachchawa Rajputs gave a daughter in marriage to the Muslims.'

'Shhh,' he said. 'Not so loud.'

'But I know, Kumar Mama Sahib. Our ancestor Man Singh gave his sister in marriage to Emperor Akbar.'

Kumud Mami Sahib's epileptic fits had worsened over the past month. Every time I saw her, it seemed to me that the blue half moons under her eyes had lengthened their shadows. When she spoke I felt it was not to make a point but for the express purpose of irritating her husband. 'We Rajputs call ourselves warriors,' she said, 'but the only killing we can do is during tiger hunts. That too, from the safe distance of an elephant howdah. Oh yes, we can also behead helpless goats tied to the stake for Durga Puja. For the last three hundred years we haven't fought a single worthwhile battle.' (What I always found amusing about my family was the way they never calibrated time in months or years — they measured time in centuries!) 'It has been one bloodless coup after another. We have been solving our territorial disputes by marrying our enemies. What we did with the British was the most laughable of all. Since we could not marry the king, as he was way above our station, we gave ourselves up for adoption. That is why we are called the princely states.' Kumud Mami Sahib's laugh was not pleasant; the hoarse squawk of a seagull in distress.

Kumar Mama Sahib turned away from her and pretended to sleep; obviously he didn't want to squabble with his wife. But he couldn't help muttering, 'Be grateful that our hand-over to the Indian union was a bloodless coup. Otherwise you would never have got your precious Independence.'

When Kumud Mami Sahib screamed at her husband the bulbuls flew off the branches of trees and I could see the deep well of her throat where her tongue began. When she finished her tirade she was taken to her apartments and held down by vas gharianis who forced opium on her. But her words still hung in the air. 'You could have done nothing! You laughable bunch of overdressed jokers! All the rajas put together are not worth Nehru's or Gandhi's little finger! I say you are not even Rajputs, you are eunuchs!'

Maybe it was her words that pierced his pretence of sleep, for Kumar Mama Sahib reacted for the first time in their married life not with indifference but with hurt. It could have been the new loss of identity I knew my elders were suffering from, that accounted for his bizarre encounter with Babban the Barber.

It was a strange day. Full of the freshness of a spanking new Independence we were still unaccustomed to. Ma had received a letter from my father requesting her to stay on at Sirikot for a few more months. Dhairwar was in a period of transition, he was busy with the hand-over of the state and it was not safe to travel.

The month-long celebration of Independence continued with full fervour. In the morning, schoolchildren in green uniforms stood before an audience of courtiers wearing turbans dyed in the colours of our new flag. The children sang patriotic songs and sweets were distributed to everybody. Yuvraj Mama Sahib sat with his courtiers. They were awkward and uneasy, men who did not know what to do with their new independent time. The harem balconies were mostly empty.

Earlier in the day, I had accompanied Yuvraj Mama Sahib in his Chrysler Windsor. Two cars full of bags of rice and pulses followed. We took them for distribution among fleeing Pakistani refugees who had settled in the outskirts of Sirikot. The government had constructed a village of mud huts for them but had forgotten to make any provision for food. Every few days or so, we drove up to the village with rations from the granary. Never have I seen such excitement over a bag of rice. Our vas gharianis were clad in silver. Those who were not farmers received employment for themselves and their families in the palaces. I have seen beggars, but never such pitiful abjection for a fistful of pulses.

Later, I had gone to Kumud Mami Sahib's apartment for lunch. I don't know whether Lalita had orchestrated the invitation. She may have, because I had not really got back to her since the night of my mother's revelations. Besides, the events of Independence had swept us up in a way that precluded the relevance of everything else.

We were whispering out of earshot, in the hall outside Kumud Mami Sahib's rooms. I knew we were having sweet tomato chutney fried in garlic and rye. I could smell it from the kitchens. Kumud Mami Sahib, unconcerned about mealtime activities — like most other women who ran the zenana — lay reading her book of poetry in bed, her hair fanned out on her pillow. Kumar Mama Sahib, permanently stationed in his easy chair in Kumud Mami Sahib's courtyard, was presenting his finger nails to Babban the Barber. He had just finished shaving Kumar Mama Sahib and had already cut his toenails. 'I had a feeling it was your Yuvraj Mama Sahib all along. He walks as if he carries the weight of the world on his shoulders,' Lalita was saying perched on a wide marble desk. I was watching her reflection in the giant Belgian mirror mounted on teak foot-stands when we heard the screams.

The shrill shrieks were Babban the Barber's. The roars were Kumar Mama Sahib's. As if on cue, we all filed out to the courtyard to see what had happened. The backs of the screaming men were towards us. First, I thought Babban's hand was on Kumar Mama Sahib's thigh and Kumar Mama Sahib was holding it in a vice-like grip. But the angle of their bodies was wrong. I moved forward for a better look and joined in the screaming.

'Do you have any more statements to make about Rajputs?' Kumar Mama Sahib was shouting at the whimpering barber.

The servant's face grimaced in pain, sweat poured into his eyes. 'No, huzur, my father, my baap. Save me, save me, my baap, I'm going to die.'

Babban's hand and Kumar Mama Sahib's hand were stuck together on Mama's thigh. The whole thing was a bleeding mess of bone and flesh. The barber's eyes rolled and I thought he would lose consciousness but his litany did not stop. Kumar Mama Sahib's moustache was dank with the sweat pouring off his forehead. I turned away, knowing that, like me, all the women present were feeling faint. We had quite lost our appetite for lunch.

It was only after Kumar Mama Sahib's hands were bandaged and the squealing barber was led away that we learnt what had happened.

Babban the Barber had been cutting Kumar Mama Sahib's fingernails with the ustra, a sharp blade-like instrument that barbers use to trim nails. He was talking nonstop about Independence and its effect on the village. Barbers are known for their incendiary gossip; a silent barber is a dishonour to his profession. Kumar Mama Sahib was, sensibly and as usual, not paying him any attention. When the barber nicked the cuticle of his index finger a drop of blood oozed from his fingernail. Rising from his stupor, Kumar Mama Sahib snatched his hand back and said, 'Watch it, barber.' At which Babban taunted Kumar Mama Sahib — as those of the barber profession are at liberty to do — 'Kumar Sahib, you, a Rajput, cannot withstand the pain of a slight cut? You call yourself the son of a warrior race?'

Kumar Mama Sahib was not supposed to react; no man responds to the mockery of his barber. Our caste system has allowed them the right to feed us, as if through an intravenous drip, a monotonous stream of insults, flatteries, taunts and gossip while they shave us and clip our hair. It is a mild hazard of personal grooming. But Kumar Mama Sahib did not take his taunt lightly. Maybe he was still hurt by his wife's tirade against Rajputs, maybe in the new national scenario he needed to justify his race. Whatever the reason, Babban's statement cut him to the quick.

'Hand me your ustra,' Kumar Mama Sahib told Babban.

'Why, huzur?' The barber was pleasantly curious.

'Hand me your ustra,' Kumar Mama Sahib repeated. When the sharp instrument was handed over, Kumar Mama Sahib lifted his dhoti exposing the wiry hair on his thigh. 'Put your hand on my thigh.'

The unsuspecting barber obeyed.

Kumar Mama Sahib placed his own hand over the barber's and then drove the ustra in. The ustra went right through his hand, the point pricking the back of the barber's palm below his own, but not even breaking the skin. 'If it caused me so much pain,' the barber told us later, sitting on his haunches and holding his head with his hands, 'just having my hand under his, imagine how much pain it must have caused him.'

The story became a legend. Kumar Mama Sahib's daughters were henceforth called the 'Children of the Great Warrior of Sirikot'. Some people said Kumar Mama Sahib had lived up to the name of his ancestors. Others said he was just a stupid Rajput.

~

In October, Durga Puja came to Sirikot and was ceremonially attended. Forced by history and habit, Sirikot cleaned out its armoury. Guns, cannons and swords were oiled and worshipped. For the last time, the Sirikot army, in full decorative show, choreographed the famous Sirikot swordplay. In dutiful observation of the year-long mourning period of Nana Sahib's death, and in deference to our new status in the country, the celebration was subdued. But the temples were busy with the innumerable pujas of our ferocious but beautiful goddess, Durga. As patron saint of the Rajput community, she had a prominent place in the Hindu pantheon. She gave us courage, spurred us to valour and taught us the art of killing for Absolute Good.

Goats were worshipped and then sacrificed to the goddess. As on other similar occasions, I had tried again to free the dazed animals tied in the temple courtyard. They wore the ritual marks of vermilion on their foreheads and waited, heads bowed, in stoic trepidation, for the axe to fall. As usual, I was shepherded away amidst much dialectic to the zenana quarters and a vas ghariani was posted on guard till the sacrifice was over.

Yuvraj Mama Sahib fumbled through the ceremonial beheading of the goat. The palace joked that when he brought down the axe on the goat's neck he lost his concentration because his dhoti came undone. Since the cut wasn't clean, Yuvraj Sahib was forced to have another go at it, causing much discomfiture to the poor goat. Yuvrani Mami Sahib made a coarse remark about his dhoti and Yuvraj Mama Sahib shut her up with a playful glare. Ever since the death of Nana Sahib and Nani, and especially now after the declaration of Independence, I noticed how prone to juvenile, even childish, behaviour my elders had become.

All evening the sacrificed goat was offered to the goddess by Yuvraj Mama Sahib and the rajpurohit in secret rituals; the giant temple doors shut to curious onlookers. The meat was to be cooked and eaten at dinner as the goddess's blessing, her prasad. The family would gather for the feast in Yuvrani Mami Sahib's courtyard. But dinner was still a long way off and the evening stretched for Lalita and I. For lack of anything better, we peeled off pistachios in the zenani bagh fountain and went over Nana Sahib's murder again. My heart was not in it.

'I don't know what would have been worse for your Nana Sahib. His murder or this Independence,' Lalita said, trying to provoke me.

'I know,' I concurred. 'What would he have stayed alive for? I think his death is better than Yuvraj Mama Sahib's life.' How unnecessary his father's assassination had turned out to be; how blighted the purpose seemed now.

'But to kill your own father, isn't that a bit drastic?'

'Lalita, his whole existence is drastic. He is damned, whatever happens. Cheated by his own life, cheated by his father's death. There is no need for retribution.'

'What bothers me is the incredible risk Yuvraj Mama Sahib's assassin took to poison Nana Sahib ... there were too many people ... the chances of getting caught were too high ... who knows, maybe it wasn't even him ...' she said and suddenly insisted we go once more to the 'crime scene' and see for ourselves how it had happened. The proposition excited her.

Especially since Yuvraj Mama Sahib was away at the temple and we would have the whole Chandramahala to ourselves.

~

Blue fumes of dusk gathered in the unlit room. I could feel its lengthening fingers probe my powers of reasoning, searching to unlock the key to a mystery that had still not been completely solved for me. The dark furniture in Nana Sahib's room looked sombre and spectral in the condensing twilight. 'This is where Nana Sahib was lying. On the left side of his bed. Really, I wonder how Yuvraj Mama Sahib can sleep in the same bed,' I said with a shiver.

'Leela, your ancestors have died on these gold beds for generations. Some have given birth in them. What is so new about that?'

'True, but still,' I said and then began pointing out the sites: 'That is where the milk was lying, on the right side of the bed, untouched. There, by the corner of the door stood poor Ganesh, like a deaf-mute, holding Nana Sahib's brushing things. On the floor sat Potol holding his head and rocking to and fro. There were only two ways Nana Sahib could have been poisoned. The tooth powder and the milk.'

'If it had been his tooth powder, there would have been some discolouration or something in his teeth or gums.'

'Ma made the rajvaidya test the residues of Nana Sahib's phlegm in the basin. There was no trace of poison.'

'Then the only way it could have been done is through the milk,' Lalita concluded.

'I think so too. And remember what Nana Sahib said... "Black" and then "blood". The poison carried through the blood. It had to be ingested. Only ingested poisons and some injected poisons move via the blood.'

'Black, Leela. My goodness, Leela, I just got it! Black was the black lotus that the assassin had used!'

'Don't be silly, Lalita,' I snorted, sitting on the bed, feeling its bounce under me. 'How would Nana Sahib know what poison the assassin had used?'

But Lalita stuck to her silly theory. Undaunted by my exasperation, giving me argument for argument, she and I walked into Nana Sahib's latrine. Three thunder-boxes were lined in a row with silver spouted cans full of water waiting on the left sides. The only sign of beauty in the room was the presence of the painted enamel jug and basin in the corner of the room where Nana Sahib washed his hands after using the thunder-box. On the far end of the latrine, as in all other latrines in the palace, a small door led to the mehtar's corridor. Its entry and exit within the walls of the palace prevented us from ever seeing the mehtar.

'Of course,' I said. Realization came to me in a cool rush of happiness. 'That's where the assassin came from! From the mehtar's corridor!'

Lalita looked at me as if I were a genius fallen fully formed from the sky. 'Of course! My god! He could come in any time he wanted and wait for an opportune moment to plant his poison. Leela, how come nobody thought about it?'

'Because in our minds, the mehtar corridor is so insignificant that it doesn't exist.'

There was nowhere to sit in the latrine so I sat on the edge of one of the thunder-boxes. A faint smell of flatulence hung in the air. 'Ganesh was there. But with Nana Sahib's back to the bed when he washed his face and hands the assassin could easily have crawled up from behind the huge headboard of the bed and poisoned the milk.'

'Let's go to the mehtar's corridor and see for ourselves.' Lalita's eyes glistened.

'Don't be silly, Lalita. The door is kept locked from the outside. The duwari has the key. He only opens it to the mehtar during the four-hour shifts.'

'So how did the assassin enter?'

'He probably spent the night in the corridor. Or if the assassin was a vas ghariani, she probably slept with the duwari and he gave her the key.'

'This theory is getting more cock-eyed by the minute. How do you know it is not Ganesh or Potol? Why would the assassin go to all this trouble in the first place? Why not just poison his lunch, or dinner, or breakfast, or slip it in his alcohol?'

'Because, my doltish westerner, he was a teetotaller unlike you drunkards in Gujarat.' I tried to yank the mehtar's door open. 'And don't you know that Nana Sahib's kitchens and the zenana kitchens are closely guarded by generations of brahmin cooks? As for Ganesh and Potol, they were the first ones to be interrogated. If Ganesh and Potol committed the murder, then half the palace must be involved, because there were so many witnesses who vouched for them.'

'Then there is only one conclusion to make,' Lalita sulked at the twists and turns of confounding reason.

'What?'

'It wasn't done the way we think.'

'I was getting a sneaking suspicion myself,' I confessed.

~

We pushed the door. After a stolid groan, the small door to the mehtar's corridor gave way, yawning open as if inviting us into the darkness beyond. Lalita and I stared at each other. Suddenly our hearts were beating fast. My recollection of the next few minutes is confused. On hindsight, I think we may probably never have ventured into the corridor had it not been for the snake.

It was the longest one I have ever seen. As black as only the most regal king cobra can be. I was momentarily mesmerized by its sinuous grace. It had probably reached Nana Sahib's toilet from one of the cracks in the basement below. They said that the basement was so full of snakes slithering over the broken furniture and discarded trunks of old stuff that the servants refused to clean it. Later Dakshyayani asked me whether I saw the gem shining on the cobra's forehead. The gem, or legendary mani, is a calcified deposit on the forehead of only the oldest of king cobras — supposed to be evolved beings who guard treasures and saintly men. But I only remember my lungs reverberating against the walls of the narrow corridor, the sound and smell of Lalita's rough breathing beside me and the slap of our feet against a floor made mysterious to us because we could not see it.

The darkness was suffocating. The air was stale and oppressive. But it was the smell that frightened me more than the darkness and my imagined vision of the cobra slithering on towards us to claim its victim. It was the smell from an evil man's afterlife, the sickly sweet stink of ancient shit emanating from the respective hells of my ancestors.

If we died of snakebite here nobody would ever find us, I thought, my mind crazed with panic. Oh no, I thought again in relief, the mehtar would, in an hour or so, he could rescue us. But what if he didn't come? We could be trapped for days in the serpentine coils of the bowels of the palace.

We kept running and groping our way to feel the continuity of the walls. Sometimes the continuity broke and the corridor branched off in different directions to other latrines in the palace. Blindly feeling the ends of the walls we yelled to each other to decide what route to take. Our voices sounded tinny, as if echoing from inside an airless coffin. We thought we heard the hiss of the cobra behind us. We agreed that it was too dangerous for us to take the detours to other latrines. What if the door leading to the latrine were shut? No, it was better to miss the breaks in the corridor and keep following the walls to the exit outside the palace.

'What if the exit door is closed?' Lalita's high-pitched tremble sounded very much like my own.

'Then we'll keep banging on the door till a duwari hears us,' I replied grim in the face of prospective death. In truth, I have never been so conscious of my mortality as on that day.

'I see a light!' I shouted in relief, empathizing with all the seafarers I had read about who screamed 'Land ahoy!' My body relaxed. I would not die today after all! I was safe from the giant jaws of the snake that had by now taken on mythical proportions in my fevered mind. I can't remember whether we hastened our steps towards the sliver of yellow light peeping from the exit door or whether we slowed our progress knowing that deliverance was at hand. My entire being focused on yanking open the exit door. It did not budge and all my previous panic rushed back to refill the niches of my body.

'Push outwards,' Lalita shouted.

We pushed the door again, with renewed desperation, and it grudgingly yielded to the pressure. Blessed light! Even though it was from a fading sun. And blessed air! Sweet, unfettered by walls. We squinted against the light and drank in the air in deep lungfuls. A torch burned next to the crude door of corrugated iron. Standing on an unenclosed landing that led off the door we looked about hopefully for a human presence. I was not familiar with this side of the palace. Moreover, it was getting dark.

The landing descended to the ground by means of a steep flight of crude cement stairs without a railing. This section of the palace wall opened into a courtyard that was unkempt and unadorned. Puddles of old monsoon rain were left undisturbed. It was evident that nobody really cared about how this area of the palace looked. What we saw next was so disgusting that even today the image of it brings to my mouth the warm taste of vomit.

Their backs were towards us. They walked side by side as if they were strolling in a pleasure garden. They were obviously paramours and this was their favourite meeting point. We had stumbled onto a lovers' rendezvous. They carried pans in both hands that from our vantage point of the landing, looked ready to be taken for cleaning. The filth around them did not bother them a bit. Slowly, they collected the white chamber pots in a corner. Then he sat down on the steps to light a beedi and she hugged his shoulders. Her hair was loose, her face bright and smiling.

It was Shanti and the mehtar.

~

Standing awkwardly in the landing like two astonished jack-in-the-boxes ejected from the palace walls we stared at them in horror and revulsion. At first I did not know his face, but then it clicked in my mind like pieces of a jigsaw puzzle neatly fitting together. I was struck by the cruelty of fate. He was the mehtar from the untouchable colony. He was the same man I had seen once prostrate before Nana Sahib in a full pranam. And though his teeth were white with smiling now, he had cast on me a glance so full of venom at the time that I had shrunk backwards. The memory of that look had stayed with me. It had been a look of intimacy, of a hatred that came from knowledge. More, there was more. He was the same man who had lifted a handful of dirt and cursed Sirikot when I fell from my mount. I could feel my breath rise and fall within my body. Quiet and unnaturally still.

A question came up in my mind and I knew only Dhaima would be able to answer it.

Like two colourful parakeets we stood rooted to the spot on the landing, frozen with fear that the lovers might turn around and see us. But they didn't. Shanti was too busy wantonly enjoying her womanhood. The mehtar was too busy letting her womanhood stroke him, making him the man he knew he was; wanted to be. They kept touching each other.

Seeing my grandfather's handsome night-soil bearer in a moment of physical intimacy with a desiccated middle-aged woman who bloomed at his touch filled me with a sweet and peculiar dread. To my young puritan mind her hair falling on his smiling upturned face was more perverse, more sensuous, than all that I had seen of Yuvrani Mami Sahib's erotica. It was profoundly dirty.

The lovers were oblivious of our presence. Dangling the dirty pans in their hands as if they were flowerpots they simply walked away. Open-mouthed at the wonderful strangeness of life, unmindful that the steps before us had been walked on by dirty, barefoot mehtars, we sank down on them in silent awe.

'He's got very broad shoulders for a mehtar,' was all Lalita had to say.

~

The first thing Lalita and I did on reaching the zenana was to take a bath. After that, much against my remonstrations, Lalita insisted on questioning Dhaima immediately. We found her lying in a huddle in the far corner of the zenana. Lalita marched her to the zenani bagh and questioned her under a banyan tree. The leaves above us rustled as if the ghosts inhabiting the tree were complying with us. Lalita told Dhaima that if she lied to us we would find out anyway, but she would be cursed to die and haunt the very same banyan tree we sat under.

'Who are the parents of Shanti's lover, the mehtar?' Lalita asked again and again. At first I thought Dhaima would not give in to our tireless questioning. She looked through us blank-faced, irritating us with her rhythmic tobacco chewing. Just when Lalita was about to give up she relented, telling us what we already knew.

'He is the son of the black brahmin and his wife.'

'Does he know?' I whispered.

'Of course he knows,' she snapped. 'He always knew, ever since he was a child. And your Nana Sahib'- the smouldering anger, which a vas ghariani usually hides so well, flared — 'he always remembered. Every time your Nana Sahib saw him carrying away his night-soil, the truth lay between them.'

'Your Nana Sahib could have spared him,' Lalita looked at me accusingly.

'The truth doesn't do anybody any good, child.' Dhaima's wide, excessively-kohled eyes looked through us sadly, the anger gone. 'And now it doesn't matter. They will marry. There is nobody to stop them. I tried hard, but I couldn't. I console myself by thinking that blood finds its level. After all, he is of noble birth.'

'But he is a mehtar,' Lalita lamented.

'He is a brahmin.' Dhaima gritted her teeth and then started crying, tears clogging the coarse lines of her cheek. 'May your Nani Sahib forgive me ... I couldn't do it any better. I tried to find her a good match. But what could I do? I'm just a vas ghariani. But it doesn't matter now ... nothing matters now.'

I was beginning to feel uneasy. I remembered the red sari in the untouchable colony, the horse bucking, the ache in my shoulder.

'Does Shanti visit the untouchable colony where the mehtar stays?' Lalita pressed.

'Visit?' Dhaima grunted. 'She practically lives there.'

So it had been her. She had tried to hurt me, dissuade me, kill me, or all of the above. I felt I was being beaten with a stick. *Let me go, or let me die*, the words popped inanely in my head.

'Come on, let's get out of here,' I tugged Lalita's arm roughly.

I wasn't sure I wanted to know the truth.

Fifteen

When one reaches an age like mine and looks back, it seems that one has lived for the sole purpose of watching people die; their deaths have been like milestones marking my way.

That Diwali was the brightest I had ever seen in Sirikot. The entire palace was made brilliant with earthen lamps. The silver lamp-stands and rukhadiyas were cleaned out and lit in every room, even the bathrooms and hallways. The flames leapt just a little higher before they died out. We would never see the grandeur of so much light again. Sirikot was defying darkness one last time.

Dhaima died soon after the Abolition, as if in protest against the new-fangled Independence. For many years afterwards, Kumar Mama Sahib claimed that she haunted him, lifting his mosquito net in the middle of the night and asking for a smoke. It was about the same time that Phulwati disappeared, from the palace. Nobody really cared where she went.

After Diwali, Kumud Mami Sahib left Sirikot for all time with Lalita. It was banishment by mutual consent. Before leaving she tied the rakhi — the sacred thread, bonding brother and sister — around Kumar Mama Sahib's wrist. I do not know whether she felt any remorse at leaving Sirikot. I think her mental and physical illnesses had not left enough blood in her body for remorse. Though Lalita and I remained in touch and forged a friendship that would abide over many decades, Kumud Mami Sahib never returned to Sirikot or to my uncle. My aunt and uncle did not divorce. They met briefly at their daughters' weddings in the city and stayed in separate guesthouses. Their daughters grew up to be surprisingly mature and balanced, quite unscathed by their parents' eccentricities.

After a few years of reclusive seclusion in Sirikot, in which Kumar Mama Sahib did little of his usual hunting, drinking and womanizing, he suddenly took to religion. He locked himself up in the Sirikot library and pored over books on philosophy and spiritualism. God is another name for peace, he said. He wrote me a feverish letter saying that, after him, I must try to preserve the treasures of the Sirikot library. There is an entire bookcase full of the parchments of taalpatras, he wrote in his neat, square handwriting. Spiritual novitiates and practitioners of secret ritualistic practices had noted down their experiences and philosophies in the local language on these taalpatras for hundreds of years. Please see that they reach the right people, his letter said. You are close to the city and know more people than I do. I had just got married then and lived in a little eastern hill station close to Calcutta.

Kumar Mama Sahib's favourite quote was from the Bhagvad Gita: 'You grieve for things you should grieve not for, O Partha, because everything has a beginning and an end.'

In later years, Kumar Mama Sahib attracted legends like a magnet. There is another one my children love to hear. Kumar Mama Sahib took upon himself the idea of the fast of silence, the maun vrat. At mid-morning sharp every day he would wash his hands and feet, take out his japa mala, and with folded hands sit cross-legged wherever he was, to take the name of god. This habit continued for a while causing a great deal of inconvenience to him and annoyance to others. When the clock struck twelve he would simply drop whatever he was doing. Once, he was sitting in a machan in the neither dense nor sparse scrubland of the Vaitary forest. The machan is a raised wooden platform fitted into the sturdy branches of a tree. It is positioned to face a clearing and give vantage to an approaching animal. Apparently, the day did not augur well for the superstitious party because the first animal they spotted on entry into the forest was the inauspicious 'minister', the rabbit.

The hunt had started early in the day. The hakua was conducted by the forest-dwellers on foot. In groups of eight or ten they shouted out their animal cries and beat their drums to corner the tiger and herd him towards the direction of the waiting machan. By around eleven thirty, the others of the royal party on the machan could sense the sound of the hakua steadily moving in their direction. They gripped their twelve-bores and tensed their shoulder muscles. Very soon the tiger would be breaking out of the scrub into the little clearing before the machans.

Trouble struck at twelve o'clock. It was not time for the tiger but definitely time for Kumar Mama Sahib's vow of silence. Kumar Mama Sahib was in a dilemma. He could either postpone his fast or do a quick religious shortcut, sitting where he was, holding the twelve-bore gun in his sweating hands. Surely god wouldn't want him to risk his life just to take his name? But what if the tiger did not break out into the open till much later? Then wouldn't it be unfair to god to deny him his time just because he was having a cowardly moment? And wouldn't it be churlish to take the safer route of not washing his hands and feet and bowing to the ground, but putting his weapon aside and finishing his fast from the machan? That would be insincere. He would be cheating god of his dues, like a moneylender driving a safe bargain. He did not want god to get the impression that he valued his life more than his devotion to His Name. This was a test and it was time to keep his vow.

As the onlookers watched aghast, Kumar Mama Sahib climbed off the machan and walked to the clearing holding a flagon of water in one hand and his twelve-bore in the other. The hakua sounded closer. Any moment the tiger could break cover and enter the clearing. Kumar Mama Sahib put his gun aside and washed his hands and feet. He bowed to the ground three times and sat cross-legged on the ground. He folded his hands, prayed for a moment, and then took out his japa mala. He shut his eyes and prayed. Those watching him knew that he would not open his eyes for the next half an hour.

'That was the moment,' his cousin recounted later, 'that I knew the line between saints and madmen is a thin one.'

Nothing happened. The tiger was late. It sauntered in at two o'clock and caught a bullet between its eyes.

Kumar Mama Sahib's son-in-law adorned the tiger skin on his drawing room wall like a medal. 'My father-in-law liberated that tiger,' he liked to say.

Kumar Mama Sahib died ten years ago in a hospital in Benares. Ma was close by, visiting her sisters in Lucknow. His sisters subconsciously felt the tug of a heartstring coming loose and rushed to his side. Cousins converged from all across the country to the hospital where he lay. Strangely, none of his real brothers attended his death.

Before the light went out of his eyes forever they rested on me. I stood across the glass panel of his hospital room, watching, not daring to enter. He looked at me with a look of such knowledge that it cut me into two.

He, who, when I was an infant, had held me squealing upside down over the pond and laughingly asked Ma, 'Should I drown this expensive wedding?' He, who consoled me for weeks when I wept over the little carcasses of my first duck shoot. He, who called me 'his little gauraiya' and taught me how to hold a steady eye over the rifle. He, who locked himself in a bathroom during my wedding when I left my parental home for good. A lifetime of tenderness is too excruciating for only one person to bear.

While his sisters put tulsi leaves and ganga jal on his tongue and placed him on the floor whispering their guru's mantra into his ears, I tried to shatter the glass panel with a scream that never left my lips.

I feel it still. Trapped inside me.

~

After Independence, like other erstwhile rulers of the princely
states, Yuvraj Mama Sahib decided to stand for elections. He
put all his salvaged wealth into the campaign, certain that his
people would not let him down, never once considering the
possibility of losing because a win or a loss that comes as a result
of competition was an alien notion for a man led to believe that
he had already won the most important competition there was
at the time of his birth.

There were other contenders for the Congress ticket so
Yuvraj Mama Sahib stood as an Independent. Sirikot was
situated at the borders of his constituency. The people of Sirikot
voted for Yuvraj Mama Sahib, whom they still believed to be
their raja, but even so he lost by a narrow margin. Yuvrani
Mami Sahib never forgave him for his defeat. And my uncle
never recovered from it either. This alien notion, worse than
Independence, mocked him into stupidity, teaching him the
taste of ashes on his tongue.

The First Family of Sirikot deteriorated in a way that made
my mother turn her face away in shame. Shame, our most
significant virtue. By the end of their lives, Yuvraj Mama Sahib
and Yuvrani Mami Sahib were quite inured to it. It did not take
long for them to reach the bottom. Just a few decades, the time
it takes for hair to go completely grey, for a mother to become
a grandmother.

Years later, in my paternal home in Dhairwar, a wandering
ghatag was put up in the outhouse with much hospitality. He
had come to Dhairwar to broker my younger sister's marriage
and had brought proposals from eligible boys from erstwhile
ruling states. Ghatags were the most efficient carriers of gossip
besides in-house barbers. The death of their profession is sorely
missed for this reason more than any other. The story he brought

from Sirikot and the intimate narrative style in which he told it left such a vivid impression of Yuvraj Mama Sahib's decrepitude that I can practically smell the stale rum on my supposedly teetotaller uncle's breath. I see him clearly ...

~

He is at the railway station.

The shock of seeing Yuvrani Mami Sahib hits him like a decapitating blow. She stands below, waiting patiently for a train in a crowded railway platform. Alone. His leg twists awkwardly on a broken stair of the foot overbridge. Coolie flab hits him with a second force. Knocked soundlessly against a broken railing he catches a wayward fragrance of clean sweat. He keels over the railing with an ease that surprises him till he remembers that he isn't young any more. 'Of course, I'm sixty and shrunken,' he thinks.

He falls into thin air and the immobility of the present moment. Humanity rushes towards third-class compartments on both sides of the platform. It seems to him they are watching him from the back of their heads. The suspended station clock gives time with digital objectivity. 4.06 a.m. Yuvrani Mami Sahib turns slowly, so slowly, as if first in space, then in time. During his long descent he notices the thick kohl of an infant's eyes over his father's shoulders, the word 'welcome' spelt wrong on a tea vendor's mud green T-shirt and the mustard yellow of her sari which he has seen often in his dreams. He watches her gaze move up to see him, or maybe not. He has suffered too much for it to matter. Violently crimson lips betray her terror of old age. She smiles. The changing light and shadows from his free-fall give her lips the shade of burnt roses.

He hits the floor and feels no pain. What happens next does not surprise him because at sixty he is beyond surprises. The red eye of the clock blinks in an eternal hiatus. His life flashes before him and most of his memories are of her.

He is standing next to his doe-eyed, moon-faced rani on his wedding day. His freshly married sisters and his mother hold their breaths. The exactly aligned emerald kalgi on his pachranga safa lends a certain phallic appeal to his otherwise pious persona. Yuvrani Mami Sahib looks from under thick brooding lashes at his pale hand resting manfully on the family sword and wonders how to convince him that she is an untouched bride. That night he cherishes a woman enough to make it a creed.

His father's corpse lies in state. The rajpurohit adorns him with coronation jewellery. His young, almost white body, as if tarred by a brush, reflects the light of the stones. The priest asks him as per custom: 'What should I do with the rotting cadaver lying in the opposite room?' Before the tremble of his chin takes on kingly proportions, comes a whisper in a bedecked ear: 'It is custom for you to say, "Take him away and burn him." Kingship is eternal and unimpeded by human death. You too are just a vessel ...'

The gigantic doors of the palace temple are shut. In the white hot June afternoon even the Lord is resting. Her bare feet burn from the long walk to the inner sanctum where she finds the lantern-jawed rajpurohit and makes love to him. She takes her two sons as alibi, the eldest only eleven years old. She makes them wait under the ample but hot rump of a stone statue of Nandi, in the shade of a banyan tree. In the sanctum sanctorum the rajpurohit lays her down among crushed puja flowers and the ash of incense and the dust of faithfuls' feet. He leaves to nurse a cut lip tasting of his blood and her sweat. Bathed in the sweet chill of release she reaches home early with Raghavendra and Yogendra. She finds Yuvraj Mama Sahib arranging her lipsticks on her dresser, still in post-coital bliss from the night before, wearing the electric-blue satin pyjamas she likes so much. He listens to her excuses sitting by her mirror, his face sewn shut. 'You are the Yuvrani of Sirikot and my wife by tradition. You are also the focus of my benighted existence.'

He does not look at her for fear of what he might see.

He sees his jealousy growing within him like a badly brought up child, aging him. The coarse faces of her many lovers torment his long evenings in the fading grandeur of the Chandramahala. They magnify his defeat. Defeat in the elections, defeat as son, brother, husband, raja. Defeat of all that is good and true. He can no longer struggle against so much defeat. Only she remains, a symbol of what could have been, should have been. He must hold on to her. What else is there? But her egalitarian preferences move from brother-in-law to family jeweller, doctor, estate manager, driver. 'Cuckold,' his friends from the city say. A steady trickle of rum down his throat bleaches his skin to the colour of warm ashes. The colour of defeat; the colour of Independence.

He sees the first sale of a family heirloom, a wall-to-wall mirror mounted on African tusks. After the first dull pang of remorse subsequent sales bring only residual pain, like serial murder. Chandeliers, carpets, crockery, silver, ivory, jade chess tables and first editions of the *Britaniccas* crowd the spaces of the palace with their absence. Sold to provide her boyfriends with clandestine love gifts, sold to pay his rum dues. Old teak pays for her interminable telephone calls. A jade fountain dismembered piece by piece pays for grocery bills in instalments. The statue of his mother, canonized for committing sati, fetches a good sum.

He sees the black cars with tinted windows he bought every time she acquired a new lover. He paints his father's Chrysler black. Empty of fuel, a convoy of darkly upholstered vehicles wait in his porch.

'The trouble with that bastard,' she spits at her grown-up sons who are equally full of bile, 'is that he hasn't done an honest day's work in his life.'

He takes off a Nepalese khukri from the wall and impales his cotton hosiery socks between his toes. 'I'll stab her in the stomach and then kill myself.' My mother's letters advise restraint, a wildness he must cope with. 'Men from good families protect and respect their women, whatever they may be.' The rum is dark and deep but does not stop the knife cutting open his innards.

He sees himself in hospital strapped to beeping monitors that listen to the tragic beating of his heart. Alcohol induced tachycardia, the doctors pronounce their verdict. Catatonic pancreas they say. He is living on borrowed time, what can they do? He smiles bitterly; even time is not his own. Only a miracle can save him, and it does. She responds to the crisis with the animal ferocity of a protective mate. She brushes his hair and teeth, feeds him with her hands, sleeps on the floor and doesn't eat for days. Her new dignity makes her round face almost beautiful. 'Of all the men in the world only you are my husband,' she says. The rhythmic scrawl of the heart monitor steadies, hospital bills soar, a bracelet is sold and they are home to start a new chapter that is still a continuation of the old ...

Prostrate on the station floor deceitful photographs swim before his closed eyes. Silver frames encircle the doting couple and their two smiling sons with downy moustaches who watch their mother's pornographic videos on the sly. He sees Yuvrani Mami Sahib composing forlorn music on the harmonium. Paintings in watercolour and oil depict ornate balconies and ships at sea. He knows that the love poems written on folded scraps of paper under mattresses and pillows are not for him.

This too doesn't last.

She flaunts a new love, an obese film maker. She declares that during the month of the new moon soulmates will find each other as prophesied in the local calendar and she will unite with her lover in a blaze of light.

He buys another black car.

He consults an obscure tantrik who lives on a hill behind the palace. The tantrik prescribes a fire sacrifice with her hair and the blood of a horse. The last undernourished occupant of the neglected Sirikot stables is suddenly remembered. He shivers under the razor's edge. Yuvraj Mama Sahib wears a talisman of her hair and the horse's blood around his neck but it does not conquer her great appetite for sex.

He stops her food and money. She gets her meals from a local temple and mysteriously acquires funds for expensive purses and saris. She develops an addiction for tranquillizers. She sleeps all day. The raja hammers iron nails on all four sides of the palace gates to ward off evil and posts a guard. He makes a garland of eleven cloves and offers it to Shiva for eleven Mondays. In the evening, when he is drinking in the Chandramahala, she exchanges giggles with her sons in dark corners of the garden crowded with lovers in repose.

He comes home late to see her legs vulgarly apart in a nightdress, smoking a beedi with the guard in the guardroom. For the first time in his demented life he hits her. He says he will divorce her, throw her out, kill her. She prepares to subject him to a final punishment. She drinks a bottle of phenyl.

In the Sirikot hospital Nana Sahib had founded, she recovers to a new sensation of eggs in a clear stream of vomit pouring out of both her nostrils. She rises to a power over life, death and love. Yuvraj Mama Sahib's hands shake with the fear of losing her. She doesn't have to see it to know its every tremor. From a great expanse of contempt she looks down at him with a pity that leaves him breathless with longing. 'I'll drive you mad,' she tells him. 'Even if I go mad doing it.'

Lying crooked and supine on an empty cigarette packet on the platform floor, in the periphery of his dim vision, he sees the yellow of her sari approach. The red eye of the clock remains shut. The sentinels of time are taking a long while to change guards. An unseen hand seems to crank a shaft and spew out the dregs of his remaining life.

Raghavendra immigrates to London. He takes off the sacred thread that has always girdled his body and throws it into the Thames. He re-christens himself George and vows never to leave London. His parents never see him again. He is as good as dead. Yogendra starts a fishing trawler business in the nearby fishing port of Paribada. The famous cyclone that hit Orissa and smashed the myriad coloured glass panes of the Sirikot balustrades spits out Yogendra's broken and lifeless body on the shore.

The death of his son leaves him numb with its inevitability. He sees the day Yuvrani Mami Sahib finally leaves, riding pillion behind the obese film maker on a scooter. A serpentine row of black cars waits in his porch. With red streaming eyes he haunts an empty palace. He searches for salvation among decaying palace library books and his forefathers' diaries. Silverfish holes on the pages make the language strange and unreadable, as if it follows a decadent alphabet. He spends his days reclining uncomfortably on the marble throne in the veranda in dirty pyjamas, chewing cheap tobacco, staring at nesting pigeons cooing on the broken beams of the ceiling.

Years pass before a friend brings news of her to the palace that now lies open because many of its doors are sold. She has been caught in a police raid in a hotel.

There is no money for a new car. He sells brass utensils but it is not enough.

For the rest of his days he sits in his study on the only chair by the only table left in the palace. In the opposite end of the ruined palace his brother also lives out his life alone, poring over religious books that he once read. But he, he waits for her unblinkingly under the harsh glare of a naked bulb because the light shades have been sold. It is an endless wait, like the last blank white pages of a cryptic book.

His life is emptied out now. His mind has cleaned out its pockets. Her yellow sari closes in. She stands near his feet and looks down. In an airless gasp he sinks in a billowing yellow that smells and tastes like her. He drowns choking in a seamless sea of her yellow armpits nostrils hair legs navel knees and stomach. He falls deep into the waterless depths of its viscosity. He prays to his ancestors to help him surface. A dark rope, a lifeline drops down into the melting yellow but the more he clings to it the thinner it becomes.

His eyes open wide to look up at her. He is amazed at a life that can be broken down in a minuscule moment to a few incidents, one woman and the interstitial blankness of long waits.

He looks at her quizzically and sees on the shrivelled maternal fat of her face the transformations of his love. It moves from the infatuation of his youth to the jaded bitterness of his middle life to the habitual acceptance of old age.

She smiles like an ancient friend. He sees her radiantly young, compassionate even, only the faintest hint of malice in the slant of her head. After a silence that could have contained many years of solitude she speaks. 'You look tired,' she says.

He stares at her with no feeling and no expectation. 'Sixty years is a long time,' he says. Her eyes seem very light, almost grey.

'We only know one hundredth of the reasons why things happen.' Her voice has the quietness of a breath. He is not convinced. He feels the burden of age. Silence is heavy with the weight of memories.

'It doesn't matter.'

He does not know who says that. He feels a faint sensation of fingers on his brow even though she hasn't touched him. For one last time he fights the forgiveness he knows is descending on them.

'But it did once,' he says unable to bear the luminosity of her eyes, which shift into the distance, breaking the glance that keeps them captive.

'There is another place I must go ...' she stammers looking vague and disconcerted. He wants to reach out and hold her hand the way he remembers it, fair, long nailed and shaped like a slender paan leaf. A train whistles and starts a lingering chug on its tracks. He sees her standing at the compartment door of the train. She is gliding away from him. He knows he'll never see her again.

In the distance, when his eyes are just about to lose their power to see, she turns and waves. She is turning again, turning wheeling turning again in the sadness of a last goodbye. She looks at his face and doesn't understand the purity of her own tenderness. He feels their souls shredding for the last time, a final moment with their darkest sides...

He did not die that day. The ghatag who had come to the station to receive him saw him fly off the overhead railing and fall on to the ground below. By Yuvraj Mama Sahib's side within moments, he was relieved to see him open his eyes from a mild concussion. It was 4.07 a.m.

On the way to the palace, the ghatag repeatedly denied his persistent queries about whether he had seen Yuvrani Mami Sahib at the station. There was no woman in a yellow sari who looked even remotely like his wife. No, she was not standing by his flattened body conversing with him, he should know since he was the only one by his side all along.

'You spend too much time alone,' the ghatag had said, when Yuvraj Mama Sahib told him his story.

~

People reacted to the holocaust of Abolition in different ways, according to their temperament and upbringing. Some gave in to the decadence of nostalgia. They stayed immobile in their glorious past, like Baby Uncle, without the strength to face an adverse world. It is difficult to wipe a slate clean when there is too much written on it, especially when it is written in gold lettering.

Those who were more practical — who had received an education abroad, or had had some exposure outside the anachronistic palace walls — fared better. They found a place in public life and moved into the freshly painted corridors of new power. Others had enough wealth to tide them over a few generations. Although the days of harems and canine weddings were over for good, they could afford to hang on to a shadow of their previous lifestyles and do so still, even today. They have liquefied their lands and jewellery into fixed deposits, the accruing interest enough for their children and their children's children. In fact, the fixed deposit has saved the lives of princely states. For a race that had never held a job or understood the meaning of work, the interest on a fixed deposit was the closest they would ever get to the concept of 'earning money'.

But that may be an overly unjust generalization. There were other zamindars and talukdars who saved some of their lands and earned money by farming. Others went into businesses of stud farms and the hotel industry. Business is alien to the Rajput's belligerent and confrontationist nature, my husband says. But there have been many who have flourished. I tell him it's because Rajputs are natural administrators. Tourism saved the royalty in Rajasthan and Gujarat, mainly because of its geographical closeness to Delhi and Bombay. Lalita's parents did well for themselves by converting their palace into a heritage hotel. Even though profits suffered in the first few years because demanding customers were met with affronted stares.

But in the remote forests of Orissa and Madhya Pradesh, small states like Sirikot quietly curled up and died. Rich in heritage and history but asphyxiated by their loss of land holdings that came about by the Abolition of Zamindari Act they were left penniless in their magnificent palaces. There are many factors for their utter and complete degeneration. Many had not received a formal education, imperative for any society with strict rules of survival. Used to deep coffers they did not know the art of economy and thrift. Their privy purses and liquefied assets were consumed without thought or restraint. They had never heard of working within a budget. Used to sitting on thrones they did not understand the etiquette of a society in which everybody was equal. Many were simply devoid of common sense. They had never needed it. It was too common.

Baby Uncle sold his chrome ore and gypsum mines for ten rupees. He called it a distress sale! There was a time when his adopted grandfather, driven by urges of generosity, gifted mines on birthdays. Today his grandson works as a security officer in the same chrome mine they once owned, which was later nationalized by Indira Gandhi.

When I took my daughter to the Lapater summer house in Cuttack she was impressed by the gigantic ornate gateway, like the doors to a fairytale kingdom. But she was shocked to see how my distant uncles lived inside the crumbling mansion. The ripped-out bucket seats of an ancient Rolls-Royce made a presumably fashionable sofa set. A small, conspicuously placed fridge was the post-modern centerpiece and chickens clucked over the threadbare Persian carpet. The old raja had tied his bed to the beams of the ceiling with ropes. He thought it was a terribly smart thing to do. 'When the house crumbles and falls,' he said, choking through his throat cancer, 'I'll be safe.'

The squalor in their rooms was worse than the bug-infested quarters of the vas gharianis' houses which I had secretly visited against my mother's remonstrations. Scantily clad children ran about with snot dripping from their noses. The Lapater summer house was a study not of genteel poverty, but of a people who are at a loss for what to do with themselves.

In a railway station I spotted the scion of a talukdar from Uttar Pradesh whom I had often met at weddings in my younger days and who had achieved an uneasy notoriety in my time as a 'zulmi zamindar', Gandhiji's term for a cruel ruler. I had heard that villagers who could not pay lagaan were taken to his garden and forced to stand with a pot of water on their heads while he used the pot as target practice *a la* William Tell. I saw him in a railway station. He was not alighting from the third-class compartment as many of my relations embarrassedly do. He wore a red tunic and hoisted other people's luggage on his head. He was a coolie.

Like him, there are others who have embraced penury as if it is the most natural devolution of status. They live in hovels and own six lockers in expensive banks to keep their jewellery. The women are draped in gold-embroidered chiffon saris inherited from their grandmothers but accessorize it with

the cheapest rubber slippers from the local market. The men are
gentle and gracious and drink country liquor and drive around
on scooters. The women however are forbidden to be seen in
public riding pillion. They are courteous and polite and serve
their guests tea in broken Dresden china. Sometimes even in
plastic cups.

First, I thought their slovenliness was a vindictive gesture
against their situation. They had turned their backs on beauty.
Then I realized that they were unable to look for beauty the way
ordinary people could and find little ways to enhance it. During
state rule, there was so much beauty around them that they did
not know it existed. And now that it is gone, they do not know
the loss of what they never had.

Yuvrani Mami Sahib once wrote and complained to Ma that
Yuvraj Mama Sahib had sold an entire trunk of old silver in the
store-room to a stainless steel vendor. Her husband brandished
what he had earned in exchange like a victory trophy. It was a
stainless steel tiffin carrier. He brightly informed her of the
ruthless bargain he had struck with a vendor.

Old silver for a brand new, 'modern' tiffin carrier!

But almost all of the royalty I knew — the poor, the rich, the
practical, the foolish, and the Darwinian survivors — never
stopped addressing each other by their titles. All letters were
sent and received by Raja Sahibs, Rani Sahibs, Yuvraj Sahibs
and Rajmatas. Indira Gandhi had delivered her famous quote at
the time she took away the royal titles. She said, 'I'm doing you
a favour by taking your titles away.'

What a shrewd woman she was; how canny. She knew how
ferociously we clung to our appellations; in spite of all her efforts
she could not eradicate the coat-of-arms on the envelopes of royal
wedding invitations. We clung to emblems as if they were phantom
ships in a stormy sea. Soon after Independence, when we were
ridiculed as 'museum pieces', we hung on. Over the decades of
oblivion we became ornate dinosaurs who clung to our glorious
appendages. And now that the media seems to enjoy addressing

us this way, we are becoming open about it. We wear our titles with more impunity.

We have little else.

~

'It all vanished like diffusing camphor...' Ma had said, eyes glazing dreamily.

She died seven years ago at a ripe old age. I was with her during her last moments.

A few days before she died we talked about the night of her revelations; about the secret she would carry to her afterlife, and I to mine. There were too many wrinkles on her face to show emotion. 'It is just as well,' she said. 'We all go when the time comes. Murder is just the means.'

A month earlier, Ma had had a stroke while screaming at an old crippled vas ghariani she'd retained as her maid. Ma died within hours. I don't remember much of her death. I only remember what the maid said: 'Her screaming killed all the bugs in my ears.'

Beautiful, angry, vivacious Ma; larger than life; full of grace; Dare I talk about it now? About the secret shame my mother carried? A shame whose burden I helped share, and therefore inherited.

The truth is my mother and I were no different.

'I am doing you a favour,' Indira Gandhi had said, when she took our titles away.

'Jai Monarchy!' was Nana Sahib's last rallying cry before he died.

'Patricide?' Ma had demanded of Yuvraj Mama Sahib. 'Such a big crime for such a small state?'

'I'll be good, Ma,' I had wept. 'Don't send me away for adoption.'

'Forgive me,' were Nani's last words to Ma, 'I am doing what I believe in.'

'It all vanished like diffusing camphor,' Ma said, unable to forget her fairytale life.

'It's all over,' Dhaima had announced, as if it were an epitaph on a tombstone.

'Kingship is eternal,' the rajpurohit had admonished. 'You too are just a vessel.'

'I am doing you a favour,' Indira Gandhi said, when she took our titles away. Time is witness, she too was just a vessel.

Whether it is forty-five minutes, or weeks, or months, or centuries, what difference does it make? When it is over, it is over. But how we clung on...

Ma always joked that the state band which stood by in preparation to play at the birth of a boy was sent away when she was born. 'It's only a girl,' they were told. Only cheap sweets were distributed, and no shots were fired.

'But that didn't stop you from thoroughly enjoying your status as First Princess,' my son would rib her, and she would agree with a bitter smile.

Yet, she had a sister who was born before her who never grew up. The knowledge saddened her but did not destroy her.

Not as much as the knowledge that she had a sister who was born before her, who grew up into something execrable.

That knowledge did destroy her.

~

'Why is Shanti blackmailing you?' I had demanded the night of the revelations.

'Because,' my mother had said, lying brokenly in her bed, 'it is not I but she who is the First Princess.'

The medicine bottle felt heavy in my hands and I put it down.

'Ma had a daughter before me, during the time of the Menda Mas case, when the Sirikot files were lying in the Court of Wards. Baba in a fit of fury demanded that the girl be strangled.

Ma lost consciousness. When she awoke she assumed Dhaima, who was the midwife attending to her at the time, had killed the child. But she hadn't. She had hidden the child in a store-room of winter carpets and linen close to Ma's birthing chamber where she was convalescing. She hid her in a steel trunk left ajar and fed her cow's milk. Ants ate into the child's cheeks. Dhaima needed to attend to other duties and couldn't check frequently on the baby. Haven't you noticed the scar? Shanti still has it. Ma told me that she used to hear a child crying at night but assumed that it was the ghost of the baby she had murdered. I don't know why Dhaima didn't kill the child. Maybe she had more humanity than my parents did. Maybe it is easier to say than do. I imagine it is not simple to kill a child; to stuff the mother's placenta down its throat or whatever the standard practice is. But whatever it was, she had the presence of mind to confess to the rajpurohit and make him sign a document that he was a witness. They even managed to take a photograph of the girl. In a few days Dhaima exposed her to the public and said she was the daughter of a distant cousin who had died during childbirth.' My mother's voice was flat, her face to the wall, a dead person talking.

'There's still no proof, Ma. She and the rajpurohit could be collaborating together,' I said in desperation.

'Even if they did, they were only exploiting the benefits of the grave sin my parents had committed. We cannot kill our bad karmas, Leela. They rise from our graves. God has his ways. But I don't think Dhaima and the rajpurohit and Shanti have plotted this. Why, Leela, why would they?'

'For personal gain Ma, like you said,' I tried to console my mother. Yet, in spite of the heart-rending story she had told me, I was more worried about my mother's title of First Princess; and the blasphemous thought that a woman like Shanti, brought up in the squalor of the dhai quarters, was actually Ma's elder sister. Not an illegitimate whelp like so many others, but the first-born of the Raja Sahib and Rani Sahib of Sirikot. 'And because they knew that when passions had cooled they would be handsomely rewarded for her existence. But if Shanti is really the First Princess why did Dhaima wait so long to come out with the truth? Surely, she could have done that in a few months?'

'Fear, child, fear.' Ma hid her eyes in the crook of her elbow. 'She had countermanded a regal order, and a very important one at that. She did not know what retribution would befall her if she told them the truth. But the other more important reason was that as the child had been nurtured in the servant's quarters — she was already contaminated. Her chances for a royal life became remote. She has not simply grown up as a dhai's daughter. She is, in fact, a dhai's daughter. What would she have said? "This ragged child who stoops before you so her shadow does not besmirch you is actually the First Princess?" A good life is like the flight of a swan. One wing flies on our birth, the other on the nurture of our environment. A bird in flight needs both wings. One without the other and you have a broken winged swan. It cannot fly.'

My ankles felt swollen. I sat down at Ma's feet and addressed the dark hollows under Ma's elbow, 'Then why now, Ma? Why has she come out with the secret now?'

'Many reasons. Dhaima could not produce a son from Baba. She had no hope for land or property. She became ambitious. She probably wanted to use Shanti as a retirement plan. But most importantly, Dhaima is dying and she doesn't want to take a secret such as this to her grave. There are other reasons. Shanti had grown into a troubled personality even though she was ignorant about the truth of her birth. Dhaima didn't know who and how to get her married. She had brought up the First Princess, but the decision to marry a girl of royal birth is too big a decision for a servant to take. It was Shanti's romantic associations with the lowest levels of the palace hierarchy that made Dhaima panic. When Shanti started illicit connections with cooks and guards, the way so many servants do, Dhaima told her the truth.'

A deafening silence clapped in my ears. 'What did Shanti do?'

'What could she do? Put yourself in her position. She has been my companion. She has cleaned my shoes, and eaten the leftovers of my plate. She has slept on my floor and pressed my feet, accepting it as we all do our station in life. Suddenly to be told that you are not a servant, you are actually senior to all the royal children who have spat at you and made you the butt of their jokes, what would you do? She went to Nana Sahib and demanded justice.'

'How do you know?'

'Because he told me. Not in so many words but subtly. He told me about the wings of the bird. I knew what he meant.'

'Did he give her justice?'

'No. How do you give justice to a child you have never known? Even the bastards he has produced, who wear his parentage like a badge, have spoken at least two sentences in their lives to their father. Baba knew they existed. We are a family of eight brothers and sisters. She was supposed to be dead. He wanted to compensate her with land and property but she wanted none of it. She wanted his respect and our respect. She wanted a public declaration and full honours and the title of First Princess. She was very clear. It was either that or nothing. Either that, or she was happy to be in the dhai quarters.'

'Oh, Ma. How terrible. How terrible for her.' I was surprised my cheeks were wet. She was my aunt after all. Not that my biological aunts and uncles did not populate half of Sirikot. But she was different. She was not another example of the bastardization of Sirikot. She was royal blood through and through. What malefic influence, of what black planet, must have blighted the hour of her illustrious birth?

'What could Baba do? She was supposed to be dead. I know Baba had mourned her. He told me so the night before he died. He said the decision came as a momentary lapse of reason. He said that he had grieved for her every day. He had given special tarpan to her each time he made his oblations to the ancestors. But he refused to accept a child who instead of being dead grew up as a petty-minded servant. He said he preferred her dead because that is the way he remembered her. She even came to Rajraj and me.'

'Did she go to Nani too?'

Ma brushed my question away, as if it were an obstruction in her stream of thought. 'But what am I supposed to do? Why should I suddenly accept as my elder sister and First Princess a woman who has arranged my clothes and helped me with my bath? What will your father say if he finds out?'

'Why didn't she go to Nani? Nani was the best chance she had.'

The shadowy hollows of Ma's eyeless face were silent. 'She did. Dhaima told her soon after we arrived in Sirikot. You remember how withdrawn Nani was during her last days? She had softened towards Shanti but I could not understand why. I don't know what transpired between all of them but Baba ended up dead.'

It was my turn to be silent, my mind a furious buzz of inverted deductions and retrieved memories. I remembered tears flowing down Dhaima's craggy face the day Nani had spat into Shanti's hand. Maybe that was the day Dhaima decided to tell all. I remember Shanti's finger a mess of bleeding pin-pricks the day Ma and Nani discussed her own death in front of her.

'On the day of Ma's sati,' — Ma's speech had taken on an incessant, compulsive quality — 'only Dhaima and Shanti were present during her last moments. I cannot help thinking that that was no accident. I think her sati was an act of protest against the injustice meted out to her child.'

And then Ma took out from the folds of her blouse, a warm-as-skin, heavily folded letter. It was the one that the rajpurohit had handed to her, sealed, after Nani's sati.

The letter was short. It didn't take me much time to read.

'I hope that with my death, your father and I shall atone for the sins we have committed. Swear by the ashes of your dead mother, you

shall reinstate your sister.' It ended with Nani's signature and the imprint of her seal.

I thought of Nani's gentle swarthy face and the long cascade of her hair as she sat in the courtyard putting her jewellery back on, just before Nana Sahib had been cremated. Savouring a few more moments before widowhood claimed her. Smiling her revenge. It is possible to lead a full life and still be empty. It is possible to be within a big family and still feel alone. Alienated, lighting her pyre of anguish, immolating her flesh, burning to ashes. She was at rest now, cleansed, as good as gold. She had been purified by the test of fire.

'It was Ma's last wish that Shanti be reinstated as the First Princess.' My mother's voice broke. A teardrop, like a furtive eye, slipped from under her elbow into her hair. 'But I can't do it.'

'So it was Shanti who killed Nana Sahib?'

'Yes,' said Ma casually concluding weeks and months of my agonizing over Nana Sahib's murder. 'Dhaima confessed to me later, during the course of my investigations. The night Shanti spoke to Ma, Ma had said, "We shall see." Shanti had taken it as a refusal. Ma had been her last card. But I know my mother. Ma would have done her best to reinstate her. Shanti had gone to the right person. If only she had waited.'

'How did she do it?' I was the questioning parent, she was my child. On another day, Ma would probably have never made these confessions. The combined press of her nervous breakdown, her guilt and a weak moment had made my mother say more than she would ever have said otherwise. I know this for true. Women of her times, contrary to popular myth, had a great capacity for secrets. Lord only knows what truths still hide in their closely guarded hearts.

'Dhaima said that she had dried and powdered the stems of black lotuses. She put the powder in Baba's milk. Shanti had come early in the morning and given it to him. Baba probably could not refuse her because he now knew she was his daughter. He must have drunk the milk obediently and handed her the empty glass.'

'But, Ma, he hadn't even been to the latrine.'

'When your time comes, you walk half way towards death. You don't wait to take a shit.'

'Your sister, my blood aunt, she could have killed all of us.'

'No, she couldn't. Black lotus is not a slow-acting poison. I've found out.' Ma sat up on her bed and pressed the knuckles of her hands against the hollows of her eye sockets. 'If only she had waited. Maybe a day, maybe two. What a dreadful waste. How utterly, utterly wasteful.' Ma's rocking to and fro distracted me.

'Ma, whatever the time for the poison to act may be, there were too many probabilities for her to ignore. There was too much risk of getting caught.'

'What does it matter?' Ma shouted at me. 'They are all dead! What does it matter how and when she poisoned them? They are dead, Leela, all dead; burnt to ashes. And I have nothing left ... not even my identity. Shanti stole that too....'

My mother got up agitatedly and started banging the open trunks shut. She looked wild, unhinged. My own nerves were shot.

'She did it.... She took everything ... and now my mother wants me to give her my title ... That's it. I've told you more about the family than a girl your age should know ...' She turned away from me. Ma suddenly looked puny, as if exhaustion had shrunk her. I could not bear to see her so miserable.

'Ma,' I said firmly, as if I were about to command her to take her medicine. 'Hand the letter to me.'

I took the letter and I fed it to the flame. Like misfortune, it caught fast. The letter contorted, blackening in agony. The fire devoured it in a single lick. And I swear by the gods, that from the ashes that littered the carpet I caught the faint whiff of burnt human flesh.

How many times have I told myself over the years that I shouldn't have. We should have ... we shouldn't have shamed ourselves so ... how useless it was ... how falsely precious ...

As pathetic as Baby Uncle sitting under a naked bulb, behind his only chair, waiting for monarchy to return.

Sixteen

My mother did not want me to marry into royalty. 'No fat rajas for you,' she said. 'I want a son-in-law who is "working".' It was a revolutionary decision on my mother's part because of its lack of precedence. 'We need new blood,' my mother said, but I doubt whether she knew the extent of the relevance of her decision. There are maybe fifty thousand blue-blooded Rajput families in India, definitely not more than a lakh. We, like other Hindus, strictly follow not only the 'gotra' system but also prevent marriages between the same subcastes of Rajputs. A boy and girl from the same gotra cannot marry because they descend from the first seven sages categorized by Manu in his shastras. But the gotra system follows the patrilinear bloodline and does not take into account the mother's gene pool.

In the same way, prohibition of same-subcaste marriages does not prevent consanguinity because the girl's subcaste along with her gotra changes after marriage. She adopts the patrilinear gotra and subcaste. What traditional geneologists forgot was that her mother's gene pool and bloodline does not change.

There are many Rajput subcastes, each claiming a more illustrious bloodline. The Rathores and Parihars are considered pure Suryavanshis claiming descendency from the sun. I am a Kachchawa from my mother's side, claiming descendency from

the moon. The Chauhans, like my sister's husband's family, are
Agnivanshis. Their origins do not go back to the Scythians and
Persians like the others but to the marauding Huns of Mongolia.
Agnivanshis were the fringe elements of the warring communities
that settled in ancient India and were incorporated into the
Rajput race. Our blood must have seen a lot of intermingling
during medieval times. Rajput women received peripatetic
soldiers, tribal chieftains and foreign settlers. But for the last
hundred years or so, when the need for traditional warring
strategies started to die down, the boundaries of the Rajput
communities became less porous. Deprived of hybridity, we
became close-knit and therefore more consanguinous.

Though in Orissa marriages between third and fourth cousins
have been known to happen, even other royal Rajput marriages
occur closer to their bloodline than they think. I have discovered
that most Rajput families, though spread out across the country,
are somehow related to each other.

I now understand the reason for my mother and grandmother's
paranoia about deformities. After my fall from the horse they
were obsessed with the fear that a bone might be broken. If it did
not heal I would be deformed, they said. My mother rejected two
marriage proposals from eligible boys on grounds of deformity.
One had a sixth thumb and the other a slightly enlarged knee
bone. My mother's fears had a sound genealogical basis. The
Rajput community's consanguinity, like all in-bred ones, suffers
from two, most-dreaded congenital diseases. Insanity and physical
deformity.

We've had our share of lunatics in our family. Kumud Mami
Sahib slipped into a comfortable state of madness after leaving
Kumar Mama Sahib. She died in her sleep in her mother's
house believing she was the reincarnation of the legendary saint
Meerabai.

My wedding was arranged to a boy from a nouveau riche
industrialist family whose father couldn't trace his lineage beyond
his parents. He came from a village of belligerent, stick-wielding

Rajputs and his father never tired of reminding me that as a child he walked five miles everyday to the nearest school.

My reaction to the arrangement of my wedding was much like my reaction to Abolition. I was indifferent. It was neither good nor bad. I was neither glad nor unhappy. Though when I look back at my years of married life I pray to god that in my next life I should be born very poor or very rich, but please lord, not in the middle.

It was easy for me to face economic poverty but difficult to understand the pettiness of my in-laws' impecunious value system. Their biggest grouse against me, as a daughter-in-law, was that I did not get up early in the morning. 'Why should I get up early in the morning?' I asked my husband. 'Do I have to go out into the field to take a shit? Are there no bathrooms in the house?'

A daughter-in-law is not loved for the strength and delicacy of her demeanour but for how well she massages her mother-in-law's feet with oil. Unlike in our system — where the wealth and property of the rani is separate and is bequeathed after her to the rani of the next generation with the men in the family having no say in the matter — the women own nothing. In my husband's family the women spend their time scrubbing and cleaning even though there are four servants for the purpose; and their faces shine like an imbecile's when their cooking is complimented. What I found most shocking in my early days of marriage was the sight of my father-in-law walking back from the vegetable market with a bag full of brinjals and cabbages. The revulsion I felt dried my bones. What an unnatural thing to do. Buying vegetables everyday from the market. I have still not understood why he did it and have expressly forbidden my husband from following such inane habits. It is like stitching your own clothes before wearing them. What are tailors for?

~

My husband was a good man with a ready laugh and an even temper. He put his arms around my shoulders one morning, in the winter of 1972, as I sat on the frost-blue rexine seat of a train that seemed to be hurtling towards a foregone nemesis.

We had boarded the train the night before. It was an overnight ride to Calcutta, to Ma and her urgent desire to see me as soon as my son's school holidays began. Potol, our only reminder of Sirikot, had been retained in my mother's staff. He would be waiting at the Howrah station in the morning. Potol had come a long way from shooing pigeons. Now he handled all my mother's affairs outside the house.

Our berths were in a coupé in the first-class compartment. The coolie fitted our luggage beneath our seats and I tried not to think about the Uttar Pradesh talukdar who would never again take potshots at hapless villagers. My husband and son opted for the two upper berths and left the lower berth for me. The lower berth opposite me was empty; the passenger had still not boarded. I did not voice aloud my irritation at sharing the compartment with a stranger because I knew what my family would say: 'Oh no,' they would laugh. 'HH is upset again.'

HH, or Her Highness, was an old sobriquet I did not know whether to live up to or live down. My son and husband settled into their seats as easily if it were their living room. They opened their Robert Ludlums and peeled their oranges. I peered out of the horizontal bars of the train window, enjoying the sensation of movement in the platform and the quiet anticipation of destination in the flurry of comings and goings.

I am not sure when she entered the compartment and took her seat. But when I turned around it did not take me time to recognize her. I didn't know whether she recognized me. My predilection for food and the trauma of childbirth had inclined me towards obesity. I was a far cry from the thirteen-year-old girl she had last seen me as. But Shanti was the same, only more withered. My heart lurched at how closely she now resembled Ma.

Our eyes met, like stones colliding, and we both turned away. From the corner of my eyes I observed her closely. Her small overnighter was cheap and had visited the repair shop. She pushed it defiantly under the seat and settled down beside the window, staring out of it resolutely to avoid my gaze.

Her sari was inexpensive but well maintained. Old age had been kinder to her, rubbing out the bitter lines around her mouth. I made a quick estimate of my travelling companion's social position. She was wealthy enough to afford a first-class ticket but miserly in the rest of her lifestyle. I had heard that Shanti and the mehtar had married unopposed in a quiet temple ceremony in Sirikot. They had accepted the compensation of a few acres of land Yuvraj Mama Sahib had granted her, only to sell it shortly after and move to an unknown city.

By the calmness in her features I knew they were doing well and were happily married. She probably had children, my first cousins. But I was not going to ask her about them, just as I was not going to tell her about my family.

The monotonous clattering of the train and the dark blur of the countryside whizzing past the window finally shook my inhibition from its mooring. The fact that our necks ached from studiously facing away from each other, also contributed.

'I'm Leela,' I offered finally, confronting her. The quietness of my voice carried over the shrieks of the speeding train.

'Oh?' She looked into my eyes and her face twisted into a familiar bitter smile.

My son and husband looked up from their books in momentary surprise and then returned to their positions of reading. The lack of curiosity in the male gender never ceases to amaze me.

She could have said more, but she didn't. I had a lot to ask her but I couldn't. Can a train bridge two decades of indifference? There was nothing more to do. I self-consciously shook my family out of its inertia and insisted to my husband and son that we make our beds. We went through the elaborate ritual of tucking in our bedsheets in the unlikely corners of the train beds. I felt exposed in front of her observant eyes. I was uncomfortable that she knew what my pillowcases looked like, even though there had been a time when she had seen the colour of Nani's spit in the cupped palm of her hand.

The train lurched to a sudden stop and I fell against her. She smelt of hardworking sweat and harsh detergent. But she also smelt like Ma. Shaken, I staggered back to my seat.

Our attendant, travelling in the third-class compartment, brought me my favourite railway station chai. Tea in an earthen cup, thick and sweet, smelling of baked soil. Shanti gave me a mocking stare, as if deriding me for still maintaining attendants. She got off the train at the stop. I peered out into the wide glare of the busy station. She filled her water bottle from a public water tap in a cement tank then she gargled and spat roughly on the platform in a way that saddened me.

She got on the train just before it pulled away with the adeptness and ease of a seasoned traveller. She did not make her bed. She put her handbag under her head, switched off the bed light and slept.

In the shifting darkness of the hurtling train compartment I slept fitfully. I dreamt of Sirikot. I often dreamt about Nana Sahib and Nani Sahib. The terrifying images and forms of my dreams were the pieces of the puzzle I still tried to fit together in my rational waking hours. Over the years, the face of Nana Sahib's murderer and the murderer's modus operandi had become clearer and clearer. I had had a lot of time to deliberate on it. Rolling against the motion of the train, this dream was new yet oddly familiar.

Shanti spat at Nani. Nani's face melted in red gobs of fire. I was running down a dark tunnel and a cobra hissed after me, the crimson jewel on its forehead gleaming like Cyclops' eye. At a dead end I turned and faced the cobra. It was twice my size. Its yellow eyes became the venomous stare of the mehtar. The snake moved to strike and in my sleep I experienced its poison course up my legs and rush to my head. I fell off a cliff into a powder-black abyss below. I tensed for the impact but a mocking Shanti received me in her arms. She put me down gently and rolled her head back to laugh. Nana Sahib stood behind her, resplendent in his finery, not a hair out of place in his beard. He looked at me the way he always did, like a doting grandfather, and chided me gently, 'Leela Ma, you are so slow.'

My eyes strained open, but my mind was still caught in a different space-time dimension, befuddled and sleepy. I couldn't stop the word jettisoning from my mouth. 'Shanti!' It was an involuntary cry for help.

The word I said must have sounded like a question because beside me on the opposite berth a reply came that I had not expected.

'Yes?' It was a reply that was more a painful appeal. She was awake, needing to talk. Dawn stalked the racing train and cut its way into her horizontal figure. I wondered whether Shanti had slept at all. Across and above, on the two upper berths, my family slept the sleep of the innocent.

'I know how it happened.'

As if on cue the train screeched to a halt.

'How?' she said. Her tone betrayed no expression.

'It was the avdust, wasn't it?'

She was quiet. She turned towards me and rested her head on her elbow as if settling down for the long anticipated moment.

'The avdust.' I said. 'The water in the can on the left side of Nana Sahib's thunder-box. He, the meht — your husband — was Nana Sahib's night-soil carrier. He knew Nana Sahib's bowel movements better than Nana Sahib did. He knew Nana Sahib suffered from constipation and haemorrhoids. It was the water in the avdust Nana Sahib used to wash himself which had been poisoned, not the milk. It was the dead pigeon that led me to the truth. It lay dead at the foot of Nana Sahib's bed, unnoticed in all the commotion. It must have been poisoned by the water, because pigeons don't drink milk. It had wandered into Nana

Sahib's bathroom and died at the foot of his bed. And the poison? Was it the black lotus?'

Shanti was still silent. She looked up once to see whether my family was listening in. They were fast asleep.

'It probably was,' I said. 'The meht— your husband— always had a motive to kill Nana Sahib. What Nana Sahib did to him and his family was unconscionable. Nana Sahib's lust for his mother was reprehensible. He murdered his father and permitted the child of a brahmin, a twice-born, to be brought up in an untouchable colony as a mehtar. Wherever he may be I assure you he is paying for his sins. We all pay up, sooner or later. I am surprised he did not commit the murder sooner. Tell me, did Nana Sahib know that the night-soil carrier was his keep's son?' Her silence was making me say more than I should have. I needed her to speak, to stem my onrush of words.

'He did,' she finally said. 'My husband believes that. He felt that Raja Sahib always observed him very closely ... followed him with his eyes ...'

'The black lotus doesn't lose its power when it is diluted...' Her participation had cast its spell and now I could finally revel in the disclosure of a mystery that had haunted me enough to inform the way I viewed the world. 'It takes two minutes for the poison to take effect. Your husband put the poison in the avdust at night, safe in the knowledge that nobody except Nana Sahib would use the toilet. When Nana Sahib washed himself, the poison acted on his haemorrhoids and worked up his bloodstream. It took two minutes. Enough for Nana Sahib to wash his hands and walk into his bedroom. That is why there was no discolouration on his fingers. He had washed it off. That was why so much blood came out of his rectum and why his anus was discoloured.

'Your husband was standing behind the mehtar's door all along, even as Nana Sahib lay dying and the uproar began. While Ma was busy flaying Phulwati, your husband quietly walked into the bathroom and removed the chamber-pot and cleaned

out the avdust water. He even cleaned the water in the basin.
That is why when we entered the room all the thunder-boxes
were open, as if they had not been used. Your husband
disappeared through the mehtar corridor. When the palace duwari
was questioned, he said that, unaware of Nana Sahib's condition,
he had opened the mehtar's corridor an hour after Nana Sahib's
death. That is when your husband slipped out. It must have
been a long night for him.'

'Go on,' Shanti said, as if fascinated by my discoveries.

'Nana Sahib knew. Black he had said. It meant the black
brahmin, or the black brahmin's son. Because the minute the
poison started to work he must have realized who was responsible
and how. Khoon, he said, meaning his death was a murder and
not natural. It also meant that the poison carried through his
blood and was not ingested or consumed in the tooth powder
as people might believe.' I forced myself to be quiet, desperate
now for acknowledgement.

Neither of us had moved from our reclining positions, as if
enraptured by the sordid resolution of a lifelong puzzle. She
complied, after a pause. 'Interesting,' she said, as if commenting
on a book.

'It's true,' I said. 'He did it for you.' I did not say it like an
accusation, because I did not consider it to be one. 'I know because
it happened at the time you declared the truth about your birth
to Nani and felt rebuffed by her. Nani was your last straw. A few
days later Nana Sahib was dead. Your husband must love you a
lot. He did not revenge his own tragedy but waited for yours.'

'We have a special bond, my husband and I,' she said softly.

'A bond special enough to kill.'

'That's where you are wrong, Leela. You are right about
everything else except the most important part. He was not the
one who slept in the mehtar corridor that night and mixed the
poison.'

'Then who?' I said. The edifice constructed over decades
crumbled. I had been so sure.

'It was Pushpa.'

'Pushpa?' I said stupidly.

'Yes, Pushpa.'

'Why?' My body suddenly felt deflated, out of air. Pushpa, privy to all our conversation, cowering under the bed, eyes rounded in horror. Pushpa, my idiot childhood companion.

'Really, Leela,' my mother's older sister chided. 'I have always thought you intelligent, such an observant thirteen-year-old. Did you never notice what a special family ours was? My husband brought our family even closer. We filled each other's empty spaces. For me, Dhaima was the mother I never had. For Dhaima, I was the blue-blood she never was. For my husband, I was the mother he never had. For me, Pushpa was the sister I never had. And for Pushpa, I was the real Jemma, the only First Princess. She was companion only to me, to you she was in service. I was the only royal patron she would be loyal to. My husband and I had deliberated over the murder, planned it, discussed it many times. But I didn't want to do it. He was still my father. I could not, would not, kill the only father I had. My husband didn't want to stain his hands with the blood of another. His parents were brahmins, he said. They would not wish it. But Pushpa saw my anguish; the anguish of the real Jemma, the actual First Princess. She was the only one in the crowded palace who gave me my due.'

Morning had broken. Vendors were climbing onto the train, waking up sleeping passengers with their ringing announcements of chai. They looked alert, so wide awake, just like us.

'And so the mighty are brought down,' I said strongly overpowered by the desire for a long restful sleep. 'In the basest way, by the lowest instruments of their own creation.'

'That's how justice works. How our destinies work,' Shanti surmised.

'Where is Pushpa now?'

'Oh, she's happily married. Her husband runs a small dairy. She has three children.'

The rest of the journey went in a blur. I don't recall when Shanti got off or who came to receive her. I don't remember when we packed our things and alighted. I only remember my husband putting his arms around me and shaking my shoulders and the curiosity in the staring faces of the people I crossed as I walked from the station to the waiting car. I remember Potol grabbing my luggage and his distracting tobacco-stained smile.

'Rajeshwari' Dhaima had wanted to christen Shanti, meaning 'queen'. Nani had considered the name presumptuous and changed it to Shanti. Irony, the curl of a woman's lip.

Pushpa had been absent the morning of Nana Sahib's murder. I had looked around for her to find my slippers but she wasn't in the room. She had spent the night in the mehtar's corridor, waiting her chance.

So it was Pushpa.

Pushpa, who dropped the lamp when Yuvraj Mama Sahib mentioned Shanti's name. Pushpa, who wanted to take a piss just when my discussions with Lalita veered dangerously close to the truth. Pushpa, who yawned during Nani's sati. It was not shock as I had presumed, it was lack of sleep because she had spent the night in the mehtar's corridor. It must have been Pushpa who leaked my romantic picnic to the elders. Pushpa, who tattled to Kumud Mami Sahib to make us stop our investigation. Pushpa, who was not a tabula rasa at all, but a book of poison written in invisible ink. Pushpa, who was never afraid of ghosts.

'Don't be scared of ghosts, Jemma Sahib,' she had said. 'They are only air.'

My idiot childhood companion, Pushpa.

'She's trying to solve a murder mystery,' she had informed Lalita shyly.

How she must have laughed.

Epilogue

The Toyota Qualis waddles like a fat-bottomed woman over the bumpy turnoff to the entrance gate. The stone lions guarding the Sirikot palace are blackened with time. As the motorcar reaches the gate it leaves a chocolate wake of muddy sludge. Discarded polythene bags of many dirty colours lace the road; the virulent filth of the Indian countryside. Before we enter the palace it is necessary to cross the granary, its magnitude reminiscent of the once opulent natural richness of the now impoverished state of Orissa. The Mangala mountain behind the palace looks like the head of an old bald man. The green cover is now only sparse scrubland. We can see scattered villagers scrounging for firewood at the elevated distance of the mountain, like lice on the old man's head.

At the foot of the Mangala mountain, the Sirikot palace is still picturesque; its decadent beauty in contrast to the starkness of the surrounding villages. As the motorcar moves through the overgrown greenery skirting the driveway, the palace waits regally, still arrogantly unabashed, its head steeped in the clouds of memory. The palace was built in three distinct architectural styles: Indo-Saracenic, Mughal and British. Now, only the last, the British facades and the east and west wing, are structurally intact — a cancerous tumour that continues to live after the host body has been destroyed.

The boundary walls are broken in many places where the village cows come through to graze. The towers in the four directions are silent. No drumbeats of the nagaras signal the changing hours. Time has forgotten Sirikot.

The ten acres of garden separating the motorcar and the palace front are studded with life-size statues of rural men, women and children in relief. Time frozen in white, they look tired, haunted even. The meandering driveway takes us to the lily pond languishing in invading green, muddied by sad memories. Just ahead, the summer house, though still bravely holding up its ornate arches, lies empty and broken. An era has passed here too. No Sirikot beauty enjoys the evening breeze. Most of them are old and away, grappling with harsher realities.

I get off the Qualis and walk up to the palace ramparts. The steps I had flown over as a girl are an arduous climb for my aching knees. I have grown old with Sirikot.

The BBC documentary film crew gets busy in the chaos of organizing a shot. They tell me they are making a series of documentaries on old Indian palaces. They promise to give Sirikot 'good footage'. I laugh.

The only wing of the palace still standing is the one containing the Chandramahala, the durbar hall and the banquet halls. They lie open. The ivory billiards table is gone. The thrones went long ago. The halls are so empty. The durbar hall has been given to the local village bank. They have turned it into a dark airless government office. Yuvraj Mama Sahib had sustained himself on its minimal rent in his old age.

The zenana is uninhabitable and broken. The forest has encroached through windows and cracks in the walls. The air is thick with the stench of bat shit. Their excreta have marked the walls like a viscous coat of paint. A weathered and faded teak ottoman in Nani Sahib's courtyard is a single forgotten piece of furniture. Its stuffing has been ripped out, possibly by a black-faced Sirikot langur. The cotton is dirty and reminds me of the decomposing viscera of a gutted animal. On an earlier visit to

Sirikot I had asked Yuvraj Mama Sahib's sole attendant where all the furniture was. 'The expensive ones are sold,' he had replied.

'And the rest?'

'The rest I used as firewood.'

'Firewood?'

'Yes, Jemma Sahib. Teak makes good firewood. It's like making a bonfire of matchsticks. And the food smells really good,' he had said.

~

'Madam, your shot is ready.'

The boy who has wires and cables hanging about him runs to fetch me. They make me sit on the marble throne. It feels overused, warm from the touch of Yuvraj Mama Sahib's helpless energy. I am uncomfortable. 'Tell me,' the girl beside the camera says. She is pretty, but has the hardened face of the city bred, 'What does it feel like, to lose everything?'

The generator has packed up, someone yells. He is a slouching man who surfaces from behind a blinking instrument of what appears to me like a tape deck. I find their jargon amusing. Packed up, as if the generator was a traveller who was in a hurry to catch a train. The girl swears and apologizes to me. I smile. She doesn't know I've heard worse. If I told her all the swearwords I knew, her ears would burn.

I wander into the Chandramahala and look down at the spot where the gold bed used to be. Nana Sahib had died in that spot. Yuvraj Mama Sahib had died in that spot too, but as alone in his death as the old in the United States. Anonymous, away from his children and family, forgotten, discarded. His attendant found his thin wasted body the next day. Nana Sahib had died better, even though he was murdered.

I walk towards the pernicious verdure that was once the pleasure gardens. I look at the dense overgrowth and cannot imagine that once fifty gardeners nurtured flowers of all seasons

here. The wind rustles through my hair. I feel the ghosts of
Sirikot walk past me. Cowdung has stained the wide, faded
expanse of the tennis courts. Tufts of grass grow where the
boundaries used to be.

I walk into the open library. There are only two bookcases.
The matted oak of their wood mocks the neglect around them.
Layers of dust blind the glass panels of the bookshelves. It is not
locked. I open one.

The taalpatras. Oh no, I think. Kumar Mama Sahib had
wanted me to preserve them but I did not have the time. I pick
out one. The lettering is buried in dry dust. The parchment is
thin. I sit down on the floor feeling heavy, as if I am carrying
a backpack of stones. I weep without tears. God is another name
for peace, Kumar Mama Sahib used to say. Centuries of ecstatic
spiritual experiences written down in the hope of posterity but
lost now, all lost.

Surely, the wisdom of our sages could have been retained.
Surely there is a place for the eternality of human seeking. Or
is that too an obsolete notion? Is the search for truth over? Is
there no need for it any more? I think of our sages and the
knowledge they had passed down in the local dialect, from
memory to word, from experience to knowledge. Kumar Mama
Sahib, I chide, you and your naïve hope that their treasures
would be awaited, that there would still be need for gospels after
everything is gone.

I am averse to opening the second bookcase but I do. The
Sirikot diaries. Written by eighteen generations of rajas. Letters
and lessons to future generations of royalty. Words of experience
for those who might need it. The spine of the journal cracks like
a breaking bone when I open one. Silverfish run for cover from
the open pages. Shunning light, shunning touch, consuming the
words of my ancestors. I shut the journal and dust flies off the
covers. The silverfish would be grateful. I put it back on the
shelf. These I will leave behind. But the taalpatras I will put in
a cardboard crate and take with me.

I pay my last respects at the Sirikot mausoleum. Seventeen cenotaphs of marble samadhis rest in uneasy peace. Yuvraj Mama Sahib's samadhi is made of cement. Eighteen generations. The circle has come round again. The snake has eaten its own tail. A curse has been fulfilled.

A tiny wisp of smoke wafts up from Nani's neighbouring sati mandir. The unburnt moth-eaten edge of her sari lies weighted by a rare and auspicious right-whorled conch. Some Sirikot brahmin somewhere is still burning earthen lamps at her altar.

The light is fading. The film crew has decided to pack up and return the next day for the rest of the shoot. It is a two-hour drive to our hotel in the city. They hurry.

Nobody wants to be left behind in a palace ruin after dark.

Acknowledgements

I must thank the casual conversations between my mother and grandmother that first set my imagination on fire. But maybe even before that are the numerous princely states of India and the uneasy legacy they carry. I hope one day they will put their ghosts to rest. I would like to acknowledge the work Ashok Chopra and Nandita Aggarwal have put into the book, without them this book would not exist. Ashok Mallik, Ira Pande, and Ankita Mukherjee for their encouragement and Franklin Rogers for the most important advice he gave me: 'Don't try to write a great book,' he said. 'Just write.'

I thank my father Mahendra Pratap Singh for first teaching me how to read and my father-in-law Brigadier S P Bhattacharjya for believing in me. My sister Sharda Singh and brother Shivendra Singh who probably think that even my email messages are masterpieces. I thank my sons, Neel and Vivek, for so graciously sleeping in the afternoons so I could write. And always, always my husband Joy Bhattacharjya, for keeping the faith.

Photograph by Hari Nair

Shivani Singh, a descendant of the royal family of Madhupur, grew up in Ranchi, in Jharkhand. She abandoned a doctorate in philosophy to take up film making and subsequently abandoned that, too, to become a full-time novelist. She says that she has completed only two projects of note: the first, to take her twin pregnancy to term, and the second, to finish the manuscript of her first novel, *The Raja Is Dead*. She lives in Gurgaon with her husband and twin sons.